CW01085388

Eggs, Butter, Suga

By

Alicia L. Wright

Tannbourne

Eggs, Butter, Sugar and Disaster

ISBN: 978-0-9567852-1-3

First publication in UK by Tannbourne Limited 2011

Published by
Tannbourne Limited
49 Westleigh Avenue, Coulsdon, Surrey CR5 3AD
www.tannbourne.com

Text and cover design Copyright © Alicia L. Wright 2011

Alicia L. Wright has asserted her right under the Copyright,
Designs and Patents Act, 1988, to be identified as Author of
this Work.

All rights reserved. No part of this publication may be
reproduced, stored in a retrieval system, or transmitted in any
form or by any means, electronic, mechanical, photocopying,
recording or otherwise, without the prior permission of the
publisher.

British Library Cataloguing in Publication Data. A catalogue
record for this book is available from the British Library.

Printed and bound by CPI Group (UK) Ltd,
Croydon, CR0 4YY

To my family and friends all over the world -
I wouldn't be the person I am without you all

<u>Warning:</u> To anyone impressionable, please do not imitate any of the things Sera does in this book, namely:

a: Drink anything strange and yellow.

b: Take things from stores without paying for them or wander onto other peoples' property, even if no-one sees you.

c: Start a cult.

Thank you.

<u>To my family and friends:</u> It's not my fault. Mythology is really like that.

CONTENTS

VANILLA FLAVOURED TROUBLE

Seralina pelted up the stairs, ignoring the rumbling that shook the castle and the roars coming from outside, trying desperately to remember which room her bag was in and which way it was. The castle may have been finished, but it hadn't been furnished yet; the glowing, white corridors all looked the same. As she rushed along, checking room after room, she wondered how on Ear- how on *Midgard* - this had all happened. She'd just wanted to help people. To make them happy. To give them pudding. It had seemed like a good idea at the time. She'd never suspected that being a goddess would be just like being a human. Only worse.

If Seralina had known what was going to happen, she never would have drunk the stuff.

Ambrosia. The Drink of the Gods. Thick, syrupy and vanilla flavoured, for some reason. It also contains enough calories to kill a mortal on the spot, so it's just as well that mortals are no longer mortals by the time they finish drinking it. Like Seralina, for example. She hadn't really meant to become a god. She hadn't taken the warning 'This will make of ye a god' seriously. It was her general policy not to trust any claim beyond 'It tastes all right, really'. She certainly didn't trust anything that sounded made-up or used words like 'dynamic'. Going round trusting words like 'dynamic' could get you into trouble. As it turned out, so could ignoring warning labels.

It was a hot day and Seralina was Lost. It was the

1

special sort of lost achieved by someone insisting to themselves and travelling companions that they weren't, that their destination would be visible any minute now and that cutting through that bit of trees was 'a shortcut'.   After almost an hour of 'We're nearly there now!' from Seralina, her friend Meena's patience was starting to wear thin.

Then, like an oasis in a desert, they saw the café.

Their enthusiasm faded significantly when they saw it was closed, as cafés are in these situations, but their hopes were marginally raised by the sight of the two vending machines outside that seemed to be working.   One had nothing but cans and cans of 'Idunn's Finest', a drink neither of the girls had heard of before, whereas the other had a wide selection of chocolate.   Meena pulled her face at the gaudy, golden cans and bought two bars of chocolate. Seralina on the other hand had no choice but to stick with 'Idunn's Finest', because she had recently become allergic to chocolate and was desperate.

"You sure you don't want one?" Meena waved her second chocolate bar under Seralina's nose "I wouldn't drink that if I were you, it looks foreign to me. It's probably made of turpentine or something."   Seralina scowled at Meena, waved away the chocolate bar and squinted at the back of the can.

"Says here it's made of apples" she replied "and... vanilla, apparently." she added, squinting even harder.   The writing seemed to be in English, but it was really hard to read.   It seemed to be in two different scripts at once, like one of those holographic cards with two pictures that are useless because you can't see either one and looking at it gives you a headache.   "It also says... 'Warning: This will make of ye a god'.   Whatever that means." she finished sceptically.

"Yeah, *right*." Meena retorted "Must be some sort of

sports drink or something. Whatever it is, it sounds dis-*gust*-ing." Meena replied, tucking into her chocolate. Seralina sighed and sipped her drink. It tasted more like vanilla milkshake than anything else. She watched Meena with growing resentment. It wasn't as if she'd even liked chocolate that much. It was just that now that she couldn't have it on account of it making her head explode, she realised she DID like it. It was like a friend you liked but didn't often visit suddenly moving to the other side of the planet without saying goodbye.

"What's your vanilla turpentine like?" Meena asked, opening the second bar.

"It's not bad, actually." Seralina replied, taking another swig "It actually kinda tastes like melted chocolate would taste, if it tasted like vanilla. If that makes any sense."

"It doesn't." Meena replied, breaking off a piece of her new bar "Anyway, you just *want* it to taste like that. It's probably like that whole 'tastes like chicken' business."

"No, really. It's quite nice. It's really weird-" Seralina started and then... pop! She was gone. Meena suddenly realised that she knew exactly where she was and exactly how to get home, although later she inexplicably couldn't remember where she'd gone and who she'd gone with and was thought by all to have gotten drunk and taken a taxi home and was grounded by her parents for a week, even though she was twenty, for being so stupid as to get blind drunk by herself on a nature walk in the middle of nowhere in the middle of the day. And everyone involved had this nagging feeling that they were forgetting something...

Seralina was confused. Confused and sitting on a cloud. Definitely a cloud. It was quite clearly, unmistakeably a cloud and that, down there, was most definitely the ground. Way down there. Way, *way* down there.

"Um." she said thoughtfully to the Universe in general.

"I *told* you, you shouldn't leave that down there!" an angry voice said, its owner materialising behind her left shoulder, making her jump "I bloody *told* you!"

"Look, *no-one* should have been able to find it!" a woman's voice replied, equally exasperated, appearing on her right "It takes nearly an hour of getting Lost for a mortal to find it!" It occurred to Seralina at this point that the word 'mortal' was not a good word to be around. It is a word after all, that implies you can die. In fact it doesn't just imply it; if you don't get the hint, it points it out forcefully and announces it to the whole room in a loud voice.

"You're going to be in big trouble, you are!" the man chided, shaking his finger "This sort of thing isn't supposed to happen anymore!" He was wearing black shorts and a short sleeved, pale blue shirt. He was also wearing a flat, black hat and most notably, winged sandals. He looked tall and gangly. He was possibly medium and gangly. It was hard to tell, because he was floating in mid-air. Or at least, he was trying to float in mid-air, but he had to keep shuffling about to keep from falling out of his sandals. They looked like they were at least one size too big for him, and his feet kept slipping about, meaning he had to keep shoving his feet into them periodically to stop them falling off. It made him look like he was trying to balance on two invisible poles. He was also wearing the ugliest socks Seralina had ever seen. They were lumpy and a filthy shade of grey.

"I don't have to take that from you, *letter monkey*." snapped the woman, causing him to cringe. A stark contrast to the lanky youth, the woman was tall, well proportioned and glamorous. She had long, thick, blonde hair. She wore a figure hugging, hot pink dress. It didn't have any sequins on it, but it looked like it should. She wore big gold bangles, two

4

on each wrist and ruby red lipstick. It looked like she'd never heard the phrase 'tone it down' in her life. The youth opened his mouth to retaliate, but couldn't think of anything and shut it again.

"You!" the woman tapped Seralina on the shoulder "You are now a goddess. Congratulations, blah, blah, blah." she waved a hand in the air and then indicated the boy, who was still sulking "This letter monkey here will look after you." She handed Seralina a blank, shiny card. "Here's your card. I'm sure you'll be going to see *her* first." The woman pulled a face. "Well, ciao." she finished with a shrug, turned, and vanished into thin air.

Seralina just gaped. There wasn't much else she could do.

"Well, now she's out of the way..." the youth pushed his black hair back out of his eyes and extended a hand "The name's Hermes. Or Mercury, actually. Take your pick. Just don't call me something stupid like Hercury or Mermes." he pulled a face "Or *letter monkey*. That was Idunn, by the way."

"Right, right." said Seralina dismissively "My name's Seralina. Run that by me again?" Hermes looked annoyed.

"I said don't call me-" he started.

"No, no. Not that bit. The other bit." she said.

"Er..." Hermes frowned "You still remember your own name, right? You just told it to me. I mean, I know in these sort of situations, people can get rather confused, sometimes they lose their whole memory even, but you just said-" he rambled. Seralina cut him off mid-babble;

"No. The *other* other bit." she replied firmly.

"Congratulations, you're a goddess?" Hermes said hopefully.

"Yeah, that bit." Seralina nodded.

"Oh. Well... that's it." Hermes shrugged.

5

"Oh." Seralina finished. There wasn't really much else to say.

"Right, well now that's cleared up, we'll have to go and see the boss." Hermes said, grabbing Seralina's wrist and pulling. The stunned Seralina allowed herself to be led through a thick mist over what appeared to be some more cloud. She wasn't sure how she was managing to walk on a cloud, but she decided not to think about it in the hope that the universe wouldn't either. They emerged out of the mist onto a rainbow, at which point she shut her eyes, because rainbows have even less substance than clouds on account of not really existing at all. After a while, there was a change in the atmosphere and Seralina dared to open an eye.

They were standing inside a huge corridor, made of something like marble, in front of some equally huge mahogany doors with more fretwork than was necessary or decent. The doors and indeed the corridor were all rather tall. It was like someone had taken the place and stretched it out upwards. One of the doors was half open. There were people everywhere. Quite a lot of them appeared to be drunk. Either that, or Seralina was drunk. She wasn't entirely sure.

"I'll just go in and tell her about you. Then I'll come and get you. Stay here." Hermes instructed. He flew rather erratically through the open door.

Seralina decided it was time to pinch herself. It hurt quite a lot. It didn't help that a bunch of men, singing loudly and badly, bumped into her as she did it.

"Sorry luv!" one of them said and waved a mug at her. Then they started off again and lurched down the corridor, leaning on one another for support and waving their beer in unison.

"And don't come back!" a woman's voice shouted from

beyond the doors "Stick to Valhalla from now on!" and then "Yes? What do you want?" There was a brief pause "*Really*? Haven't seen any of *that* in a while." Then the owner of the voice swept through the doors, with Hermes in tow. He bobbed along after her like he was on an invisible leash. Perhaps he was. Despite her confusion, Seralina couldn't help thinking that Hermes would probably look a lot better if he didn't keep appearing alongside such glamorous women. Although whilst Idunn's glamour was gaudy, this woman's glamour was not. She wasn't quite as tall as Idunn; she wore a simple white dress and wore her long hair curled and pinned. It was exactly the colour of sun-ripened wheat. Draped over her shoulders was some kind of cloak made of feathers, it was pale brown flecked with black and white. It wasn't very big, it was almost like a boa or a small shawl.

"Lady Freya, this is Seralina." Hermes waved in Seralina's direction. "She's new." he added helpfully.

"Right. A new girl, eh?" the woman addressed as Freya began "I know *just* what to do with *you*. I'm Freya by the way. I'm pretty much your boss for the time being, but don't let it bother you. I wouldn't." She smiled and waited for Seralina's response with her hands on her hips and her head tilted.

"Freya, the Viking goddess of Fertility?" asked Seralina cautiously "That Freya?" Freya pouted a little.

"Is that all anyone remembers of me these days?" she sighed "Oh well. A day in the sun must turn to dusk."

"So you really are then?" Seralina had finally found a rock to cling to after being swept away and wasn't letting go in a hurry "You're really a goddess and this is really Valhalla?"

"Well, no this isn't Valhalla, this is *my* hall, Sessrymnir. Valhalla is up the corridor, third on the left. Probably. Over there somewhere, anyway." she waved a hand in its general direction "Oh, and 'Viking' is just a rude word for pirate, so it's better to say 'Norse'." she thought for a moment "But yes, I really am a goddess. So are you. You *were* told weren't you?" She gave Hermes a hard look.

"Yes, I was. I think there must have been something funny in that vanilla-flavoured stuff or something." Seralina replied "This sort of thing doesn't happen. Especially not to me. Nothing *ever* happens to me."

"It used to happen all the time." Freya shrugged "Not always using Ambrosia, though. But now Idunn makes that, too. She's got the market cornered."

"That pink woman?   *She* made me a goddess?" Seralina frowned "*Why*?"

"Pink woman?" an amused look flitted across Freya's face "That's Idunn, all right.   But no, *you* made you a goddess. You drank the Ambrosia. It used to be Idunn's apples, but she makes it into canned drinks these days so you can carry it round with you without it going wrinkly. Funny thing really, they grant eternal youth but they go sour like nobody's business." Seralina finally panicked.

"But I don't *want* to be a goddess!" she protested.

"You *don't*? Don't humans want to be gods?" Freya asked, puzzled "I thought they were all for quests for eternal youth and so on?"

"Only if they're insane or completely self-absorbed!" Seralina explained desperately.

"You mean they aren't? I always thought they were both, to be honest." Freya shrugged "Oh. Well, there's nothing we can do about it now."

"Nothing?" Sera sagged.

"Nope.   Now let's get you some armour." Freya finished and led Seralina into Sessrymnir. Seralina looked around for Hermes to thank him for his help, because she

8

might have gone insane, but that was no excuse for being rude, however he seemed to have fluttered off elsewhere. She thought she heard him curse as the door closed, it sounded rather like he'd banged his elbow on something. Then again, she was now insane, so it was probably the start of all that 'voices in your head' business.

An hour or so later after rummaging through a surprisingly small and poky armoury, Seralina finally had some armour. She felt like she was wearing half the contents of a kitchen, including the sink. She looked at herself critically in the mirror.

"I look like I'm wearing a bunch of pan lids." she said "*Stylish* pan lids, I'll give you that, but still pan lids." Her armour was constructed of many circular bits of metal overlapping each other. Underneath all the armour somewhere was a simple, toga-like, white dress, made out of enough material for three, which made it quite heavy on its own. Seralina felt like she was wading everywhere through her own clothes. In addition to the pan lid armour, her forearms and shins were encased in worn, metal bracers. Someone had clearly decided that that was enough of that, because her shoes were thick leather sandals and her helmet was merely a circlet with a lot of feathers stuck on it. If someone wanted to chop off her feet or her head, that was fine as far as the armourer was concerned, as long as it looked good. Which, despite having pan lids in its ancestry, it did. Not beautiful, but good. Even though Seralina was fairly short, had boring hair and was nearly a stone heavier than she'd like. She was impressed. Now if only she could move without something going 'clank' and pinching her, being a goddess might not be so bad.

"Do I have to wear this all the time?" Seralina asked.

"No." Freya replied "In the evenings you wear different

armour. It's all thin and has a lot of gold on it and it's as much use in battle as a chocolate teapot."

"Right. Er..." Seralina began, worried "I'm not going to have to do much battling am I?" Seralina would try anything once. Provided she thought she'd have the chance to do it again if she wanted to.

"Well, valkyries generally pick up people who are dead, and they're not likely to feel like having a swing at you." Freya replied.

"What about everyone else?" Seralina asked.

"Well, I would imagine they'll be too busy fighting each other. Anyway, you shouldn't be seen by anyone unless you want them to." Freya replied "Unless you're caught by surprise or just aren't concentrating. It's a bugger when that happens." she added. Seralina frowned.

"How do I know where I'm going and stuff?" she asked.

"Well, I lead the valkyries out when there's a lot needs doing. But there's not much like that that we deal with these days." Freya replied "Mostly you'll be working evenings. Until we find you a permanent job."

Freya had explained while they were looking for armour that usually girls who became goddesses started off as valkyries because it was the Asgard equivalent of a barmaid-slash-taxi driver, and not many pantheons had spare places for ex-humans in any case. Anyone could get the hang of it with a bit of training, she'd said. The world had rather a lot of gods and goddesses right now, so until they could find something better to do with her, basically, she might as well be a valkyrie. Freya offered to go with her on her first few jobs until she got the hang of it.

It wasn't long before they were flying off to Seralina's first job. Freya had needed to look for a while before she found anything, but was insistent that Seralina should have done what she called 'real work' before she started the evening shift, whatever that meant.

The journey to Earth, or Midgard as Freya kept calling it, involved jumping off the end of a rainbow that jutted out from Asgard, which she suspected was where she'd just come from. Then there was a lot of rushing scenery until they got close to the intended destination. It was like bungee jumping without the cord or the extremely tall building.

Seralina was quite surprised how well she was taking it all. She was basically just getting on with it, one of the effective ways humans deal with things they don't like, the other being the famous ignoring-it-and-hoping-it-goes-away tactic, which wouldn't work in this situation because gods make themselves hard to ignore. Once they got to the general area though, they had to search by themselves. Freya had told Seralina that if they knew an actual battle was happening they just turned up early and hung around.

They ended up on a ship. As soon as they materialised, Sera tripped over a pile of rope and landed in a heap. As she was helped to her feet by Freya she saw they were in a narrow corridor above deck, lined on one side by the ship's railings. Life boats lined the corridor on one side as far as she could see. It looked to be some sort of huge cruise ship.

"This doesn't look like a battle." Seralina said, looking around nervously for any signs of sudden warfare "People aren't going to suddenly fall out with each other and get thrown overboard or something are they?" It looked safe enough. She was both relieved and concerned; relieved because she didn't want to have materialised in the middle of battle with people chopping other people's bits off and concerned because she didn't want people to *start* chopping each others' bits off in the middle of the ocean. She couldn't swim very well and it had never bothered her, but there was a difference between swimming in a pool or at the ocean's edge knowing you can stop anytime you like and being stuck in the middle of nowhere with several fathoms below you knowing you can't.

"We're just here for one person." Freya nodded towards the deck "He seems to be down there." She set off down the corridor.

"How do you know?" Seralina asked hurrying after Freya.

"You just *know*." Freya replied "It's part of being a goddess." Seralina, who currently felt as if she'd never known anything, ever, said;

"What if you *don't* know?"

"You wing it."

"*Wing* it? *Goddesses* wing it?" Seralina was shocked.

"It's practically in the job description." Freya said over her shoulder "If it goes all wrong, you just say 'I meant to do that' and no-one's going to argue with a goddess, are they?" She stopped suddenly. "There he is."

If there had been more than one person on the deck Seralina would have wondered who she meant. As it was, there was only one rather old man on a red and white striped deck chair, snoozing with a book over his face.

"It might just be me." Seralina began "But he doesn't *look* like a battle hardened warrior."

"Well, with battles being a lot more political these days and mostly involving nasty comments and embarrassing photographs there isn't much work around for us these days. That, and no-one believes in valkyries any more." Freya explained. She sighed. "*And* they think I'm just a fertility goddess." she added sadly.

"He doesn't look like he believes in valkyries either." Seralina paused and frowned "If you aren't a fertility goddess, what are you?"

"You can never tell what someone believes just by looking at them." Freya replied, flicking her hair over her shoulders "Besides, these days people don't necessarily *need* to believe in us. They just need to *want* to."

"Isn't that a bit... *wishy-washy?*" replied Seralina sourly. She'd grown up being told that just because you want doesn't mean you get. It seemed unfair. She *wanted* to believe she'd lost some weight since she'd become allergic to chocolate and stopped eating it. It didn't make it true.

"Well, we have to take work where we can find it these days." said Freya sadly.

"Hang on a minute." Seralina started again, puzzled "My knowledge of Viking- sorry, I mean Norse mythology isn't that great, but don't you have to die in battle to get taken to Valhalla by a valkyrie?" she hesitated and her puzzlement became concern "Someone isn't going to come and chop that poor, old man's head off, are they?"

"No, no." Freya reassured her "Nothing like that. He's going to die peacefully in his sleep."

"Oh. Well that's all right then." Seralina replied. Then her ears caught up with what her mouth had just said- "Wait, no it's not! Is he really going to die?" Freya gave her a pitying look;

"No-one knows anything about the Norse pantheon any more, do they?" she said sadly "That's what valkyries *do*. That's why we're here."

"But that's so sad..." Seralina started, trailing off. Freya just shrugged.

"You've got to die sometime." she said matter-of-factly "Unless you're immortal. Then you have to find something to do to keep yourself amused until the end of eternity. That's what causes most of the trouble."

"I see..." Seralina replied sadly. Then logic kicked in. It had a treacherous way of doing it when it would most make Seralina look like a cold-hearted cow. "But strictly speaking, he's not dying in battle, is he?" she added sceptically. Freya shrugged again. "Would you *rather* someone came and chopped his head off? We could probably arrange it."

"No!" Seralina replied quickly.

"Well there you are, then." Freya replied. "He *is* dying in battle anyway." she added "It's just not the conventional, run-at-your-enemy-and-scream battle we're famous for handling."

"Oh?" Seralina couldn't imagine what kind of battle the old man could be in, aside from a battle against old age, in which he seemed to be faring pretty well. He looked like a typical British tourist. He'd gotten slightly tanned, he was wearing a terrible combination of a yellow t-shirt and red shorts and he was wearing white socks with his sandals.

"I believe he's called Thomas Turner. It seems that he met up with an old school friend a few months ago and they got to talking about all the things they'd planned to do when they were young." Freya explained "And he got rather fired up and decided he was going to do all those things after all."

"I don't see how that's a battle." Sera replied, frowning.

"Ah yes, but then his friend said 'Not at our time of life, you won't' and he said 'Wanna bet?'. And so his friend got fired up too, and they're having a competition to see who can go the most places and do the most things. Apparently you get extra points if it's something particularly crazy." Freya finished.

"I see." Seralina replied, not bothering to ask how Freya knew all this "It's not an actual battle as such though, is it?" Freya merely shrugged.

"There are many kinds of battle." she answered vaguely.

The old man gave a snort and woke up.

"Who's there?" he demanded "Oh." his tone softened on seeing the two women "What are you ladies doing up 'ere?" He took in their unusual attire. "Are you part of the entertainment? They goin' to do an opera today? It never said anything about them doin' an opera." His eyes misted over in recollection "I've seen some wonderful operas, I have. Just wonderful." He waved at the pair of them "I saw one once, all about valkyries and Valhalla it was, and I thought to meself, 'that's how I'd like to go'."

'Ah.' thought Sera to herself. Freya had been right. You never could tell, just by looking.

"Carried off by beautiful women to go feasting and such." he continued, and made a face "Meals on Wheels I was having before I came on this holiday. Well, I say holiday. I'm in a fierce battle, I am!" he grinned "I bet my old mate Albert that I could do more stuff than 'im this year, and I reckon I'm winnin' too."

"Good for you!" Freya said and smiled at him.

"Damn right!" the old man continued, still grinning "We was talkin' about old times and we 'ad all these plans when we was kids, but they never came to nothin'. So I said we should do it, you're never too old sort of thing. And 'e said, 'Knock it off, you daft old codger!' but I wouldn't listen and anyway, he came round. I reckon we can die happy now, the both of us. You should 'ear what 'e's been up to!"

"I'm glad to hear that." Freya replied.

"Yep. I reckon I can die happy now... Best few months of my life, these last few months have been. Been all over. Tried all sorts." He smiled. "Best few months of my life." he repeated.

"Well, we have good news and bad news then, Mr. Turner." Freya began and then nudged Seralina. "Go on."

"Er... well..." Seralina began. She wasn't sure how you told someone they were dead. It wasn't something you would expect to have to do. She decided she may as well just be direct. "Well, I'm sorry to say that you are, in fact, dead."

"I am?" said Mr. Turner and looked around "Oh. So I am." It was then that Seralina noticed that there were *two* Mr. Turners in front of her. One, the Mr. Turner lying on the deckchair with a book still over his face, and the second, his remarkably solid ghost sat up talking to them. He looked so real she hadn't noticed. But now that she *had* noticed, he also seemed to be younger than the Mr. Turner on the deck chair. In fact, he seemed to be getting younger all the time. She also couldn't help thinking that some poor soul was going to get a nasty shock when they lifted up that book. "What's the good news?" asked Mr. Turner cautiously "Unless that *was* the good news?"

"The good news is that I am, in fact, a valkyrie." Seralina answered "And that you are invited to Valhalla."

"Well, blow me down!" Mr. Turner exclaimed "I reckon that takes the biscuit! Ol' Albert ain't been to Valhalla, I know that much!"

"Well, shall we be off?" Freya asked. Mr. Turner nodded.

"You know it's a shame though." he said, solemn all of a sudden.

"What is it, Mr. Turner?" said Sera, as kindly as she could.

"That bugger'll never know I won!" he shouted.

On the way back to Asgard, Mr. Turner talked to them at length about his family, his cruise and the things he'd done and seen, including the operas with valkyries in them. He was vaguely disappointed that they hadn't turned up on a white horse and that there was no singing, but other than that he was surprisingly happy. By the time they got there, he was a strapping young man with a mane of red hair. He strolled off to Valhalla humming to himself and grinning at anyone who came past. They grinned back. It looked like everyone in Valhalla was sharing the same private joke.

Somewhere, a gong banged. Three times. Seralina looked round in alarm.

"What's that?" she asked "It's not some sort of alarm, is it? We're not under attack or anything, are we?" Seralina had been trying to remember everything, or indeed *anything,* that she had ever learned about Viki- the Norse. But all she could remember was that battles were important and mentioned a lot. Battles and dying. Usually both together. It was their favourite pastime, or something.

"No." Freya replied "It's just time for the evening shift."

"Evening shift?" Seralina asked "What do we do in the evening?"

"Well, you know all the food and mead and so on for feasting in Valhalla?" said Freya.

"Yes?" replied Seralina, a little cautiously.

"Well it doesn't serve itself." Freya finished.

It turned out that there were two parts to being a valkyrie... well, three parts. The first part was collecting the dead. The second part was serving the fallen warriors - or delighted ex-pensioners - with platefuls of meat and gallons of alcohol. The collecting of the dead Seralina was more-or-less prepared to do. The serving of a hall full of drunken men and the occasional woman - "What with equal opportunities these days" as Freya had explained - was tolerable because basically she had to just ditch massive plates of food and

17

huge pitchers of mead and beer on the available space on the massive, long, tables that ran the full length of the hall and smile politely at any of the men who grinned at her and gave her a thumbs up. But she wasn't prepared to put up with the third part. It wasn't the sort of thing you could put up with.

In short, what it amounted to, was being a 'lady of the night', which might well involve working at night, but is not very ladylike at all. Needless to say, when Seralina found out she was less than pleased.

"I'm supposed to do *what*?" Seralina demanded of the valkyrie who'd dragged her out of Valhalla to stop her smashing an entire pitcher of beer over an einherjar's head.

"It's what valkyries *do*." shrugged the blonde-haired woman who'd pulled her away "Don't you know anything about Norse mythology?" Seralina was livid.

"Yes! But I didn't know that!" she yelled.

"If it's any consolation, you won't remember in the morning. It's part of the whole eternally virginal thing."

"The whole *what*?" Seralina said, exasperated. She hadn't signed up for this. In fact, she hadn't signed up for *anything*. "Look, can I talk to Freya about this?" The valkyrie shrugged.

"Knock yourself out." she said, and bustled off back into the hall.

Seralina stomped off down the hall and then realised she'd forgotten where Sessrymnir was. She wandered aimlessly along the corridors until she saw a sign.

'Sessrymnir Grand Re-Opening!' it said, then in smaller letters underneath it said 'A modern approach to the Norse Afterlife! Ask about our two year package!' There was an arrow. Seralina followed the signs until she saw Freya's hall. There was a huge billboard outside proclaiming more of the same. Underneath was a smaller sign that read 'We no longer serve beer. If you want beer, go to Valhalla. Vegetarian meals available on request.'

The doors to the hall were closed. Seralina knocked on them. Nothing happened. She tried to push one ajar, but it wouldn't budge. She leaned all her weight on it, but it didn't move even one millimetre.

"What's the deal with this stupid door?!" Seralina yelled, losing her temper and kicking it. Just then, it opened.

"Did you just kick my door?" Freya asked sternly.

"Yes." Seralina admitted, slightly ashamed "It wouldn't open." she explained "Also, I was mad."

"Sessrymnir is impregnable unless I, personally, open the doors." Freya explained proudly, swelling a little. Then she asked "You were mad?"

"Yes." said Seralina sharply, remembering why she'd come in the first place. "I was mad about... the other part of being a valkyrie. The bit that isn't picking up dead people or serving drinks."

"Hmm." Freya thought for a moment "I think you'll be perfect for my hall."

"What do you mean?" Seralina asked suspiciously "Is this something to do with those signs I saw on the way here?"

"That's right. Times have changed. I want to modernise my Sessrymnir. Anyone who wants to go and drink themselves silly with beer and sing badly all night is free to do so at Valhalla... but I'm turning my hall into something a little more modern." Freya threw open the doors behind her and waved a hand proudly at the inside of the hall. "Behold! Asgard's first Ginza bar!"

THE OTHER AFTERLIVES

The long, thick, wooden benches had been replaced by an area filled with little tables in their own booths with comfy looking, red plush seats. They were set into black, shiny stone. The tables were made of some kind of marble. There were little decorations on all the tables and the booths were hung with pretty materials. It all looked very classy and most of all, expensive. The rest of the hall seemed to have been made into something else...

"What's a Ginza bar?" asked Seralina.

"It's basically a Japanese, upmarket version of Valhalla." Freya replied "Only the customers aren't dead and it's not free."

"What?" Seralina was still confused.

"Look, it's like a little bar where men come and sit down and get served drinks by pretty girls. The girls sit down with them and talk to them and so on." Freya waved a finger "And no-one has to sleep with anyone." she paused for a moment "Unless they want to." she finished.

"What kind of goddess *are* you?" asked Seralina exasperated.

"I'm a fertility goddess, of course." Freya answered, smiling.

"You said you weren't!"

"No I didn't. I said I wasn't *just* a fertility goddess." Freya tossed her hair.

"So what else are you then?" Seralina put her hands on her hips. She didn't like being messed around. It happened too often and she was generally not too sure of the world as it was.

"I'm the Goddess of Sex." Freya answered, adopting a similar pose and tilting her head to one side "And War and Death. But those are just chores, really." she smiled as Seralina's jaw dropped "Happy now?" she waited a moment, to see if Sera would get her voice back, then sighed "Oh all right, Love, if you want to be a pansy about it."

"Oh. Er... well, that explains the whole valkyrie thing then." Seralina managed, going red. She rallied as best she could. "So, er... why a Ginza bar? And what did you do to the rest of the hall?" she asked, determined to change the subject.

"Like I said, a Ginza bar is like an upmarket, modern Valhalla." Freya answered "The rest of the hall has been made into a hotel. I thought I'd share our Afterlife with everyone else."

"Everyone else?" Seralina frowned "What everyone else?"

"Well, our einherjar can come and go as they please, but people in a different Afterlife would need to make a special trip... so I thought I'd make a hotel." Freya explained "You've got to move with the times. I've been thinking about it for a while."

"Wait, so there are other Afterlives apart from this one and you want to offer the people in them a-, a *holiday*?" Seralina asked, frowning a little.

"That's right." Freya nodded "For people who don't believe in reincarnation, the Afterlife can get a bit tedious. A change will be good for them." She smiled.

"I... see." Seralina could see Freya's point. She was

quite happy to stay at home and relax but she did get itchy feet occasionally. And they say a change is as good as a break. "It sounds like a good idea." she said at last.

"I'm glad you think so, " Freya replied with pride "especially since you're now one of my Ginza girls. Hmm..." Freya paced up and down a little, thinking about something. She glanced up at Seralina a few times and then finally gave her a long, hard look. "I think I'll stick with the golden armour. We've got an image to uphold after all " Freya paused "and another thing, I'm going to start calling you Sera." she announced "Seralina is far too long and it makes you sound like a pudding. Where is it *from*, anyway?" Seralina shrugged.

"My mother is a bit... eccentric. I think she just made it up, to be honest." Seralina stopped. She suddenly had a horrible feeling, like seeing the neighbour pull into the driveway and remembering you were supposed to feed their pet while they were away – but didn't. "My *mother!* My *friends!* Do they think I'm missing? Do they think I'm *dead*?" She panicked. She'd become used to living at university and basically doing what she liked, occasionally phoning people to let them know she wasn't dead or kidnapped. In her attempt to take in and adjust to her new life or afterlife - she wasn't sure what it was when she hadn't and couldn't die - she'd forgotten, as it were, to phone home. "What am I going to do?" she asked, chewing on a finger in desperation "What am I going to tell them?"

"Well in the old days, mortals knew about these things and they'd generally say good riddance or pine for a while at the loss of their loved one or whatever." Freya interrupted before Sera broke into hysterics "But these days it doesn't happen very often and people are too busy and modern to go around pining, so we generally arrange that everyone just thinks you're somewhere else."

"Oh..." Sera calmed down a little "So they're not upset or worried or anything?" she said "Well... that's all right then, I suppose. For now." Sera decided that she would see how her family was doing as soon as she could. She didn't know if valkyries got a day off or not, but she was going to find out. Most gods seemed to have too much time on their hands 'which was the problem' as Freya had put it, so she must be able to do what she wanted sometime. Or if not what she wanted, at least something she didn't *have* to do.

For a while Sera mainly worked in Freya's bar, setting up the place, serving customers with drinks and sitting down to talk to them. They were mostly einherjar, mainly the more recent ones, who wanted a bit of a change or were merely curious. But there were also quite a few gods and even goddesses who'd either had enough of Valhalla for the time being or didn't even have a Valhalla and were pleased to have the chance to visit a different Afterlife for once. She heard that Loki showed up to see what all the fuss was about whilst she'd been in the kitchen, but he'd made a scene, so Freya kicked him out. Hermes came in for a little while and hung around looking nervous; it looked like he was waiting to be noticed. Sera meant to thank him for his help, but by the time she was free, he'd vanished. After a few nights even Hera visited and talked to all the girls, curious about what it was like in Asgard and if they were treated well. Aphrodite and Eros were soon regulars, happy to have somewhere new to hang out, and flirted with practically everyone, but it added to the atmosphere and meant the girls had less work to do, so nobody minded.

During the day - that is, the day in Asgard - Sera's work was a lot less enjoyable. She didn't particularly like serving drinks, but she had plenty of people to talk to and was starting to make some friends, so she was feeling a little less lonely. But she wasn't happy with picking up the einherjar at all. Some of them were all right; some of them were just old men who'd died peacefully like Mr. Turner. But then there were cancer victims and other people who'd died of terrible illnesses and there were a few soldiers who were sad because lately all they'd wanted to do was go home and see their mother, or their girlfriend or their sick little brother... and then one day there was multiple pick up. It involved land-mines and people in bits and Seralina was sick three times and it was then she decided she really couldn't do this any more.

"I'm sorry, but I just can't do it." she confessed to Freya before the evening shift began "I've tried to be philosophical about it but I just can't do it any more. It's too sad... I'm really sorry. You've been very kind to me and-"

"That's all right." Freya interrupted, waving her into silence "It was only temporary. Most of the girls are stuck for something to do during the day, anyway." Freya thought for a moment "Would you do me a favour and stick around for a little while? I won't ask you to pick up einherjar but there are some errands I want you to run. And most of the valkyries are from the old days... well, they want to stick to what they know, so I'm short on staff." Sera nodded. It wasn't serving drinks she minded.

The next day Sera waited outside Sessrymnir for Freya. Hermes showed up before Freya did and looked a little puzzled to see her there. He looked a little better than he had the last time she'd seen him, but not much. The lack of Idunn's presence seemed to have improved his general aura; he didn't look so much like he expected to be hit at any moment. After a few minutes of awkward silence he finally said;

"You're the girl from the other day, aren't you?" he thought for a moment "Semolina, was it?"

"Sera." corrected Sera "Seralina." Hermes spluttered.

"I'm so sorry! I've got so many names to remember, what with all the einherjar, I just-"

"It's fine." Sera reassured him quickly, afraid he would bite his tongue or something "Just call me Sera." There was some more awkward silence. Finally, Sera had to ask. It had been nagging her since she'd met Hermes on her first day. "Why are you dressed like a postman?" she asked. She'd left out 'badly-dressed' because she'd been brought up to be tactful.

"Oh? Well, I suppose it's because I am." he replied, shrugging "I'm delivering some scrolls and things for Freya today."

"But you're a god aren't you?" Sera asked trying to think of a nice way to ask why he didn't look better "Can't you look however you want? Couldn't you look more... god-like?"

"You have to move with the times." Hermes replied "I mean, you work in Freya's new Ginger bar, don't you?"

"Ginza." Sera corrected "Yes, but I only just got here. Besides, I seem to have gone backwards. I usually wear jeans and a T-shirt. There's not much call for massive white dresses and armour down on Earth." 'But there *should* be.' she thought privately 'That'd show those bean-pole women.'

"Oh, I see." Hermes went into a thoughtful silence. After a while he asked "Are you waiting for Freya? Shouldn't you be out collecting dead people or whatever it is valkyries do these days?"

"Until now, yes. Freya told me she had some errands for me to do. I've given up collecting einherjar. It bothers me."

"Odd. Never heard of a part-time valkyrie before. But I suppose I'm not from this pantheon, anyway."

"Oh yeah. You're..." Sera paused, rapidly rifling through her mythological knowledge, such as it was "Greek, aren't you?" she asked "Why do you hang around Asgard so much?"

"Greek *and* Roman." Hermes answered with a touch of pride. Then he shrugged "I just wanted a change from Mount Olympus, that's all. Although there are *some* people here I could do without-" he started.

Just then Freya came through the doors with an armful of scrolls and papers.

"Right!" she said dumping them on the floor "Glad to see you're both here! I want you to deliver these posters and things to the other Afterlives. Don't worry about Mount Olympus, I gave Hera a bunch of posters when she came in the other day." she added, speaking directly to Hermes "And don't bother about any of the shut-ins, they won't be interested anyway."

"Right." said Hermes.

"Shut-ins?" asked Sera.

"Oh, you know. They don't like to admit there's any other Afterlife except theirs. There's a few of them. I mean, it's to be expected really." Freya replied, rifling through the scrolls and pausing to count under her breath.

"It is?"

"Of course. You'll never get anyone to follow you if you just say 'well, it's your choice really, there's plenty of gods to go around', will you? Although some people do manage to mix religions and get away with it. But they're generally the ones where pretty much everything is a god and you don't have to sacrifice *anything*." Freya sighed "There's no proper religions around these days if you ask me, I mean what's the point of sitting in some building and singing all solemnly? It's not a proper religion if you don't even have to sacrifice a chicken or two, if you want my opinion." She sighed again. "That's modern life for you, I suppose. No-one wants to die in a big ol' battle anymore and end up drinking themselves silly for the rest of eternity." she paused and thought about this "Which is good news for me!" she added, brightening up "Get going delivering these posters, you two."

"Oh, are we going together?" asked Sera, surprised.

"Yes." replied Freya "I think you should get out and see the other Afterlives to help you decide what you want to do. But you'll get lost without help from Hermes." She paused briefly "Plus it's his job." she added.

While they were walking over the rainbow bridge, Sera admiring the scenery, something suddenly occurred to her.

"If we're going to a different Afterlife, why are we going to Earth?" she asked Hermes, who was fluttering erratically alongside her "And do you have to fly everywhere on those sandals?"

"Does it bother you?" Hermes asked "I can walk, if you like."

"No, it just looks awkward." she shrugged "I don't mind either way, although I'm not used to people fluttering about near my head."

"I suppose I should walk. They're not very useful unless you fly straight and fast." he admitted "I usually end up bumping my elbows on walls and things, to be honest."

"So why are we going to Earth?" Sera asked again.

"Well, you can only get from Asgard to Midgard by crossing Bifrost. And you need to get to Earth to get to different Afterlives." Hermes explained "It's a little inconvenient, but it's better than going through any of the other eight worlds. Earth is sort of... in the middle of everything. You can get *anywhere* from Earth."

Their first port of call was the Egyptian Afterlife. It looked a lot like Sera imagined Egypt really looked like. Which means it looked a lot better and a lot more like Egypt is supposed to look, rather than how it actually looks. There were fields bursting with high yielding crops everywhere, a beautiful, sparkling, clear river and several huge palaces visible in the background. There were people working in the fields all over the place.

As they approached some of the workers to ask where they could find Osiris or Isis, Sera realised that most of the workers were in fact little, clay people. She pointed to them;

"What are those?" she whispered.

"Ushebti." Hermes whispered back "They're little clay dolls that are used as servants."

"Excuse me..." she waved at one to get its attention. The ushebti looked up and trotted over to them. "Excuse me-" Sera asked again "Where can we find Osiris or Isis?" The ushebti stared blankly at them for a moment then suddenly ran over to a human worker taking a break on the edge of the field. It made some complicated motions and scratched something on the ground. The worker nodded. The ushebti ran back over to Hermes and Sera and scratched some hieroglyphs on the ground. "Er, right." acknowledged Sera, who had no idea what it had written "Shall we go then?" The ushebti nodded and pointed in the direction of one of the palaces. Then it made motions to follow it.

It seemed Hermes even had trouble when he was walking. He kept having to stop occasionally and retrieve whichever sandal had flown off his foot and put it back on. Sera wondered briefly why he didn't just get a pair that fitted.

They followed the ushebti through fields and fields of perfect crops. There were little irrigation channels everywhere, making the land look like a patchwork quilt. There were lots of houses around the palaces, as if they all had their own private oases of towns in the sea of fields. The ushebti seemed to be leading them towards the nearest and biggest palace. It was huge and covered in all kinds of decorative inscriptions.

"How come this Afterlife looks just like Egypt?" Sera asked Hermes as they entered the town in front of the biggest palace. There were people everywhere, buying food, selling jewellery and generally going about their daily lives.

"Well, the Ancient Egyptians thought life was pretty good, really." Hermes explained "So they figured the Afterlife would be pretty much the same, only with better weather-" he pointed at the little figure hurrying along in front of them "-and the ushebti to help them with chores or whatever. But mostly they do it themselves, because work is a pleasure here. As long as you were good, that is. And passed a lot of trials."

"What if you were bad?" Sera asked.

"Your heart got eaten by a monster." Hermes replied.

"I'm glad I'm good." Sera said relieved, then she hesitated "At least, I think I am. How do they tell?"

"They weigh your heart against a feather." Hermes replied.

"I think a lump of meat is going to be heavier than a feather any day of the week." Sera retorted.

"Maybe it's a metaphor for the wickedness of mankind?" Hermes shrugged.

"Are gods allowed to talk like that? Anyway *they* all seem to have got here OK." Sera indicated the bustling streets full of people.

"Actually in the old days they believed everyone went to a sort of purgatory, except for Pharaohs."

"That hardly seems fair." Sera scoffed.

"As I understand it, life is unfair. I suppose it didn't occur to them to think the afterlife would be any different. But that's probably why they started believing something else." Hermes shrugged again "I know I would."

When they got to the palace the ushebti rapped on the doors which made a surprisingly loud booming noise. The doors were opened by two more ushebti, twice the size of the ones they had seen working in the fields, although they were still only half the size of a grown man. The little ushebti wrote something in the dust and the big ushebti nodded. They motioned for Hermes and Sera to come in.

They were led straight up several staircases that gradually took them to the top floor of the palace, although they were clearly used as the main staircases to access all the floors. The palace was hung with many splendid tapestries and other expensive-looking materials and there was a lot of gold.

Finally they came to Osiris' throne room. Osiris rose to greet them and clapped his hands. Human serving girls in pretty costumes immediately led them to some cushions to sit down and offered them huge plates of food.

"Welcome, guests!" Osiris announced happily "Relax a while and tell me your business. Dancers, if you please?" he nodded to some of the servants in the corner. A few of them began to play wind instruments and beat drums. The rest of the servants began an intricate dance involving a lot of banging sticks and twirling swords. The two watched for a while, wondering how the dancers managed not to cut their own arms off, while Osiris told them how pleased he was to have guests.

"Well, we came to deliver these posters, er... Sire?" explained Sera a little uncertainly. She wasn't entirely sure how you addressed a god. Hermes was like a, well, like a postman, and Freya was the 'Mama' of Sessrymnir's Ginza bar, but Osiris looked and acted like a king. She'd never met a king before. They're not the sort of person you run into every day. He was dressed in stereotypical Ancient Egyptian garb... a white robe, as much gold as he could wear without falling over, a huge crown-type hat... He was also green. That wasn't typical as far as she knew. She wondered if she should ask him about it, but thought it safer to ask Hermes later, so as not to offend.

Osiris read the posters with interest.

"Marvellous!" he exclaimed "What a splendid idea!" He rubbed his chin and read one of the scrolls, nodding occasionally. "I think I shall have to pay your bar a visit sometime. I think it might be a good idea if we thought about this sort of thing, too. Perhaps I shall arrange a meeting with Lady Freya... Would you be so good as to deliver to her a message?"

"Of course, Your Majesty." replied Hermes.

"Very good." Osiris nodded "I shall have it ready presently. In the meantime, please enjoy yourselves."

And enjoy themselves they did. The food was different to the food in Valhalla or Sessrymnir, even with its new vegetarian options. Seralina, impressed with the dancers, asked some of them to show her how they twirled the swords round without hurting themselves and had a go, almost taking Hermes' ear off when she accidentally let go of the sword in mid-twirl and it went spinning past his head.

"You're never to even look at a sword again if you're anywhere near me, understand?" Hermes complained, as they made their way back to Earth "I could have lost my ear! I'm a god, you know. That sort of thing gets about. People would start telling the tale of how I lost my ear after some clumsy girl attempted a bloody silly sword dance and messed it up. Only they'd probably make it more exciting and say I set you some terrible task or that we slept together or I cheated on you. And then my ear would float down a river and turn into the God of Moonbeams or something."

"Would it start some terrible cult where you get your ear cut off as part of the initiation ceremony?" Sera giggled.

"Probably." Hermes replied "Mortals are daft enough for anything."

"You've got that right." replied Sera, a little gloomily. "They're daft enough to drink things when they don't even know what they are, even though there's a perfectly clear warning label..." she muttered, to herself.

Sera was a little quieter for the rest of the trip. They went to several other Afterlives, even some Sera had never even heard of. But they had a long way to walk and it gave her too much time to think.

"What am I doing here?" she said suddenly, on their way out of the last head god's chamber. It was a vast Oriental-style house and the god there had seemed to be Chinese, but aside from his beautiful garden, he didn't seem to have a kingdom as such. A bizarre collection of animals appeared to live in there. A horse rambled round a corner and stopped to watch them and there was a rat gnawing at something by the gate, but it fled as they approached.

"We're delivering posters." Hermes replied, puzzled "This is the last bundle, I think. I don't know where it's for though, we've been everywhere we can go..."

"No, I mean... what's the point in me being here?" Sera said, staring into the distance "Why did I drink that stuff and end up here?"

"Oh." Hermes sighed "The eternal mortal question."

"Well?" Sera demanded "You're a god, aren't you?

Can't you answer me?"

"Well, not really..." Hermes replied, a little awkwardly. Gods don't like to admit they don't know the answer. "You're not one of my followers, after all." he scratched his nose "Anyway, you're a goddess now. *You* can decide why you're here. *And* other people, at that." he added "That's kind of the point."

"I can?" said Sera uncertainly. She'd never really thought about it before. A short time ago, she had been a Graphic Design student at university. She'd just gone to university and done a course in art because she was good at it and going to university was what you did. It wasn't really because she'd wanted to. It had taken away the fun of it all, really. She used to draw all the time before she'd started doing art at college. These days she barely picked up a pencil outside of class. And she couldn't draw what she wanted *in* class. She didn't see how writing an essay on Picasso and what he was trying to say would help her draw comics, either. In the old days, she just drew what she wanted. She hadn't been trying to 'say' anything. She'd thought about how funny it would be if she became famous, to walk into an art class where the teacher was insisting that the students look deeply into one of her pictures, of some girls eating ice cream or something, and tell them they were talking a load of old tosh and she just drew it because she wanted to draw something pretty.

"Of course you can. Just don't get too uppity and decide you want to rule over all of creation. Odin and Zeus and the others take a rather dim view of that sort of thing."

"But aren't *they* the rulers of creation or whatever? Not that I want to be one."

"Exactly. That's why they don't like other people doing it." Hermes was quiet for a while. Then he asked "What *do*

33

you want to do anyway?"

"I don't know."

"You *don't know?*"

"Well, no... I mean, I suppose I'd like to go home and just be normal, but that's not going to happen now. But even if I did, I still wouldn't know what I want."

"Well, the first thing you need to do is figure that out then." Hermes replied thoughtfully "Or it's going to be one hell of a boring eternity."

"Well, what do *you* want?" Sera asked.

"Me?" Hermes blinked "I suppose I want some respect. And a better job. Everyone else on Mount Olympus gets to just lounge around and do what they like whereas I'm just a *letter monkey.*" he spat the last two words.

"Well, why can't you just lounge around and do what you like?"

"Well, I'm responsible for communication. So that's what I do. Delivering and stuff. It's not much fun, really. Not like those buggers who are God of Wine or Music or something. Even being a God of Death might be more fun."

"It wouldn't." said Sera darkly "Trust me." Hermes shrugged.

"At least I'd get to meet new people." he replied.

"Yeah. In bits."

"Whatever." Hermes shrugged again "Oh yeah... Where are these last posters going to?" Seralina looked at the bundle in her hand. She'd forgotten she was even carrying it. Unlike the other posters, this one was tied with red string and had a note attached... Sera read it out;

"'This is a bit naughty, but could you post these around Midgard? Thanks! Freya.'" She looked sideways at Hermes. "Can we?" she asked doubtfully.

"I think it's a good idea." Hermes nodded "We can't get

into some of the other Afterlives, but their deities might be hanging around on Earth or something. It can't hurt."

The two of them put up the posters and scrolls in several locations on Earth. They had to keep going back and to over the rainbow bridge though, or else they'd have to walk miles and miles. Or even worse, they'd have to take public transport.

The posters were in a sort of universal spirit language that appeared as whatever the reader's mother tongue was, but also as itself at the same time, which made it terrible to read and made the reader think they'd forgotten their glasses, even if they didn't wear any. It was the same writing as on the cans of 'Idunn's finest'. Sera stared at the last poster with remorse.

'If the damn writing was easier to read, I might not have drunk the damn stuff.' she thought to herself. She wondered how Meena was getting on. She ought to be starting her third year of university soon. It annoyed Sera that she'd done all that work - second year had nearly killed her - but wasn't going to graduate. She suspected that being a goddess was somehow better than having a degree, but that wasn't the point. In fact, she realised, that was what she had wanted. Her degree and a job she liked. Then she'd probably have wanted something else, but first things first.

She decided to check on her family. She asked Hermes about how to do it and then sent him home. He offered to go with her, in case she got lost, but she wanted to go alone. She wasn't sure how she would react, and wouldn't be able to stand it if she suddenly burst into tears. She didn't like to cry in front of other people.

As it turned out, her family were fine and thought she was back-packing around Italy somewhere with terrible mobile phone reception and couldn't contact them. Apparently she'd decided to take a year out and had gone on a journey around the world to find herself. When she got to her house her parents were having a lengthy discussion about why she hadn't looked in the obvious place, which was down, and kept saying things like 'well, she doesn't get it from *me*'. They didn't seem angry, just rather bewildered. She didn't blame them. She'd never been the type to go and find herself. She hadn't known she was lost. That, and she was simply too lazy.

She umm-ed and ah-ed over it for a while, and finally decided to phone her parents. Waltzing into the house and announcing that she was now a goddess was out of the question and her mobile phone seemed to have disintegrated on the way to Valhalla, so she had to find a payphone. She wondered briefly why gods hadn't invented mobile phones yet and realised that that was what Hermes was for. She fumbled around for some money, remembered she was a valkyrie and didn't have any, and then picked up the receiver and glared at the phone until it decided she had some credit. Shocked that it had worked, she rather clumsily dialled her home phone number and waited nervously.

"Hello?" It was her dad's voice.

"H-hello? Dad?" Sera stuttered.

"Sera!" came the surprised reply "I thought you wouldn't be able to phone us for weeks! How is Italy? Are you having fun?"

"I found a payphone. It's er, great. I'm working in a bar at the moment. It's OK, but I want a better job. I've been, um, delivering posters for the owner today."

"That sounds interesting. Have you had any pizza?" he asked.

"Pizza?" asked Sera bemusedly, before remembering

that she was supposed to be in Italy "Oh yeah. Lots. More pizza than you can shake a stick at."

"Don't eat too much, else you'll not fit into your jeans." he chided "You're already having trouble. You'll never get a boyfriend like that, you know."

"Dad!" shouted Sera, her worries evaporating in a cloud of rage. She couldn't believe how insensitive her dad was sometimes. And she didn't even *want* a boyfriend. Well... she didn't want one at the moment, anyway. So she told herself. It was just one more thing in the sea of things that she wasn't sure she wanted or not.

"What?" Sera's father asked innocently "Shall I put your mother on?"

Sera talked with her mother for a little while. She wanted to know if Sera was eating enough, had she made any new friends and all the other usual questions mothers ask that you aren't going to answer 'no' to unless you're on the brink of suicide.

She was quite impressed at whoever was responsible for the set up, though. She had been worried that her parents would think she was dead, but they basically believed her to have gotten a job in another country, which was practically true. It just wasn't a conventional job or a conventional country.

When she was satisfied that her parents were okay and weren't more worried than any parent whose children have gone rambling across the world with no mobile phone reception, she headed to the library. She wanted to read up on some mythology just in case she was in for any other nasty surprises.

Sera spent an instructive few hours learning that gods, whilst pretending to be all high and mighty, mostly went around acting completely off the rails and doing whatever they darn well pleased. It seemed to Sera that gods were in fact very much like humans... they were vain, arrogant, kind, generous, prideful, loving, cunning and artful, sometimes all at the same time. Gods got away with doing what humans wanted to do but couldn't, on account of gods forbidding them to.   It seemed that what gods were most, was hypocritical. And what they mostly seemed to do for humans was cause them problems by having arguments that resulted in mountains being split in two or doing stupid things like trying to commit suicide and flooding the Earth in the process.   Some of them apparently aided in creating the human race, or at least some of it, but then they didn't really do much about it. Mostly what gods did was to argue with each other or sleep around. Or both. Sera was surprised to learn that Hermes was apparently an athletic god, patron of some arts, travelling, herdsmen and whole host of other things and had done most of the things that gods were good at doing - i.e.: sinning - and then some, some of which he did right after being born. And then had the cheek to say he couldn't have, on account of just being born, which made him a liar as well. Sera made a mental note and decided to ask him about it when she got back. She was also concerned about Ragnarok, which she'd thought was the end of the world. It turned out it was the end of the gods mostly and was a great, sudden battle resulting in the death of most of the Norse pantheon. It didn't sound like fun at all and when she got back to Sessrymnir she asked Freya about it.

"Ragnarok?" said Freya, raising an eyebrow. She paused to smile and wave goodbye at the last few customers to totter out the door. "Why do you want to know about that? It doesn't concern you, because you aren't Norse."

"Well, it's apparently happened already, according to some theories. Something about all the gods getting killed in a big epic battle and there being about three left. It sounds bad." Sera explained.

"Yes. It *did* happen already, actually. Happened... oh, about... I don't know, a couple of hundred years ago? Something like that." Freya shrugged "Is it a problem?"

"Well, not really. But...well, why isn't everyone dead then?" Sera asked matter-of-factly. She'd decided it was better to just be straight with gods from now on, in case they got the wrong idea. And to avoid sarcasm. Definitely to avoid sarcasm. She'd been surprised to learn that not many languages actually had sarcasm, so she wasn't risking it. Unlike with humans, pretty much all gods and goddesses - and giants and dwarves and other Afterlife residents - had at their disposal the celestial equivalent of concrete shoes and a deep river.

"Do you remember that thing a lot of you mortals were worried about a while ago?" Freya paused, and made a circling motion in the air with her finger, trying to remember what is was "Something to do with a calendar. It hit 2000 and there was some big problem or other with that."

"Y2K?" Sera answered and looked a bit bemused "When there was a problem with the counters on computers or something?"

"Yes, that's the one." Freya nodded "People thought planes were going to be falling out of the sky and people were going to lose all their money and Midgard was going to explode and all kinds of crazy things."

"Yeah?"

"And all that happened was that there were a few glitches and some people had built themselves nuclear bunkers for nothing?"

"Yeah?"

"Well it was a bit like that." Freya finished.

"I see." Sera stared into the middle distance for a while "Freya? If you don't mind me asking, what do *you* want the most?" Freya looked a little taken aback and then her expression became sad. Sera hadn't yet seen her look sad. She'd been all shades of anger through ticked off to bloody furious at various customers from Valhalla who'd gotten the wrong idea and one particularly mistaken gentleman had had to be shown the error of his ways by the medium of being hit in the face with a vase of flowers. She'd been happy and merry and joyful and also drunk, but she hadn't been sad.

"I want my husband back." she said quietly. Sera bit her lip. The gods she'd asked in the bar had said things like 'Right now, more wine!' and 'For my wife to stop reminding me about that bloody affair I had with a water nymph nine-hundred bloody years ago'.

"I'm sorry." Sera managed.

"What?" said Freya, coming back from whatever memories she'd been staring at "Oh, don't worry about it. It's not like it's your fault. Why do you ask?" she added, her tone suddenly sharp.

"I just don't know what to do." Sera replied "So I'm asking everyone."

"Well, you can do whatever you want." Freya replied, relaxing again "Do you want a husband?" she asked, brightening up "I bet I can find you one."

"No thanks." replied Sera politely. If there was one thing she hated, it was people trying to find her a boyfriend. It made her feel like she was being criticised for not having one.

"Suit yourself." Freya shrugged. Something gleamed amongst the feathers of her cloak.

"That's pretty." Sera brushed some of the feathers out the way so she could see it better "What is it?"

"Thank you." Freya smiled "It's the Brisingamen." Freya was wearing a gold and black choker with a spectacular decoration on it. It was vaguely in the shape of a butterfly; it was made of gold and jewels, blended in such a way that it looked like imprisoned fire. The colours shifted and gleamed at even the tiniest movement.

"It's gorgeous." Sera said admiringly "Where did you get it? Did you make it?"

"No. I got it off some dwarves." Freya answered.

"Was it expensive?" Sera asked. There was a thoughtful pause.

"That depends on your definition of 'expensive'." said Freya carefully.

"......you slept with someone, didn't you?" Sera asked accusingly. Sera had spent several hours in that library and had regrettably learned that the most common currency amongst gods, or at least goddesses, was sex.

"Four people, actually." Freya answered and shrugged "But the expensive bit was getting into trouble about it afterwards. Stupid Loki." she grumbled "I'll get him back, one day. Mind you, I did throw him out quite spectacularly the other night."

"*You* got into trouble?" Sera exclaimed, amazed "Whoever with?"

"Odin." Freya shrugged again "He was only mad because he fancied me himself." she pulled a face "He had that little creep Loki steal it and said I could only have it back if I took on the responsibilities of War and Death as a punishment."

"So did you?"

"Well I couldn't *un*-sleep with four dwarfs, could I?" Freya complained "That might be worth remembering, by the way." she added.

"Not to sleep with people for jewellery?" Sera raised an eyebrow.

"No, not to get *caught*." Freya replied, waving her finger.

"By the way-" Sera said, suddenly remembering something "That's your falcon skin coat, isn't it?" Sera indicated the mass of brown feathers draped around Freya's shoulders.

"It is." Freya confirmed "You've been reading up, I see." She sounded impressed.

"Could I borrow it?" Sera asked, a little tentatively "Just for a bit?"

"I don't see why not." Freya replied. She unhooked the cloak and handed it over. "By the way Sera... you asked me what I wanted, but...what do *you* want?"

"Like I said, I don't know." Sera shrugged "I'm going to find out." As Sera reached the door she hesitated.

"Something wrong?" Freya asked.

"Er..." Sera hesitated "Does being turned into a falcon hurt?"

LEARNING TO FLY

Freya had said that Sera should take the next morning off, seeing as she had something important to do. Sera had tried to say that it wasn't all that important really and she could go tomorrow, but Freya wouldn't hear of it. Sera made her way to Bifrost with mixed feelings. So far, the only thing goddess-like she'd done was to bully the payphone into pretending she had credit, which was practically a mortal thing anyway; she'd managed it a few times in high school when the payphone had gone funny and thought two pence coins were twenty pence coins.

Sera stood at the top of Bifrost and thought. If she hung on to her mortality, would she be able to become a mortal again? What would happen if she did? What if she missed Freya and the others and could never go back?

'No.' she thought to herself 'There must be something I can do here. Something good. There must be *something* I want. I just don't know what it is yet.' As she stood there thinking, someone silently came up behind her.

"Oh, it's just you, Miss." came a deep voice "I could hear someone thinking and I thought it might be an intruder." he sounded a little disappointed. Sera jumped.

"Oh! I didn't see you there!" she explained, trying not to blush. She always felt so stupid when people managed to sneak up on her.

"Is there something wrong, Miss Valkyrie?" he asked,

concerned "You've been up here thinking a long time."

"No." Sera tried to remember all the things she'd read in the library "You're... Heimdall, aren't you?" she asked cautiously. Of course, she'd seen him on the bridge before, but never stopped for a conversation.

"That's right Miss." Heimdall nodded "I guard the rainbow bridge, Miss." he added, in case she needed extra information. He was very tall, well built and, there was no other way to put it, very beautiful. He was like a romantic painting brought to life. His hair was so blonde it was almost white, and he himself was very pale, like a porcelain doll. He almost shone. White and gold was definitely his colour scheme. He was wearing a white tunic, with a large leather belt and long, furry-looking brown boots. The belt was adorned with a gold decoration and gold filigree, similar to the doors of Sessrymnir. It also had a huge horn hanging from it. Similar to Osiris, he looked like he was wearing as much gold as he could manage whilst still being able to move. A lot of it was actually white gold, Sera noticed, which was a lot better in her opinion because it looked less glaring, even if it still wouldn't stop a sword. Now she was watching him as he spoke, she realised his teeth were also made of white gold. She found herself wondering how on Earth he kept them so clean and what dental floss would do to them.

"-ou thinking about?" Sera suddenly realised she'd been staring and hadn't been paying attention.

"I'm sorry?" she said.

"I said what were you thinking about for so long, Miss?" he repeated politely.

"I was thinking about my family on Ear- I mean, Midgard. I don't know whether I want to find a way to get back there, or if I want to try and make a new life for myself here." she explained.

44

"I know what you mean." Heimdall replied sympathetically "I'd like to go and see my mothers and my grandfather sometime."

"Why don't you?" asked Sera and then mentally backtracked "You have two mothers?" she asked.

"I have nine." replied Heimdall proudly "They live in the sea down on Midgard. Off the coast of Norway. It's lovely down there in the summer." He sighed. "But I have to guard the rainbow bridge. Or else the giants will invade Asgard."

"I see." Sera nodded sympathetically "Do you miss your mothers?"

"A little." Heimdall replied "I used to be able to go and see them more often... but since Ragnarok, well... there are other people wanting to invade Asgard besides the giants."

"Heimdall... what do *you* want the most?" Sera asked.

"Me?" Heimdall thought carefully for while "I think... I'd like a day off once in a while. And a really big, soft, cushy bed." Sera gave him an odd look.

"That's really all you want?" she asked, which surprised her as well as Heimdall. Surely knowing what you wanted was better than not knowing, especially if it was something so simple.

"Well, just because I don't need to sleep a lot doesn't mean I don't *want* to." he said plaintively "Would a lie in some mornings really be too much to ask?" he carried on "I mean, there's more than one god responsible for death and war and birth and so on, but there's only me to guard the rainbow bridge. And if I stop guarding it for just one day, we'll all get invaded and it'll be all *my* fault. I don't call that fair, do you?" he complained. Sera shook her head. She felt compelled to say something else, so she said;

"I'll ask Freya if we can do something about that."

Heimdall brightened up considerably.

"Would you?" he said enthusiastically "That'd be champion. I'm sure Miss Freya would try to do something about it for me." he smiled "I got her favourite necklace back, you know. I duelled Loki for it. Kicked his arse, too." he added proudly.

As Heimdall strolled back to his proper post, Sera made a mental note to stop asking what gods wanted in case they got the wrong idea. But she couldn't help wanting to help Heimdall. He put her in mind of a big puppy, faithfully waiting by its master's gate and wagging its tail hopefully when they walked past, wanting a pat on the head. It would probably be quite a large and deceptively innocent puppy, with a lot of gold armour on, though. She wanted to help Freya too of course, but she didn't know anything about husbands and it probably wasn't her business to meddle. A nice bed and a day off once in a while didn't seem too hard though. Sera decided to work on it when she had the chance.

'Maybe I could be some kind of Goddess of Happiness.' she thought vaguely as she put on the cloak. Then she realised she didn't know how to use it. She wrapped the cloak around her as tightly as she could manage. Nothing.

"Abraca-falcon!" she shouted, and then felt like an idiot. Still nothing. She got the feeling that she should just pose dramatically and it should just go 'whoosh!' and *work*. She looked around surreptitiously and then posed dramatically. No such luck. Sera sighed and closed her eyes. Maybe she had to *think* falcon. Sera concentrated and tried to think about being a falcon.

Open skies, the land rising and falling below... carried by updraughts, feeling the pull of gravity and defying it... swooping, racing other birds... the rushing wind-

Sera hit her face on the floor. She struggled to get up and realised she was having so much trouble because wings aren't designed for that. She managed to get upright after a few false starts and flapped her wings experimentally.

She fell over again. Backwards.

Heimdall heard the noise and came to help her up. She tried flapping her wings again, a little more carefully this time. She tried to fly a short distance but messed up the take-off. Heimdall helped her up again and then did a surprising thing. He turned into a falcon himself. He did a few take-offs, going only a very short distance and then he dived right off the edge of the rainbow bridge and swooped about under it. Then he came in to land, flapping his wings to slow himself down so he didn't crash. He gave her a nod that said 'now you try'. Sera imitated Heimdall, launching herself off the ground and trying to take short flights across the bridge. She was clumsy, but she managed it. When she'd gotten relatively good at it, she'd headed for the edge of the bridge. She peered cautiously over the edge and made sure she wasn't going to dive head first into anything. She wasn't sure what there would be at this height, but she wasn't taking any chances. In an Afterlife, *anything* could be *anywhere*. Then she leapt.

People say that baby birds learn to fly when they fall from the nest. That shows how much they know, because actually they spend weeks exercising their wings by flapping like crazy on the edge of the nest and by hopping from branch to branch and have as much chance of learning to fly by falling as they do to learn tap dancing. Baby birds that do fall from nests are usually eaten by cats or in some fortunate circumstances, get rescued by humans who get pecked for their trouble. Even the careful ones can launch themselves perfectly, only to smack into something after five feet or so.

So it was lucky for Sera that she was so high up. It started off as a would-be elegant dive that succumbed to gravity very quickly and became trying to fall with style and failing. Finally, as she came near enough to Earth to catch its updraughts, she managed to glide down to the ground.

Or she would have, if she hadn't crashed into a tree.

Small birds - and to her surprise, a red squirrel - panicked and fled as she 'landed'. She managed to grip a branch after crashing through several. She shook herself and looked around. She could hear children playing nearby.

'I must be in England then' she thought to herself. Then she thought 'Or Scotland.' She spent a few more minutes trying to remember where the hell there were any red squirrels left and made a mental note to smite any grey squirrels she happened to see. It wasn't that she didn't like grey squirrels, it was just that she liked red squirrels better and they were rare now. After a few more minutes she decided she'd just... carry them off and put them somewhere with more grey squirrels. She was too much of an animal lover to actually smite anything. Then she was annoyed with herself for being so soft.

It was then she saw the two children staring up at her.

"Wow, that's awesome! Look at that hawk!" shouted the little boy and pointed with his ice cream, sending bits of it flying off everywhere.

"Don't shout, you'll frighten it away!" shouted the second child, a little girl, just as loudly "Anyway, 's *not* a hawk, 's a *falcon!* Stupid!"

"They're the same thing, anyway!" retorted the boy, sticking his tongue out.

"Are not!"

"Are too!"

"*Mu~m!* Timmy's being stupid and saying that a hawk

and a falcon are the same and he's going to frighten the *falcon* away!"

"*Mu~m!* Jessica's *lying!* Come and look at this *hawk!*"

Sera wanted to fly away, but she had the horrible feeling she wouldn't be able to. She had a terrible vision of launching herself, crashing after a few feet and being set upon by the two children who would probably try to feed her ice cream. It's the sort of thing small children try to do to wild, potentially dangerous animals. She shuffled about to get a better purchase on her branch. At least she was safely perched on a branch now, instead of painfully sprawled across several. Her other option was turning back into a human, which she currently had no idea how to do, and if someone saw her she could be in trouble.

Consequently, she spent the next hour or so, stuck in the tree, listening to the goings-on in the park. It was just outside a woodland, and an effort had been made to make it part of the woodland by planting as many trees around it as possible. There were also 'obstacle courses' for the squirrels with nuts at the end as a reward. Not that she saw any, because there was, after all, a falcon sat in a tree only ten feet away. She listened to the troubles of the people in the park. In such a small area, there were so many... they made accidentally becoming a goddess seem like nothing. Sera had a roof over her head, she didn't have to pay for food - or anything, come to that - she just had the eternal dilemma of what to do with her life. At least she *had* one and could choose what to do with it, more or less... On the other hand, she was annoyed that some of the people in the park seemed to be wasting their lives. It was like the gods... what possibilities there would be, if they would only work together and make things better... It occurred to Sera that the God and Human worlds were a lot alike... the good actions of a few were nearly swamped by the bad or merely indifferent actions of the majority. She mused over it all for a while.

'Maybe I should try to balance that out... That's what religion's supposed to be *for*, after all...'

Sera waited until there was no-one around and flew down from the tree, managing not to crash this time. She had to hop or take short semi-flights, like some kind of lethal chicken, until she was out of the woodland. Now she needed to change back...

'Well, thinking of being a bird changed me into a falcon... maybe thinking of human things will make me change back.' she thought to herself. She closed her eyes. 'Let's see... a hairbrush, *clothes*, I'd really *like* some clothes right now...ice cream, shoes, opposable thumbs...'

When Sera opened her eyes, she was sat in the middle of the sparsely vegetated ground not far from the edge of the park. She was in her valkyrie outfit, much to her relief. She'd had a horrible feeling she was going to turn back naked. It was *Freya's* cloak, after all. She remembered reading a children's story once... a legend about some fairies or swan maidens or something that were bathing in a pool, when some punk snuck up and stole their feathered robes. Sera wasn't going to be bathing in any pools, but she remembered how she and Freya had rummaged around for ages trying to find clothes that fitted. Perhaps celestial robes were scarce. She decided she'd better not lose or damage her valkyrie outfit. She might not get another one, and she rather liked it. It seemed like it was meant to be worn by a woman with a bit of weight, rather than some anorexic beanpole. A lesser woman would probably crumble under the weight of the *dress*, let alone the armour. It was probably something to do with opera.

Sera knew what she wanted to do, but wasn't entirely

sure how to do it. She wanted to fly all over the world, to see what was going on, to see what she could do. But as she couldn't even land in a tree properly, she'd have to walk. That meant she'd have to stick with one area, at least for now. It made borrowing the cloak rather pointless, but it couldn't be helped.

'Perhaps that's a good idea, anyway' she thought to herself, a little sadly 'I'm new at this whole goddess thing, after all. Rome wasn't built in a day.' Sera reassured herself, despite the fact that she now suspected it was. She nodded and set off. She knew people couldn't see her; after all, they'd be staring if they could. It wasn't everyday you saw a valkyrie walking down the street. It wasn't *any* day you saw a valkyrie walking down the street.

Sera wandered all over the place until she got tired; into schools, into libraries, into churches... after some hesitation, she even went into some houses, if the door had been left open. It wasn't something she would have even dreamed of before, but if she was going to be a goddess she would have to stop being so polite and passive, at least to non-gods. She'd been a fairly inoffensive person as a human, but had often wished she wasn't. At least she knew one thing; she knew she wanted to help people. She'd always been keen on helping people, but it never seemed to turn out how it was supposed to. She usually ended up making things worse, or getting into trouble herself. Now she was a goddess, she could do anything she wanted, or so Freya and Hermes kept telling her. She was sure it couldn't be that simple; nothing ever was. On the other hand, she'd just flown down to Earth from a rainbow, as a falcon, albeit badly, so perhaps anything was possible after all.

Sera was exhausted, so she sat down on a bench to rest and think. She couldn't be an honorary - lit.: 'not really a' - member of the Norse pantheon forever. And the other Afterlives didn't have jobs for ex-mortals. But what should she do? And what kind of goddess should she be? She wasn't very outgoing, so although she'd like to call herself something like 'Seralina, Supreme Ruler of the Skies and Bringer of Wonderment', she was going to have to try something a little more humble. She was staring into the middle distance when she suddenly realised there was a man sitting next to her. He grinned at her.

"I didn't know they did Street Opera." he laughed "Shouldn't you be riding a great, white horse or something? And singing?" he added hopefully. Sera's mind raced. Mortals weren't supposed to be able to see her. What should she do? And then the answer came to her plain as day: Lie.

"Actually I'm doing this for charity. I get paid about a pound a day for as long as I dress like this." she said as haughtily as she could manage. She didn't like the man's tone of voice. And she wasn't going to be mocked by some guy just for wearing her uniform.

"Oh yeah?" the man replied cynically "What charity?" he demanded.

"I haven't decided yet." she replied icily.

"I see." he said thoughtfully and then grinned again "How about me? I'm a right charity case, me."

"I doubt it." Sera tried to remain as icy as possible without being too offensive; she wanted to tell him to just go away if he was going to be so patronising, but she was worried where that might lead. The other gods might be able to turn people into frogs or make bits of them fall off, but she couldn't. She made a mental note to learn how as soon as possible.

"Oh?" he scoffed "And you'd know, would you?"

"No, but I can guess." she replied "I'm afraid I have to

go now." she added as nonchalantly as she dared and made to leave.

"Hey, where are you going?" he demanded "I just told you, I'm a charity case."

"I have things to do, I was just taking a break." she replied and walked a little faster.

"But I'm a charity case!" the man insisted following her.

'Oh God, what am I going to do?' Sera thought frantically as she tried to ignore the man's incessant rambling and stared determinedly in front of her. Then she saw a train station. She made a bee-line for it.

"Hey, stop ignoring me *bitch*!" the man shouted angrily as she got past the ticket booths. Then to Sera's relief, one of the staff stopped him.

"Sir, please don't shout like that, there are children around." the staff member said in a painfully polite tone of voice, the kind that suggests that if polite doesn't work they will happily skip all in between tones and go straight to the Glaring Public Humiliation tone in the blink of an eye. "May I see your ticket?"

Leaving the angry man behind, Seralina looked for a remote platform to hang around on until she felt safe. No-one took any notice of her. She wondered why the obnoxious man had been able to see her. Maybe he just wasn't a full shilling. She hated people like that. She couldn't help wondering how they didn't understand why a woman by herself would be intimidated by a sudden insta-stalker and want them to go away.

'I must have some kind of invisible sign that says 'I'm minding my own business! Why don't you bother me?' over my head.' Sera thought gloomily. She saw another way out of the train station and brightened up a little. 'I've had enough... I'm going to get back to Asgard as soon as possible.'

As she left the train station behind - alert for any more stalkers and other crazy people - she saw a house with a door ajar.

'Oh all right.' she thought to herself 'I'll try one more house. Maybe I'll find some answers in there-'

Sera pushed open the door as quietly as she could and squeezed through the gap. She shut the door behind her. It was strange, but there didn't seem to be anyone in. Sera wandered around the ground floor, peeking into all the rooms. It was a nice house; there was a newly decorated living room, a downstairs bathroom that was all posh and full of marble and a children's playroom littered with toys. She stopped in the kitchen and stared thoughtfully out at the garish, primary-coloured, plastic disaster zone that was the garden and a mini-playground. There were a few forlorn toys lying around outside, too. It looked like the parents probably had too much money and not enough time. There was no-one home. Sera wondered why the door had been open.

Then she saw the burglar.

Without thinking - she was still worked up from the obnoxious man from the park - Sera grabbed the nearest object to hand and threw it at him. By sheer luck, it was a pepper pot. The loose top came off in mid air, sending pepper everywhere. He started to yell, but was cut off in a fit of coughing and spluttering. Then Sera hit him with the only large object on the table, an ornamental teapot. It shattered and the burglar fell to the floor.

Sera stood stock still for a few minutes in shock at what she'd just done. It wasn't even her house and she'd just nearly killed someone. At least, she *hoped* he wasn't dead. He wasn't moving at all. She remembered the children's playroom and ran there to grab the skipping rope she'd seen lying on the floor.

She tied up the man's arms and attempted to tie them to his feet, but was too useless at knots to manage it. Then she phoned the police. When asked where she was, she panicked at first, but then she concentrated... and found that she really did know where she was. At least she could do a few simple godly tricks. Then she went back to the kitchen to check on the burglar. She didn't want to hang about, but she felt bad about the mess. She looked around and soon found a small notepad and pen. She left a note saying;

'I called by and there was a burglar in your house.
He should be tied up in the kitchen.
Sorry about the mess.'

Then she wondered how she should sign it. Putting her mortal name was out of the question, so she'd have to make up some kind of goddess alter-ego. She thought about what would be a thing of happiness, but wouldn't sound too high and mighty.

'What would make me most happy right now?' she thought. She looked around the kitchen and spied a tin of sponge pudding on top of the fridge. She remembered having those when she was a kid, but she hadn't had any in years. She remembered really looking forward to her pudding and custard. They didn't seem to have pudding in Valhalla, or at least, in Sessrymnir. Or crisps. Seralina would have killed for a packet of crisps. She wondered if she could pick some up before she left... She thought for another minute. Crisps were good, but they didn't sound as good as pudding.

'Seralina, Goddess of Puddings' she wrote.

'Yep.' she thought, sticking the note on the fridge with a badly-made, dough magnet in the shape of a frog

'Definitely puddings. Pudding definitely equals happiness, not too presumptuous, not too difficult. Definitely puddings. I wonder where I could get some...' As she mused about the unlikeliness of materializing money or puddings out of thin air, goddess or no, there was a groan from the burglar and a commotion from outside. She rushed to the front door and made it out just as the police appeared at the front gate. When she was sure the police had found the burglar she set off to find a good place to get back to Bifrost. A little further along the road she spotted a suitably high tree; it was a gigantic oak. It had probably been there before the town was. She was surprised to see such a huge tree still standing; there had been one in her hometown until a gale had blown it down. The tree stump had stayed behind for years too; it had been bigger than a picnic table. Sera regarded the oak tree critically for a few minutes. It was no good. She would never manage to fly up into it. She'd have to climb up first.

"Oh well." she said to herself "It's not like anyone will see me."

She managed to get one foot onto the lower main branches and was in a most awkward and uncomfortable position when a voice said;

"Young lady, whatever are you doing?" Sera was fairly annoyed at this point; climbing the tree would be difficult anyway, but climbing it wearing enough dress for three women and several pounds of armour was almost impossible. And now, someone was talking to her just when she was looking most undignified and least wanted to be talked to.

"Well, as you can clearly see-" she began in annoyance "-I am climbing this tree. It's pretty obvious." Sera hoped the message had got through. Her arm felt like a furnace and she felt like it was going to snap any minute. There was a thoughtful pause.

"What for?" came the reply.

"I've lost my frisbee. I know it's up here somewhere." Sera grabbed at a higher branch and nearly fell off when it snapped. She hastily redoubled her grip on the original branch and swung one foot up.

"That sounds like a lie, young lady." said the speaker jovially. It sounded like it belonged to an old woman.

"Fine." Sera replied irritably "I'm climbing it because it's there. Or here, rather."

"Come now." the old lady insisted "Would it be so hard to tell the truth?"

"Yes." Sera replied firmly and managed to get her other foot onto the branch, so that she now looked like some kind of celestial sloth. She'd always found it quite hard to lie, and never saw the point. But now things were different.

There was an expectant silence from the old woman.

"I could tell you, but you wouldn't believe me." Sera insisted.

More silence.

"Oh *all right!*" Sera complained "I'm currently a valkyrie, I've been a goddess for a few weeks now and I'm having a day off to decide what to do. I borrowed Freya's falcon skin cloak but I'm no good at flying, so I'm climbing up this tree so I can fly back to Asgard. I'm having some trouble. And while I'm at it, what is it that you want the most?" Sera managed to haul herself onto the branch, which creaked a little, then settled. "I'm trying to be some sort of Goddess of Happiness, because I have no idea what I want myself." Finally Sera was in a position to look around. She looked down. Smiling up at her from the base of the tree was a little old lady. She was dressed rather oddly... in a bright green, velvety suit. She was also wearing a green hat. Her hair was quite long, it was white and very wavy. She had the most vivid green eyes Sera had ever seen. They were clearly visible even from where Sera was sitting. The only place she'd seen more green was a field.

"Hmm... what do I want?" mused the old lady. She turned and stared out at the street thoughtfully for a while. "Can't say I want anything much." she concluded eventually "I've got food, I've got water... there's plenty of sunshine, what with there not being many trees around. It's a little lonely though. Could do with more trees around, really. Not too many, mind." she added sharply "Get too many trees and all you've got is a big row waiting to happen." Sera thought carefully for a minute. Being around gods for a few weeks had taught her some things.

"You're a *tree*, aren't you?" she said bluntly "*This* tree. That's why you can see me."

"Well done." said the dryad and gave Sera an approving nod "Goddess of Happiness, eh? I'm a tree, like you say, so I wouldn't know about that... trees don't want much. But I know humans do. Humans want a lot. You'll have your hands full there. But you need to know where to start and where to stop." the dryad said firmly "Humans often want something else when they've gotten what they think they wanted. And there are plenty that are never happy. I've been here a long time and I've seen it all. You'd be amazed what people stop and discuss by a big, old tree." Sera nodded. It was true, at least in her case. She hadn't really thought that far, yet. She'd just wanted to help people.

"I'll try to help you if I can." Sera said "Next time I'm here. Sorry for climbing up you by the way." she apologised.

"Oh, don't worry about me." said the dryad "No-one cares what a tree wants." she shook her head sadly "Thank you all the same, though." Sera nodded. She found it

58

surprisingly easy to climb the tree after that. It may have been that the branches were in a mysteriously easy-to-climb structure, although it was just as possible that it was because the hard part was shimmying up a trunk wearing armour.

Sera crash landed right in the middle of Bifrost. Heimdall, who had heard her coming, waited at a respectful distance until she had changed back. Then he wandered up, looking concerned.

"Are you all right Miss?" he asked, wrinkling his forehead "That man was very disrespectful to you." Sera matched his expression. She didn't like to think that she had been watched.

"Yes." she replied simply.

"Did you find what you were looking for?" Heimdall asked.

"No." Sera said slowly "But I think I understand a little better what it is I should do. I think so, anyway. I'm probably wrong." She shrugged. It wasn't a godlike attitude, but she wasn't very godlike yet and as far as she understood gods could have whatever attitude they liked.

"You're to be known as the Goddess of Puddings now?" Heimdall asked, tilting his head to one side.

"Sorry?" Sera stopped staring into the middle distance "Oh... right. No." she shook her head "I just thought it up on the spot. I just thought I should leave something to say sorry and I couldn't go and put my real name. I mean, I thought it'd be a good idea *then*, but it's just silly, really..."

"Well, I don't know..." said Heimdall slowly "I think things like that get stuck, Miss."

"They do?" Sera said and sagged a little.

"Afraid so, Miss." Heimdall replied sympathetically.

PHIN

"The Goddess of Puddings?!" Freya burst out laughing, causing several of the clientele to look round, annoyed or surprised.

"It was just the best thing I could think of at the time! And I was tired and hungry!" Sera complained, turning crimson "I just thought 'What would make me happiest right now but isn't too high and mighty?' and that was all I could think of!"

"Oh dear, oh dear, oh dear." Freya shook her head "You've not quite got this whole goddess thing down yet, have you?"

"Is it really stuck?" Sera said gloomily, staring at the table "Is it really, really stuck? Am I really officially the Goddess of Puddings?"

"I'm afraid so." Freya nodded and stifled another laugh "When you put it in writing like that... It's official."

"I can't change it at all?" Sera asked, pouting and glaring at the table.

"Nope." Freya patted her hand "You can add to it, though. You can say you're the Goddess of, oh, I don't know... 'Pudding, Chocolate and All Associated Confectionery'."

"It's not funny, you know." Sera said defensively "If I'd known I was going to make myself a laughing stock I would have put something impressive, like 'Mistress of All That Is' or something. I was trying to be non-threatening."

"Ah." Freya tapped the side of her nose "It's the quiet ones you have to watch out for. If you act threatening, people watch you all the time. But a non-threatening person can get away with all sorts before anyone even notices." Freya gave her a reassuring nod. She smiled. Sera found herself smiling back. Maybe Freya was right.

"So what should I do now?" she asked.

"Well, you'll probably want some familiars, a place of your own... stuff like that." Freya rested her chin on her hands. She looked like she was enjoying herself.

"Do you have familiars, Freya?" Sera asked. She'd read a bit about them in the library, but not much.

"Well, I have a boar and several cats." Freya replied "They pull my chariot sometimes." Seralina felt a pang of sadness. She'd just realised that she would probably never see her cat Bella again. All of a sudden she missed her a lot. Although she couldn't help wondering how cats could manage to pull a chariot. Or how you'd get them all to do it in the first place. They'd all just sit down and sulk, even if you managed to harness them. That's certainly what any of the cats she'd ever had would have done, anyway.

"I like cats." she said vaguely, suddenly lost in thought. Freya looked puzzled at Sera's sudden change of mood.

"Are you OK?" she asked.

"Yes. Definitely cats." Sera nodded to herself "With wings on. And... dragon-y bits..."

"Sounds... interesting." Freya mused, pretending to know what was going on "Very Egyptian."

"Yeah." said Sera vaguely "Definitely." She stared at the air and then started to draw pictures in it with her finger. After a while she said "Do you have some paper?"

Sera had spent the last few hours doodling her

familiars and was finally getting somewhere. They were all basically the same; cats with wings, although they were different kinds of cats with different kinds of wings. She'd tried lions, tigers, panthers, all sorts. She'd tried huge wings, tiny wings, black wings, purple wings... she'd even tried some sort of skeletal thing, but had decided it creeped her out far too much on paper and wasn't having them running around everywhere.

Finally, she had her final design. She was an art student after all. If she was going to design a familiar she was going to design it *right*. She wasn't going to make a mistake like 'the Goddess of Puddings' ever again. She wondered how big she should make her familiar. She automatically thought of it as house cat-sized, maybe a little bigger, but she couldn't help wondering if she should make it lion-sized so she'd have a steed. But a big cat would look a bit silly as a steed... besides, it wouldn't be able to fit in her room and it might even be dangerous. She wondered if it should have some sort of powers, like shape-shifting, into a human maybe, like some of the other gods' servants had or if it should be able to speak multiple languages or turn things into gold. She scribbled notes in the margins. There were a lot of '?'s.

She had just added the finishing touches when a voice said;

"That's pretty good."

"Thanks. It took me ages." Sera responded without looking round. She was too busy making sure everything was to her liking to worry about sudden anonymous voices. Besides, it had been happening a lot lately.

"So what is it?" said the voice encouragingly.

"I think I'll call it... a Sphinik. Like a Sphinx. Only not. Like a baby Sphinx. I got the idea from a computer game I played when I was a kid. There was this baby phoenix that they called a phoenik. So... you know." The voice thought for a minute.

"That's a bit rubbish, really." it concluded "Couldn't it be 'Agralea, the Mighty Beast of Smiting' or something?"

"No." replied Seralina, annoyed. Like all artistic types, she didn't take kindly to people insulting her work. "I've named it now. Who asked you anyway?" she asked, turning around.

The Sphinik looked her right in the eyes with that piercing, unblinking stare cats sometimes use when they want something.

"How do you feel about some kind of nickname?" it asked.

It had been rather disconcerting to see her pen and ink creation walking and talking. Well, not so much talking as criticising. Between them they'd come up with the nickname 'Phin'. Phin had also argued that she clearly wasn't a baby Sphinx and that Sera had to change her definition. Sera had said she couldn't think of anything right now, but would work on it. Phin had also quizzed Sera on several other things, such as why she wasn't pudding based, as would befit a Goddess of Puddings and Sera had said it could probably be arranged, at which point Phin had wisely shut up.

"And what about your castle or whatever?" Phin asked "What are you going to do about that?"

"I don't know. I haven't thought about that yet. Who says I want a castle?" Sera replied.

"*I* want a castle. Go on, go for a castle." Phin said encouragingly "You know you want to."

"Fine, fine." Sera agreed wearily "I'll get a castle. *Tomorrow*." she added firmly, climbing into bed. Phin jumped onto the bed and curled up on the pillow, where she started to purr. Despite her initial annoyance, Sera fell asleep smiling.

Sera woke up fairly early. It was largely because Phin was pawing her face. Sera rolled over and said blearily;

"Phi' wh' y' d'in'?" Phin gave her a calculating stare and then said;

"So you *are* alive then?"

"Y's."

"I was just checking."

Phin decided that she would lie over Sera's feet. She couldn't have been comfortable because Sera kept tossing and turning, trying to get back to sleep. But she lay there anyway. Eventually Sera gave up and got dressed.

"Get me some breakfast, would you?" Phin said. It wasn't even a question.

"We can go and get breakfast in the hall." Sera replied "When I'm dressed."

"But I want it now." Phin said jumping off the bed.

"Then just go now. It's not very far away." Sera yawned. It was too early for this. "I'll find you when I'm dressed." Phin considered this for a moment.

"But then I'd have to get it myself."

"Yes, I can see your dilemma." Sera couldn't help smiling, even in the face of such stubbornness. She'd missed having a cat.

"I'm getting dressed first." she said firmly "No matter what."

After a few token protests from Phin, the two of them made their way to Sessrymnir. Freya had decided that whilst Sessrymnir wasn't being used for anything during the day, she might as well use it as a canteen for the girls and even for some of the gods, if they could be bothered to get up in time. The low lighting, delicate vases of flowers and floaty,

64

translucent materials of the evening were replaced or covered up by great big portable murals of the sun in various styles and little, gold sun-shaped napkin holders. Oranges, reds and yellows filled the room. Even the sign outside was temporarily covered up with a new sign saying;

'Freya's Breakfast Bar - Full Of Sunshine!'

Freya served the meals herself for whatever reason, although a few of the girls helped by cooking the food. They were on some sort of rota, apparently. Sera hadn't been included because she was now part-time. She didn't mind. Serving drinks was all right, but she absolutely *hated* serving food. There were too many things that could go wrong. That, and she was fairly useless at cooking.

Hermes was sat by himself at one of the tables. Seralina got herself and Phin some breakfast and went to join him.

"Good morning!" he said brightly and smiled at her "I hear you've made yourself a Patron." He wasn't wearing his hat. He looked a lot better without it. Hermes was actually pretty attractive, it was just that he seemed to have left his fashion sense in the middle ages.

"Who's this jerk?" Phin asked, sitting herself on a chair and putting her paws on the table so she could reach her plate. Hermes blinked and leaned over to get a better look at her.

"What's this thing?" Hermes asked, just as bluntly "It looks like something from the feline reject bin."

"Well, you look like a badly-dressed postman." Phin retorted back, dragging her chicken off the plate and eating it on the floor "I'm a cat-dragon-bird thing." she managed to reply. Sera absent mindedly put Phin's plate on the floor, next to her. Hermes gave Sera a questioning look. Sera shrugged.

"She's a cat-dragon-bird thing." she explained "I created her last night. She's my familiar. I, or rather *we*'re trying to think of a better name for what she is."

"Does she have to be so rude?" Hermes asked, glaring in Phin's direction.

"She's a cat." Sera shrugged. It was a sufficient explanation. Phin was actually more like a small, sleek lion than a cat. She was slightly bigger than a normal cat, and mostly sandy coloured. She had the tail and wings of a dragon. Both were a pale, creamy brown, like milky coffee, and her wings were covered on both sides in thick, white feathers tipped with brown, something like a cross between a bird's wing and a bat's wing. She also had dragon 'fins' behind her ears. The final thing that distinguished her from a regular cat - as if the bits of dragon weren't enough - was the fur on her head and tail. The sandy fur covering her body was short and sleek, but she had a mane of longer fur on her head, a bit like a Chinese-style dragon, starting just in front of her ears and continuing in a line to the back of her neck. It was white, but tipped with pale brown, similar to her feathers. The same fur also covered the end of her tail.

"So as I was saying -" Hermes gave a second glare in Phin's direction "- you've made yourself into a Patron? Goddess of Puddings, I believe?"

"Oh." replied Sera gloomily "So you know about it, then?" Hermes shrugged.

"*Everyone* knows about it." he replied "New gods are really rare these days. Congratulations, by the way."

"Thanks, I guess." Sera sighed and pushed her food around her plate, which wasn't particularly wise. She'd got waffles and ice cream, partly because she felt like she should live up to expectations as the Goddess of Puddings. Sera often took the attitude that if she was going to do something, she was going to do it properly, even if she didn't like it. But it was mainly because she'd never had the opportunity to have waffles and ice cream for breakfast before and was going to take full advantage of it. Freya was expanding the menu all the time. It had started off as a traditional Norse menu, featuring the famous dish Lumps Of Meat. But Freya had soon realised that she could serve whatever she pleased, so she'd started to serve pretty much everything. Besides that, a few customers from other Afterlives had started to show up and they had wanted all kinds of different things.

Freya came over to join them when she'd finished serving.

"I see you've got yourself a familiar." Freya nodded towards Phin who had just about finished dragging her chicken all over the floor. "I thought it might be a cat."

"You did?" Sera asked suspiciously.

"Well, last night you just sort of switched off and you kept muttering 'cats, yes' to yourself and scribbling cat-shaped things on the napkins. Then you just wandered off, writing things in the air with your finger."

"Did I? Oh." Sera waved vaguely at Phin "Well, there she is. What do you think?" she asked nervously. When it came to her art, she didn't really care about what other people thought. Art is like that - unless you want to make money, of course. But Seralina had a great deal of respect for Freya. She was doing whatever she wanted but had somehow managed to do what everyone else wanted as well. It was an unusually happy arrangement with the universe. That, and she liked cats, too.

"Nice." Freya nodded approvingly "A bit odd, but nice. Mind you, there are plenty of high class, old gods and familiars where you can't tell what the Nifelheim they are."

"Hello there." Phin said brightly, jumping back up onto the chair and giving Freya a hopeful look. Freya petted her on the head. Hermes, feeling left out of the conversation, tried his best to join in;

"So you'll be moving out of Freya's hall, then?" he asked.

"Will I?" Sera looked questioningly at Freya.

"Every goddess needs a place of her own." Freya commented, earning her some dirty looks from a few goddesses sat on a nearby table who didn't have one.

"How do I go about getting one?" Sera asked.

"Well, you could try creating it yourself..." Freya began "but I recommend dwarves. You have to be careful about creating things yourself. They often go wrong." she warned "You can have some land on the edge of my realm. It's technically not allowed, but you *are* one of my girls. It's a Ginza Mama's job to look after her girls." she finished proudly.

"Wow, thank you." Sera said gratefully "Are you sure it's OK? Do you know where I can find some dwarves?" she asked.

"Oh yes," Freya answered smugly "and of course it's OK."

"Er... won't the dwarves want paying?"

"You let me worry about that." Freya patted Sera's hand "You worry about the design. Although they might be picky and think they know better. Although..." Freya fingered her choker "...they usually do."

"Oh yeah-" Sera suddenly remembered she had a job to do "Is there anything you want me to do today?"

"Well, if you're going to Midgard, you could post some more of those posters for me." Freya grinned "But I know you've got things to do. You might want to make some of your own. Do you need to borrow my cloak again?" Sera shook her head.

"I know where I'm going this time." she paused for a moment "By the way, Hermes, I want to talk to you for a bit. Do you mind?"

"You want to talk to me?" Hermes said surprised "No, I don't mind. What for?"

"Well, it's about what you said before, what you said you wanted." Sera explained.

"Well, I have things to do." Freya stood up and stretched, taking it as her cue to leave "I'll leave you two alone."

While Freya busied herself around the bar, clearing tables and swapping decorations and furnishings, Seralina explained her 'Goddess of Happiness' plans to Hermes. Phin got bored after about three minutes or so, curled up on her chair and went to sleep.

"What, you want to be some sort of fairy godmother?" Hermes remarked.

"Why not?" Sera replied haughtily "If I can be the Goddess of Puddings, I can be anything. Anyway, it's got the word 'god' in. It's close enough."

"And you say you're going to start with me?" Hermes said uncertainly "I don't think gods are supposed to have fairy godmothers."

"I don't see why not." Sera argued. Hermes thought for a minute. Sera thought he was going to argue, but then he said;

"I think you're getting the hang of this goddess thing."

"Well, I'm trying my best." Sera admitted. She took a deep breath and added "My next step is going to be telling people what to wear and how to act."

"That's the spirit!" he said encouragingly.

"Starting with you." Sera added.

"Oh." Hermes said, crestfallen.

"For a start, you look bloody awful in that outfit. You need to get a classical godly look going on. And get a better hat. And some shoes that fit, for goodness sake! And if you don't do something about those socks, I shall burn them." she announced and then paused. "With you in them." she added for good measure.

"She'll do it, too." came Phin's voice from under the table. The hint that bad things might happen to people she didn't like seemed to have woken her up.

"Fine, fine! I'll do something about them!" Hermes held his hands in front of him in an attempt to ward off the barrage of criticism.

"And another thing, you've got to stop lazing around, expecting people to respect you for nothing." Sera waved her arms, indicating the bar around them "Look at Freya. She thought about doing something new and ambitious and then she actually did it. That's really impressive, you know. If more people actually did what they thought about doing, the world would be a better place." Hermes nodded a little gloomily. Nevertheless, he was quite impressed. This wasn't the mildly stunned girl he'd met a few weeks ago. Even so, it was a rather sudden change.

"You've been thinking, haven't you?" he asked in an accusing tone.

"Yes." Sera nodded firmly.

"You've thought of all this enlightened, world-saving stuff and you've been just *dying* to tell it all to someone, haven't you?"

"Maybe." Sera replied furtively.

"She has." Phin's voice confirmed.

"How would you know?" Sera retorted "You're not

even a day old yet!"

"I just *know*." Phin replied darkly.

"Well, pretty words aren't going to get anything done." said Hermes sulkily "I don't see *you* doing anything."

"That's because I haven't done anything yet." Sera replied, shrugging "I'm going to start today. Like I said, with you. You're supposed to have a winged hat. *A proper one.* Go and dig it up from wherever it is. Get yourself a toga or something. Wear some gold. Look like you *deserve* respect."

"This from the girl who said she used to wear just jeans and a t-shirt... Looks aren't everything you know-" Hermes began defensively.

"It's not about looks. You look pretty good, but you're all...rusty. You need to chip it off or something. Fresh coat of paint. Some other metaphor involving shiny things." Sera waved a hand vaguely.

"Gods really resent being told what to do, you know." Hermes hinted.

"I know." Sera replied briskly "So do women, incidentally. But look, I mean, do you *like* looking like that? Are you really happy just doing odd jobs?"

"I suppose not... but... ...move with the times... ...got these from Zeus..." Hermes mumbled and looked at his knees.

"Well then. If you don't like the view, look somewhere else!" she finished triumphantly.

"You've been really *bored* in the evenings, haven't you?" Hermes sighed.

Sera made her way to Bifrost with a spring in her step. She was going to *do* something. She *had* done something. She was fairly sure *someone* would thank her for doing something about Hermes' socks, even if it wasn't him. She'd looked somewhere else. She still didn't know what she

71

wanted, but she felt like she was closer to finding out. Maybe she just hadn't seen whatever it was yet.

"I think you were a little harsh, back there you know." Phin said all of a sudden.

"Actually, *I* think I was too." Sera admitted, her enthusiasm deflating a little. "But I was trying not to think about it. Besides, goddesses have to be harsh sometimes, don't they?"

"I suppose." Phin said thoughtfully "Where are we going?"

"To plant some trees."

"That doesn't sound very goddess-like."

"It will be if I do it."

"...Hermes is right. You've been thinking a lot."

"How do you know anyway?" Sera asked suspiciously.

"Well, I may have only been born yesterday, but..." Phin tried to think of a suitable way to put it and failed "I just know. It's like how sometimes you hear the phone ring and you just *know* who it is."

"How do you even know what a phone is?"

"Well, for a start, *you* made me, so you ought to know why I know." Phin complained "If anything, *I* should be asking *you*. That, and I'm a cat. I just *know*. Morphic memory or whatever it's called. That thing where blue tits all learned to peck at milk bottle tops at the same time."

"I don't think cats have that." Sera said thoughtfully as they reached Heimdall half-way across the rainbow bridge "Some cats are downright thick. We had one once who thought there was another cat on the other side of the mirror."

Heimdall treated them to a twenty-four carat grin.

"Not using Miss Freya's falcon skin today, Miss?" he asked cheerfully "I see you've got a familiar. It's a good choice, a cat." he said, giving an approving nod "Miss Freya likes cats." It puzzled Seralina why Heimdall referred to Freya as a Miss. She was married after all, even if her husband wasn't around. It was probably just because he thought it was polite to do so. Either that, or Freya's reputation made it seem somehow more appropriate than 'Mrs'.

"No, no falcon skin today." Sera replied. It seemed to her that Heimdall was fond of Freya. Whenever he spoke of her, he always spoke warmly. She wondered if there was a reason. But then, it seemed like most of the pantheon admired her greatly. She had been given her own realm and hall after all. She even had her share of admirers from other pantheons, now that her Ginza bar and hotel was up and running. Several drunken customers and even a few sober ones had often waved their drink at her and slurred something along the lines of 'Tha' Freya, she'sh one schpesial lady!' and then the more drunken ones had nudged her and grinned or done the special sort of laugh that goes 'hur hur hur' and generally accompanies a dirty joke.

As the two of them neared the end of the rainbow bridge a figure stepped out of the mist that wreathed the part connected to Midgard, making her jump.

"Greetings!" said Osiris brightly, waving a few strands of mist away "You're the young lady who came to deliver those posters the other day! Am I correct?" He beamed.

"Yes. That's right, Sire." Sera replied and smiled back.

"Ah, I see you have acquired a cat!" he clapped his hands together "A fabulous choice! Cats are gods too, you know." he said knowingly.

"What are you doing in Asgard, Sire? If you don't mind me asking, that is." Sera said politely. She quite liked Osiris. He acted like a rather jolly uncle. He reminded her of one of her own uncles, who was always immensely proud of whatever she did. Sera didn't understand why he made such a fuss; she wasn't particularly proud of anything she'd done. She was *ashamed* of a few things she'd done, mostly as a child... but she wasn't really proud of anything. She'd decided that that was going to change...

"I thought I'd take up Lady Freya on her offer." Osiris explained "I think I shall enjoy a holiday. It will be most interesting to experience another Underworld." Sera was a little surprised.

"Isn't that a problem for your Afterlife-, I mean, your Underworld?" Sera asked, a little concerned "How will they manage without their king, Sire?"

"Ah, my son Horus is the king now." Osiris explained "He's doing a marvellous job, simply marvellous. I haven't been the king for some time. I don't miss it. It was a great relief to not have to worry about that sort of thing any more." He smiled and his eyes twinkled "And even kings need a holiday sometimes, dear girl."

"I see." Sera nodded "Well, I hope you enjoy your stay, Sire. I'm afraid I have some business on Earth, so I must be going. It was nice to see you again." She gave him a rather metallic curtsey and headed into the mist.

In no time they were in the playground outside the forest where Sera had crash landed in the tree. She headed purposefully in the direction of the town.

"What are we doing here?" Phin asked, sniffing the air.

"I told you, we're going to plant some trees." Sera replied "And buy a bed."

"What're we going to do that for?" Phin asked bluntly.

"Because it will make some people happy." Sera replied. They reached the town centre and Sera cast around until she saw what she was looking for. She made a bee-line for the garden centre.

Sera wasn't quite prepared for the scene at the garden centre. There were children, running around everywhere. She wondered if it was some kind of school trip gone awry at first, but once she'd adjusted to the laughter and squealing, she realised that they all looked quite similar. For one thing, they all had piercing green eyes. They all wore something resembling a school uniform, although not quite so formal. Some of them looked up at her as she entered and smiled brightly at her. She managed to smile back. She waded through the crowds of children and the occasional humans and found the plant section. Then she located the saplings. She selected four and made her way to the counter. Then she stopped. What should she do? Should she pay? She approached a counter with no line and waited for a while to see if the cashier would notice her. After a few minutes she waved a hand in front of his face. Nothing. Sera shrugged and walked past him. She felt bad for not paying, but there wasn't much she could do about it.

Sera headed down the street, the four dryad children wandering along after her, a little confused. It was a little disconcerting... four strange, silent, green-eyed children following her everywhere, watching her solemnly. They were only young, so unlike the old lady, their skin was tinged with green, just like their bark. Sera reached the area where the Old Oak was and stopped. She looked around for places to plant the trees. Luckily, there were two empty places for trees on either side of the oak. She started with those. Sera hadn't had the foresight to take a trowel, so she started to make a little hollow in the soil with her hands. Phin watched in bemusement for a few moments and then said irritably;

"What are you doing that for?"

"Well, to plant a tree you have to, you know, *plant* it. In the ground. In a hole." Sera answered in much the same tone "Just sticking it somewhere and hoping it will take root does not count as planting it."

"I know that." Phin complained "But I'm a cat, you know. I would have thought that, with you being my creator and all, you would have noticed."

"Yeah?" Sera stopped for a moment and gave her a Look "What's your point?"

"I can dig better than you."

"Oh. Well why didn't you say so?"

"I just did." Phin shoved Seralina's hands out of the way "Move."

Sera watched Phin dig the first two holes in silence. It took a while, because cats, unlike dogs, don't enjoy digging. They merely have to do it occasionally. If they had a choice, they wouldn't, because it involves getting dirty and cats are the animal world's equivalent of ladies with expensive false nails.

By now, the young trees had caught on to what Sera was doing, and they were laughing and clapping and singing. It made them a little less worrying, but not much. Sera couldn't help feeling that they belonged in a horror movie. And yet, the old lady hadn't bothered her at all. Nor had it bothered her when they were just part of a crowd of noisy children. Perhaps it was that they didn't speak to her, or the way they sounded; their voices sounded silvery and a long way off, as if they were ghosts.

'I suppose they are, in a way.' she thought to herself 'I never saw them when I was mortal.' Sera had to keep herself from thinking that she was dead. She almost always managed to insert 'mortal' into her thoughts instead of 'alive', but under the surface she could hear her 'shadow thoughts'. The dark, brooding, treacherous little voices everyone has, the thoughts that know what the words really said. The thoughts you can't change. But she could speak to her parents, and in the Afterlives, there was usually a clear distinction between the dead and the deities. For one thing, the dead were often treated a lot worse. Besides that, having read up on her mythology, she had found that gods could indeed die and did so with worrying frequency.

"Right." Phin shook her paws in distaste, sending bits of soil everywhere "Where are we planting these other two? Let's get this over with." she complained. Sera cast around for another suitable place. There didn't seem to be one.

"I don't know..." she replied, frowning "I can't see anywhere." Then she saw the Old Dryad watching her in amazement.

"You're... planting trees? For me?" she asked quietly.

"Well... I'm trying to be a Goddess of Happiness, even if it's only of puddings." Sera explained. Phin sniggered. "It still *counts*." Sera pointed out sulkily "Puddings can make people happy."

"You keep telling yourself that." Phin said cheerfully and trotted over to the huge oak "Can I scratch on this?" she asked the old lady.

"You can." the dryad sniffed "I'll only be replacing it sooner or later." Phin started to sharpen her claws "It's been a long time since anyone bothered to do anything for us. Gods have been chasing after humans for a long, long time now."

"Did you have gods before humans came along?" Sera asked, intrigued. She didn't know that trees had gods.

"Oh yes." the dryad nodded "Not what you humans would call gods. But gods nonetheless. There are no... heavens?" she paused seeking confirmation. Sera nodded. It was an extremely loose way of describing some of the Afterlives she'd visited, but still- "There are no heavens. Life stays on Earth, where it belongs. There are only so many souls to go around."

"I see." Sera nodded. It made sense. "Um... I don't think I can plant these two around here. I'm sorry, but I'd have to dig up people's gardens."

"That's perfectly all right. More for us, eh?" she patted one of the children on the head "I'll look after these two. You check up them from time to time, all right?" she pointed to the woodland "You should plant those others near the woodland over there. I can't see it from here, but I can feel it. Make sure you plant them on the edge, where they'll get plenty of sun."

"I'll do that. Thank you." Sera nodded solemnly and set off. Phin stretched and trotted off after her. The two dryad children caught on to what was happening and bade their fellows a brief goodbye before skipping off to follow them.

Sera planted the two remaining trees on the edge of the playground with help from Phin. She could see other dryads peeking out at her from the corner of her eye, but if she tried to look they disappeared. Sera supposed that not all dryads were as friendly as the Old Oak.

After she was done in the woodland, she looked for a furniture store. She couldn't see what she was looking for so she had no choice but to ask for help. She was a little worried about drawing attention to herself, but she had Happiness to Spread.

"Excuse me." she said, doing that special, bent, sideways step that customers always do for some reason when trying to get a salesperson's attention. It's as if they're checking the salesperson still has a face.

"Yes?" said the slightly unnerved assistant, who could have sworn there was no-one around a moment ago "Can I help you?"

"I'm looking for a really comfortable bed. But I've got to be able to carry it away." Sera asked.

"Er... I'm not sure we have anything like that." the assistant said uncertainly "But I can check for you."

"Would you?" Sera asked "That would be great." The assistant nodded and set off towards the desks. Then he stopped and turned round;

"Erm... why are you dressed like that?"

"I'm on my way to a fancy dress party and the bed is a surprise gift for someone."

"Right. I'm sorry, I just had to ask. Fancy dress party, eh? Odd time of year for one, but still... Nice." and off he went to speak to the manager.

After a few minutes the assistant returned.

"Well... we don't have any, but you could try a water bed or something like that? They're still quite heavy though." Sera thought for a moment.

"Yes, I think that would work. Thank you very much. Is there anywhere around here I could buy one?" she asked.

"There's a big department store not too far away. Just go straight down the road from here and turn left at the third set of traffic lights." he explained making complicated movements with his hand "You can't miss it."

"Thanks. Bye." Sera set off and headed for the department store. The assistant blinked. He looked around the store, bewildered. He was sure the girl he was just speaking to had left, but he didn't see her go out the door.

"Must have switched off for a minute..." he muttered to himself, and went to stock check the pillow cases.

HERMES' OLD GROOVE

Sera strode into the department store and looked at the floor plan. She headed for the third floor and found what she was looking for. She also picked up some rather frilly, but extremely comfortable looking blankets and some pillows.

Sera hauled the lot to the lift and hoped no-one would see her. Luckily, there was no-one around the lift area at all and it was quite close to the exit so Sera didn't have to drag it far once she got out. She wondered why people didn't scream at the sight of several pounds of merchandise dragging itself out of the door, but she suspected that once she had gotten hold of something it just became a stock error on the computer system somewhere. It worried her that that was probably what stolen merchandise also became and wondered if there was really any difference between them. She decided she'd go home some day soon and leave some more apology notes and some money at all the places she'd taken things in her pursuit of other people's happiness.

"Aargh, I'm glad I don't have to *fly* up to Bifrost today..." Sera heaved the stuff along the street with great difficulty.

"Want some help?" Phin asked, walking alongside her.

"Yes." Sera replied bluntly "But, I doubt you'd be much help. Besides that's not very cat-like, is it?"

"No." Phin replied "But I'm a cat-dragon-bird thing, remember?" Sera looked round because it seemed that

Phin's voice wasn't coming from below her knees any more and she wondered why. She saw why. Stood with her arms crossed was a woman with sleek, fiery coloured hair. She wore a fairly simple white dress, decorated with leaves or possibly feathers. She looked a lot like Freya, only with much darker, straighter hair.

"Oh." Sera replied shocked "I didn't know you could do that."

"It's something to do with what you were thinking when you drew me. You thought familiars should be able to shape shift. Basic familiar ability. I saw that design sheet of yours. I wish you'd been more careful. Honestly." she tutted "And you'd better appreciate this-" she added haughtily "-because I'm not doing it if I don't have to. Now let's grab this stuff and *go*. I want some fish."

A short time later the two of them arrived at the Asgard end of Bifrost and collapsed.

"Take this... stuff... off ...   me... right *now*..." Phin panted "And remind me... never to do anything like that again... *ever*..."

"Remind me not to do this again, either." Sera staggered as she took the whole weight of the stuff from Phin, staggered a little way and then plonked it onto Bifrost. Then she sat on it and fanned herself "I'm sticking to getting ice cream and, well, *pudding* from now on. Pudding doesn't seem such a bad thing to be responsible for any more."

"As long as I don't have to carry it, you can be responsible for whatever you like." Phin said as she shrunk back into a cat again.

Heimdall, who had heard them coming, came up to see what all the fuss was about.

"Did something happen, Miss?" he asked "You look like you've had some bother. I never heard you having any bother else I'd have-"

"No, no." Sera held up her hands in front of her "I-"

"-we-" Phin interrupted.

"-we just had to carry some heavy stuff." Sera explained, deciding to ignore the fact that Heimdall seemed to be watching her or rather listening to her when she went to Midgard "It's for you, actually." Heimdall looked surprised, then delighted.

"What is it?" he asked, inspecting the pile, lifting bits of it up to get a better look.

"It's a water bed. And some sheets and pillows and things. They're supposed to be very comfortable." Sera told him "You fill it with water. The bed that is, not the sheets." she added.

"Water?" Heimdall smiled happily "How nice. It's a little odd, Miss, but it will remind me of my mothers' place. Thank you very much." He lifted the whole pile up effortlessly "Thank you very much, Miss." he repeated happily. He strolled off humming to himself.

"He seems happy." Phin mused, tilting her head to one side "Good job, Goddess of Happy Puddings. Now how about that fish?"

Sera and Phin arrived in Sessrymnir in plenty of time for the evening meal. Unlike the Breakfast Bar, this was only open to Freya's Ginza girls. The girls were on a rota for that, too. It would be Sera's turn tomorrow.

"There you are!" Freya exclaimed as they turned up to help themselves to the valkyrie-only buffet "What on Midgard have you been doing all day?"

"Making people happy." answered Phin a little sarcastically "It involves lugging heavy things long distances. She thinks I'm a mule you know."

"Hey, you offered to help, you liar!" Sera pointed out as

she filled Phin's plate with tuna "Do you want this fish or not?"

"And she's starving me." Phin added, giving Freya a shameless, wide-eyed look. Freya merely laughed.

"I'm glad you two are getting on." she said "But I need to talk to you. You know you're working tonight, don't you?"

"Yes, I know." Sera nodded "What do you need to talk to me about?" Sera's tone became uncertain "I haven't done anything wrong, have I?"

"Oh no." Freya shook her head "It's nothing like that. It's about your castle." They reached the table and Sera put Phin's plate straight on the floor.

"So, what about my castle?" Sera asked, tucking into some tuna salad herself.

"Well, all the building arrangements are sorted. But the dwarves want to meet you tonight. They want to discuss design, payment, that sort of thing..."

"But.. I thought you said you'd pay?" Sera's fork stopped halfway to her mouth which had become an O of horror.

"No I didn't." Freya sounded a little puzzled "I said let me worry about it. I've sorted it. I'm sure it's nothing you can't handle."

"I'm not!" Sera protested.

"Well, you're trying to be a Goddess of Happiness aren't you?" replied Freya, tilting her head to one side "They said they wouldn't mind some happiness."

"Well unless they want pudding, I'm probably no good to them." Sera stopped and thought about what she'd just said "I'm probably no good to them anyway!"

"Oh, stop it." Freya patted her hand "Just see what they want. If you're really having problems, come and ask me, okay? I'm your Mama after all." she smiled.

"Well, OK..." Sera agreed reluctantly "I'll try my best. Um."

"Um?" Freya tilted her head to one side "You still don't think you can handle it?"

"No, it's not that." Sera shook her head "Actually we ran into a sort of problem today."

"A problem?" Freya frowned "What sort of problem?"

"It was awfully difficult getting that stuff up to Asgard without being able to fly. And if I'd been using your falcon cloak we still wouldn't have been able to carry it." Sera explained "It was difficult enough even with Phin's help. Um, it turns out she can turn into a human."

"Quite a lot of familiars can shape shift. Standard feature, really." Freya shrugged.

"Well, yes. But it would be more useful if she could turn into something else. Or if I could. Is there any way I could go about that? Could I... could I alter Phin so she could change into something bigger?" Sera asked.

"Oi." Phin looked up from her fish "Don't just decide to muck about with me without asking!"

"No." Freya replied "It's very hard to change something you created, just like that. Living things aren't like clay. You can't just add or remove stuff."

"Oh." Sera frowned and folded her arms "I suppose I could make another familiar, but it doesn't feel right to do that. How could I tell them they just exist to carry my stuff? And on top of that I wouldn't have anywhere to *put* them. My room is lovely and all, but it's not that big."

"Hmm." Freya drummed her fingers on the table and stared up at the roof. After a while she said

"I think there's some more cloaks in the armoury, you know."

"Cloaks?" Sera asked, puzzled.

"Like my falcon cloak." Freya held up a hand as Sera opened her mouth to protest "I don't think they're falcon cloaks, though. No-one will miss them. Most of the people here inclined to shape-shift can do it naturally."

"What sort are they?" asked Sera doubtfully "Any idea?" Sera had had enough trouble turning into a falcon. She wasn't sure what else she could handle.

"No idea." Freya stood up suddenly "Come on. Let's go and find out. Before it's time for the bar to open."

Sera nodded and beckoned Phin to follow them.

Once in the armoury they spent some time digging through various dusty pieces of cloth and being disappointed. Several promising pieces turned out to be a rather tattered valkyrie's dress, a rag rug and a bed sheet with holes cut into it.

"Is this... is this a ghost costume?" Sera asked fumbling under it trying to find the right holes. She managed to get one arm through the right hole and flapped about trying to find the other one. She dragged the rest of the sheet back over her head and peered at it critically, trying to find the other hole. "What is it even doing here, anyway?" Freya glanced over and suppressed a laugh.

"Sera, your hair is a mess." Freya giggled "I expect it belongs to one of the einherjar. They do get bored with fighting and feasting sometimes, you know."

"I'd be careful if I were you." Phin warned "If a falcon cloak turns you into a falcon, what do you think a ghost costume is going to do?" Sera paused in the act of inserting her arm into the other hole, which she had finally located. She hurriedly dragged the whole thing off over her head, making her hair even worse.

"A-HA!" Freya shouted from the other end of the

room. She'd been rooting around in a bunch of chests. She dragged out something feathery and shook it, sending up clouds of dust, making all three of them cough. When the dust had settled and they could breathe properly again, Freya peered into the chest and rummaged around in it. She picked up a few more pieces. "Let's beat the dust out of these outside, shall we?"

Once outside, they shook the dust from the cloaks and laid them out. There were four of them, each one looking sorely in need of repair. There were two similar looking ones, one made of brown fur, the other of white. The third seemed to consist of a pair of wings with two furry legs and a weird feathery cowl attached. The last wasn't furry or feathery at all but was made of a leathery, scaly material. It too had wings and an odd-looking cowl. It had large gashes at the bottom end, and the shiny scales were rubbed off or faded in patches. It looked like it was once a vivid red, but now it was a dusky, pinkish-brown.

"So, should I try one out?" Sera asked, poking the brown one with her foot "What sort of cloaks are they? Do you know?"

"I think this one is a griffin." Freya replied, indicating the feathery one "But I'm not at all sure about the other three. That pinkish one could be a serpent or something. I think someone has been raiding other Afterlives, by the look of it."

"How am I supposed to try them out if I don't know what they are?" Sera picked up the white fur and brushed it off "I used your cloak last time by thinking about being a falcon, but I can't do that if I don't know what it is." She wrapped the cloak around her shoulders. It was patchy. The fur had rubbed off in places. Freya picked up the brown cloak.

"You're a goddess. You can feel what it's supposed to be." Freya answered, draping the cloak around her shoulders. There was a weird moment when Freya seemed to go out of focus and then she was back. She took a step or two backwards on her new hooves. "Hmm. I thought as much." she mused, looking down at her lower half. Freya had retained the upper half of her body, and her dress had ruffled up where it became, quite suddenly, a bay horse. "This one must be damaged. It's supposed to be a horse, but as you can see, that isn't what it turned me into."

"Are you sure?" Sera asked, peering around Freya to get a better look "You look like a centaur. Maybe it's a centaur cloak?"

"We'd catch Nifelheim if we went around making cloaks out of centaurs. They wouldn't appreciate it." Freya replied, blurring as she changed back into herself.

"If you say so." Sera felt the edges of the white cloak and shut her eyes, trying to feel what the cloak was. She could smell mud and grass and warmth.

"It's a cow." said Phin, sniggering "If it didn't look so silly, I'd make you pick that one." Sera tried to say 'Silly, how?' but couldn't get the cow's throat to make the right noise. Instead she just started coughing.

"Oh dear, that one's damaged as well." Freya shook her head "I bet you can't see from there, but it's balding like crazy in several places. Otherwise it would have been a pure white cow." Sera changed back and shuddered, practically tearing the cloak off.

"That was horrible! I didn't have that trouble when I was a falcon." Sera said, hugging her knees.

"You tried to talk didn't you?" Freya asked, picking up the pinkish-brown cloak and trying it on "I should avoid it, if I were you. You tend to choke through not having the right

87

sort of vocal chords and such."

"I wished you'd warned me earlier." Sera complained, eyeing the last cloak with distaste.

"Oh, don't be so soft." Freya chided, blurring as the cloak took effect. She transformed into what would have been a red dragon, had time not taken its toll. The wings were ragged and limp and as with the cow, there were patches of shed scales all over the creature's back end. It looked like part of the tail had been cut off. It hissed, convulsed and then blurred, becoming Freya again. She grimaced and threw the cloak onto the other two defective cloaks.

"Some stupid, heavy-handed idiot made this one wrong in the first place!" she swore and rubbed her leg, grimacing "They must've injured the poor thing to catch it and now the pain is stuck in the cloak. The back legs are nothing but a crippling pain sensation. I couldn't move them at all. But I think the front is OK. Hard to tell though, when your legs are screaming at you. No wonder it was shoved in that trunk." Sera examined the last cloak in more detail. Now she was even less keen to try it than before.

"It doesn't seem to be too bad." she remarked, inspecting the back legs for any sign of damage.

"Oh just get on with it." Phin complained from the sidelines "I want to get this over with already! Don't be such a wuss."

"*Fine*. Geez." Sera took a deep breath and screwed up her eyes, expecting an onslaught of pain any second. Instead, she just felt strange.

"It's just as I thought." Freya announced "These were all in that chest because they're unusable. What a shame." Sera had turned into *mostly* a griffin. The bird's head was there, right where it should be, there were a lot of feathers and the wings were fine. The back end was mercifully as it should be and free from pain, but the front legs had been replaced with Sera's hands. Sera remembered just in time not to try to talk. She looked down and around, but seemed to be frozen to the spot. Then she tried to step forward and fell over when her back legs wouldn't move.

"Are you all right, Sera?" Freya asked gently. The nearly-griffin nodded. "It doesn't hurt, does it?" Sera shook her head. She cautiously lifted one back leg and then the other. They seemed to work fine. But when she tried to move forward, this time her hands wouldn't move and she fell on her face. The almost-griffin blurred and Sera was back.

"It's got too many legs! Or arms!" Sera shouted crossly "I couldn't move properly at all. It felt like I had bits missing but that I had extra bits all at the same time. I'll never be able to use the damn thing, even if you could fix it." she shook her head "I'm sorry, Freya. It looks like I wasted your time."

"No, no. It was my idea in the first place. I should have known they'd be in bad repair. Changeling cloaks are hard to make in the first place and then they're difficult to repair. Not everything makes a good cloak either. Looks like these were made by some cowboys who thought it'd be cool to turn into something different like a dragon." Freya tutted "Otters and birds have always been good enough for everyone else around here, I don't know. It was probably bloody Loki or some other idiot. Or a joke on someone. Wouldn't surprise me if they were 'presents' for some giant."

"Oh well. We'd better go and put them back then, I suppose." Sera admitted, annoyed. They could have been really useful, if only they'd been made or repaired properly. Not that Sera much liked the idea of turning into a cow or half a horse, but the griffin and the dragon would have been useful. Sera gathered up the cow and horse skins, but as she reached for the dragon-skin, Phin stopped her.

"Wait a minute." she demanded, pinning the cloak to the ground with her front paws.

"I thought you were the one in a hurry?" Sera asked, tugging at the cloak "Come on, I know it sucks, but this whole thing has been a dead end."

"No. It isn't. Let me try it on." Phin pawed at the cloak until she could get underneath it. Then she stuck her head out to complain some more "Just because you're useless doesn't mean I am."

"If you like." Sera replied, seeing what Phin was getting at, despite her irritating way of putting it. Unlike Sera, Phin was used to having six limbs. "Are you sure you want to try the dragon one though? Freya said it hurts."

"I *know*." Phin replied, rolling her eyes "I was here the whole time. *Bored*, I might add. But I have an idea." Sera said nothing, but crossed her arms and frowned. She didn't like to think Phin would be in pain. "Oh, stop pulling such a face." Phin chided, sticking her tongue out at Sera. Then she blurred as the cloak took effect. As with Freya, the dragon hissed and became Phin again almost instantly. "Ow."

"Well, I did say-" Sera began.

"Shut up." Phin retorted "I know you said. Trust me for a minute, okay?" Sera said nothing, but was happy enough with Phin trying the griffin cloak. It hadn't hurt. There was the blurring and Phin turned into the very-nearly-a-griffin. But this time, Phin's paws were where the bird's legs should have been. Phin was small in comparison to the griffin, so it gave the creature a distorted look. Nevertheless, the almost-griffin flapped its wings and then trotted round in a circle. It was made slightly awkward because of its tiny front legs, but

Phin was managing much better than Sera had. Finally it flapped its wings harder and harder until it managed to take off the ground a little. Then the image blurred and Phin fell to the ground, pinned under the cloak.

"I'll take it!" she announced, emerging from the feathers "But I need you to sew the front half of that dragon to the back half of this one, okay? You can do that, right Freya?"

"Sew them... together?" Freya mused, looking from one cloak to another "I see. The front legs of the griffin are missing, but the front legs of the dragon, plus its head are fine."

"So you'll be making a new cloak out of the best bits of the old ones." Sera summarised, nodding "What a good idea. Sure you don't fancy being half a horse though?"

"Half a dragon and half a horse? With no wings?" Phin scoffed "No thanks. Anyway, may I remind you that I'm a cat-dragon-bird thing? A griffin is a lion-bird thing and a lion is basically a cat anyway *and* a dragon is... well it's a dragon. Stands to reason that's the best thing to do."

"I was only joking." Sera shrugged.

"About sewing a horse's bum onto my noble visage?" Phin said as haughtily as she could manage, which wasn't very, because nothing containing the phrase 'horse's bum' will ever manage to sound haughty.

"As you like." Sera replied, gathering up the last two cloaks "What shall we do with these, Freya?"

"I'm sure I can think of some use for them. Maybe not that cow one, but... how about I sew it into a bag for you? It's not much use as a cloak, after all. Then you can carry around the new cloak without it getting it in the way?" Freya asked.

"Oh, thank you. That would be really helpful!" Sera

replied.

"Now I've fixed everything, can we *please* get out of here?" Phin complained, running ahead of them, rather pointedly in the direction of Sessrymnir.

"Let's." Freya replied, nodding at Sera.

It was then time to get the hall ready for its night time role as the Ginza bar. The sunny decorations were taken away and the warm oranges and yellows replaced by dark reds, blues or purples. Sera had forgotten all about Freya's talk that morning until about halfway through her shift, when Freya showed some dwarf clients to a relatively quiet corner of the bar. Sera suspected that the clients were hers and she hovered nearby nervously, until Freya signalled to her that she should come over.

"And this lovely lady is your client, gentlemen." she made a sweeping gesture towards Sera "Sera, these gentlemen are the dwarves I was telling you about this morning. Be nice to her boys, or I will hear about it. "

"As long as she's nice to us!" one of them grinned and was silenced seconds later by a megawatt glare from Freya.

"H-hello there." said Seralina nervously sitting on the one free chair. They seemed to be fairly young dwarves, although Sera had no idea how to tell. They had rather bushy hair; one was a red head, one was brown-haired and the last one was a dark blonde. They all had beards that were just as bushy. She wondered if there was some celestial template for dwarves where all you could change were the colours. They all wore horned helmets and most oddly, suits.

"So you're the one who wants a new castle, eh?" the red-haired one asked "We'll do a bang up job, don't you worry. Just you tell us what you want-"

"-and give us what *we* want-" the brown-haired one added;

"-and it'll be right as rain." the red-haired one finished.

"Well, I don't know what I want yet." Sera admitted "But what is it that *you* want?" she asked nervously. She couldn't help but think of Freya's necklace.

"Well... we want to expand our business, like." answered the blonde dwarf "We don't get hardly any customers any more, y'see. We thought you could help spread the word, what with us doin' such a good job on y' castle an' all."

"I see." Sera was relieved. She didn't know how she could help, but at least she *wanted* to. "I'm not sure what I can do, but I'll try my best. I'm sure I can come up with something."

"Tha's the spirit!" the blond dwarf said encouragingly "Now, what about this castle then?"

"Yes, do y' have any idea what you want us t' build?" the red-haired one asked "We can't build anythin' if we don't know what y' want."

"Well..." Sera began "Whether I like it or not, I'm stuck as the Goddess of Puddings. So I suppose I ought to live up to that, somehow... Look-" she stopped abruptly "Does anyone have any paper?"

The dwarves and Sera discussed the castle for a few hours, going through sheets and sheets of paper. They also discussed Sera's end of the bargain, although they were far more keen to simply get to work.

The final result would be quite spectacular. It was to be the very first gingerbread castle in existence.

Sera was both excited and worried to live in her own castle made of sweets. On one hand, it was a grand twist on a classical fairytale occurrence, which helped with the 'fairy godmother' image she was going for. It was the wrong fairytale and associated with entirely the wrong sort of person, but she felt it would work. But she was worried that she might just end up eating bits of it. The dwarves had also offered to make her some kind of artefact, a magical one, that would make food on command, provided they could hold parties at her castle and use it for free whenever they wanted as payment. Sera knew what 'whenever they wanted' was likely to mean, so she hammered them down to weekends and Friday nights. They were happy enough, and so a deal was struck.

The castle itself was to be constructed firstly as a skeleton of metal, which was to be mostly coated with gingerbread, marzipan and icing. There was to be a huge fountain of custard in the main hall and smaller fountains of white sauce, melted toffee and butterscotch. The dwarves were surprised when Seralina absolutely forbade chocolate, but they said that since chocolate fountains had already been made by mortals anyway, it probably wasn't much of a challenge and was therefore beneath them.

"Now, you mustn't eat any of your castle y' understand." warned the brown-haired dwarf, much to Sera's relief. She'd been surprised to find out that his name was Stan. She'd expected it to sound German or Norwegian and be difficult to pronounce. "That's what we're making you this artefact for, y' see? Normal confectionery won't stand up to being used as a building material y' know, so we have to treat it special, like. It's no' edible, understand?" he warned again "It'd kill y', if y' ate it."

"I understand. I'll make a sign to warn guests." she promised.

"A good idea." Stan nodded approvingly "Thinking of your guests, that's what I like t' see. Especially since *we'll* be your guests often enough." Sera thought privately that she was really glad she'd managed to put restrictions on the dwarves coming to visit. She was the sort of person who usually avoided parties, even her own. She'd always wanted to have birthday parties when she was child, but her parents could seldom be bothered to organise one. She probably got it from them.

When the dwarves had left, arguing about the best way to fortify marzipan, Sera sat by herself for a little while and thought. After a while Freya sidled up and whispered;

"You're still at work, you know." Sera jumped a mile.

"What? Sorry!" Sera apologised. She stood up, flustered. She did zone out occasionally, but not usually at work.

"Oh don't worry. Everyone does it sometimes." Freya replied "Just don't make a habit of it."

"Right." Sera nodded "Sorry. Shall I tidy up the tables or something?" Freya shook her head.

"No, no. You, my dear Sera, have a client." Freya winked at her.

"I do?" Sera said surprised. Customers at the bar could request a particular waitress, but they didn't usually bother. The clientele were mostly Norsemen after all; they weren't picky.

"That gentlemen over there -" Freya indicated with a subtle tilt of her head "- has specifically requested your presence." She grinned. Sera glanced over and saw who Freya was talking about. She didn't recognise him.

He was a man of medium height, but he *stood* tall. He looked slightly bronzed. His outfit screamed 'I am a god'. He looked like the male equivalent of a valkyrie. The predominant colour was white. He wore a plain, white tunic that came down to his knees. Wrapped around his waist like a belt was a long, thin band of a coarse, brown material. Large, leather arm bracers, decorated with gold filigree covered his forearms and he was wearing sturdy-looking dark leather boots. The toe caps and soles were coated with gold, and they were winged. The wings twitched a little. On his head, keeping his thick, black hair from getting in his eyes and presumably to top the whole thing off, was a winged leather headband.

The man made his way to Sera through the mine-field of tipsy guests and errant Ginza girls and gave her a hearty grin.

"What do you think?" he asked. Sera's jaw practically hit the floor.

"*Hermes*?" she exclaimed.

"So it looks good then?" he said, still grinning. Freya eyed him up;

"I think... we might have to start employing some men in here." she said thoughtfully "Well, I have guests to entertain, drinks to serve." Freya beamed and swept off to see to the other customers "Have fun, you two." she called over her shoulder.

Hermes nodded to Freya and then turned back to Sera.

"So?" he asked cheerfully and waited.

"I didn't recognise you at all!" Sera blurted out. She really hadn't. This certainly wasn't the Hermes who flew erratically everywhere like a chicken trying to prove gravity wrong. He wasn't the gangly looking youth who looked like he expected to be booted any minute. Sera realised that the Hermes she knew had merely been brought about by wearing several bits of poorly chosen clothing for a few decades too long. He was fairly tall really, but he'd constantly been trying to get his winged sandals under control and trying not to fall out of them, so he was always trying to push his feet toward the ground; consequently, he was always bent to some degree, which had made him look gangly and badly proportioned. The leather band was keeping his hair out of his face, so he didn't look like he was hiding behind it, nor did he have to keep squinting.

"You know, it's odd..." Hermes began "But since I decided to be all modern and move with times, I never liked myself much. And I think Zeus gave me those sandals as a joke. I think I'll have to return the favour." he said darkly "I didn't like dressing like that. What do you think of this anyway?" he asked her for the third time.

"It's great!" Sera nodded, managing to accept reality at last "It looks really good. Where did you get all that stuff?"

"Well, I am a god you know." he said. Seralina merely raised an eyebrow. "Oh fine, I threw some of my old stuff together and begged some stuff off Freya. These valkyrie's boots are great. My sandals were too light and too big for me to be able to control them properly. So were my clothes. You need some weight to be able to keep them pinned to the ground."

"I mean it, you know. It looks really good."

"Thanks." Hermes grinned "Women have been eyeing me up all day! Mind you, it's not all been good. Some of them have been making snide comments like 'Why don't you wear something from *this* millennium?' and 'Where's the toga party?'"

"Do you care?" asked Sera.

"Nope. Not at all. It's not like it's even a toga. I wish they wouldn't be so shallow, but what can you do? That's gods for you." he stretched and looked up at the ceiling "I was going for godlike, like you said. I think I look godlike, so who cares? We never did in the old days. No one cared what you wore, really." he gave Sera a surreptitious glance "It was all about what you'd look like if you took it off." Sera glowered at the glass opposite her. She found it unfair that no matter where you were, that was the sort of thing people cared about. *She* could make beautiful pictures with only her imagination and some paper and ink, which was more than a lot of people could do, but did anyone care about that? *No.* Some talentless bimbo, with less clothes on than a caveman, who laughed at everything would get more respect than her just by walking into a room.

"Where did all these empty glasses come from anyway?" Hermes asked, fingering one "You must have entertained a lot of men today, eh?" He grinned.

"There's going to be an empty glass embedded in your *face* in a minute." Sera replied harshly.

"Er, right." replied Hermes, a little puzzled but nonetheless cheerful "Are you going to get us some drinks?" he asked "I've got some business with you, Happy Goddess."

"I'm not a maid, you know." Sera replied flatly.

"No, but you *are* a waitress." Hermes pointed out "I'll have some red wine, if you don't mind."

"*Fine.*" Sera replied crossly and swept off to the bar area in a huff. 'I've created a monster.' she thought to herself 'All of a sudden he puts on a tunic and he turns into a big jerk. But, he must have been like that before he became a, a *postman*. So, he must have been a jerk before and then he became a postman and became... well, Hermes. He was quiet and polite and didn't mention people's clothes being taken off.' Luckily her muscle memory took over and she poured out their drinks on automatic, overriding her anger 'I think Asgard should have a lot more postmen.' she thought darkly as she headed back to the table.

Sera plonked Hermes' glass and the bottle of red wine on the table and sat down. She took a sip of her own drink in an effort to calm down.

"Are you mad at me?" Hermes asked cautiously,

98

picking up his glass.

"No."

"You seem mad."

"I'm fine." Sera replied, taking a bigger sip of her drink 'I'm not mad, I'm bloody furious.' she thought to herself.

"You're sure?" Hermes asked.

"Perfectly." Sera replied making a half-hearted attempt to take the ice out her tone and failing.

"Anyway -" Hermes began, reverting to the age-old tactic of pretending nothing is wrong "Since your advice is working so well so far, I thought I'd ask for some more."

"Oh?" Sera took another sip.

"Well, looks aren't everything, you know. Else I wouldn't have put up with wearing that stuff all this time, right?" he said nervously "You said I should get out and do something, instead of lazing around waiting for odd jobs to come up. So, you know, I thought you could help me decide what to do."

"Oh. Don't you know what to do?" Sera asked, her anger cooling considerably. This was more like it. They were practically in the same boat.

"Not really. I can't carry on doing my old job... there's not enough work around. No one even communicates with mortals any more, you see. Consequently, there's a lot less to communicate about on Mount Olympus. No-one is really doing anything."

"I see."

"I thought I'd do something more modern. But, well..." Hermes hesitated and looked at his knees "You've seen how good I am at that."

"Hmm." Sera looked at the ceiling and thought.

After a while, Hermes coughed.

"I'm thinking." she assured him. "The thing is... it's not

like you can send gods e-mails. That's what is largely replacing post down on Earth. Actually-" Sera stopped suddenly and remembered her deal with the dwarves. Maybe your problem could be the solution to *my* problem." she looked Hermes in the face and smiled "And vice versa."

"You have a problem?" he frowned, looking worried "You should have said. I'll help if I can."

Sera told him about her deal with the dwarves. She suggested that he could help her find more work for the dwarves and use his existing skills in the process.

"You could make other contacts, for example you could ask the dwarves if they know anyone else who wants to get marketed... hang around in the bar and in Valhalla or whatever. Go to other Afterlives and see if there's anyone there. Make leaflets for your clients. Offer to post them to prospective customers and to other Afterlives." Sera waved a hand in the air to indicate the myriad of other things he could do on this theme "Ask them what they want you to do. Get an office or something. Make some familiars. Stuff like that." Hermes finally caught up with all he'd heard.

"How in Olympus did you come up with all of that?" he asked in awe.

"All you have to do is think for a while. It's not that hard." she shrugged. She'd done graphic design; it was the sort of thing she had to think about all the time, at least art wise. A graphic design brief was basically a problem that needed solving; the first thing you did was to draw lots and lots of rough, little solutions, even if they weren't very good. The point was you needed as much to pick from as possible. Then you could pick one or two and try different things with those. And you refine them and refine them until they're perfect, or at the very least, damn good. Non-graphic design problems were basically the same, only without pictures.

There were bound to be more complications, such as uncooperative people and bits of the world selfishly being in the wrong place, but they were only non-art versions of problems such as not being able to get the right colour marker pens and the printer refusing to work.

"I think... I'm going to need more help with this." Hermes began cautiously "Would you be able to help me with it tomorrow? Just to get me started?"

"Sure." Sera shrugged "The only other problem I know about... I really don't know how to fix. Plus, it's probably none of my business." Sera made a mental note to find out about Freya's problem. She still had Heimdall's request for a day off to think about. 'First things first' she thought to herself 'I started on Hermes' problem first, so I should fix it first.'

"Well, I'll see you tomorrow then." Hermes said enthusiastically "You know, I can't wait to get started. It's great, I haven't been this motivated for ages."

"Well, at this time of the evening..." Sera said thoughtfully "I think quite a few people will be too drunk to know what's what, but you might find a few clients if you ask around. Who knows, some of the girls or even Freya might want something." Hermes nodded.

"Strike while the iron's hot, eh?" he said and grinned "I'll give it a go. Thanks, Sera." And off he went. He started with Freya, who was leaning elegantly on the bar, surveying her domain. Sera saw her listening with her head tilted, as she did when she was interested, and then they sat down at a table together chatting animatedly.

Sera looked down at her glass. She may as well finish it off; it was nearly the end of her shift anyway. As she put the glass to her lips, she heard a cough.

She looked around, but couldn't see anyone in the

immediate vicinity except a woman who appeared to be most determinedly looking in the opposite direction. Sera blinked and went back to her drink... There was a louder, considerably more impatient sounding cough. Sera put down her glass and stood up to address the nearby woman.

"Can I help you?" she asked, as politely as she could manage. The woman turned round sharply, as if Sera had dealt her a personal insult. She was dressed rather oddly for a Ginza bar customer, even by Norse standards. She had long, blonde hair, tied up in a bun, with a few strands falling either side of her face. She was wearing a dress that looked like it had been plucked from the Victorian era. It was brown and white, fairly simple and it had frills on the neck line and sleeves. The woman's sleeves were rolled up and she was wearing an apron, which was also rather frilly.

"Are you addressing *me?*" she said sharply.

"Yes." Sera replied bluntly. With that sort of attitude, the customer was always *wrong* as far as Sera was concerned. Sera had worked in retail, and for long enough that she knew what was coming. She'd dealt with many customers to whom the term 'retail staff' was the same as 'peasant'. "Can I help you?" she repeated.

"Oh." the woman paused and considered how to deal with this travesty "I doubt it, but wonders never cease." she said snootily and sniffed "I'm looking for someone. I believe they work at this... establishment."

"Who is it you're looking for?" Sera asked, her politeness dropping to base level, the tone that isn't *quite* rude, but indicates that the speaker is only asking to get you to leave faster.

"The valkyrie Semolina." the woman replied.

"Seralina." Sera corrected automatically.

"So you know her, then?" the woman asked.

"I am her." Sera replied, cursing her inner teacher.

"I see." the woman replied grimly "I have a bone to pick with you."

"Is there a problem?" Sera asked, raising an eyebrow. She was sure she'd never seen this woman before. She would have remembered the snotty attitude even if she hadn't remembered the clothes. The woman stood out mainly because she *didn't* stand out. She was like a plain clothes policeman in a police station. Most of the other gods made damn sure they stood out, which meant they didn't. It was like trying to stand out by wearing feathers and sequins at Mardi Gras.

"Yes, there is a problem." the woman sniffed "You're in my way."

"I am?" Sera was genuinely surprised. It was clear she was not in the way in the physical sense and people who said you were 'in the way' in the other sense were usually some sort of super villain. "I don't think I've even seen you before. Who are you?"

"I -" the woman paused for effect "- am the Domestic Goddess." she looked down her nose at Sera "And you have encroached on my territory by your claim to association with puddings. I demand that you rescind it immediately." Sera scratched her head.

"Well, I'm afraid I can't do that." she replied. She thought briefly about explaining the situation properly; that it was an accident, that she hadn't really wanted to be the Goddess of Puddings anyway... but she stopped herself. Who was this woman to give her orders? Sera knew there was some sort of hierarchy amongst the gods, but as far as she knew, only very few gods were above others. There had been a woman like this at her old job. She had constantly bossed Sera about, as if she wouldn't do her job unless pestered all the time, whilst doing a sub-standard job herself. Sera had a healthy respect for hierarchy and order and she was quite happy to be ordered about by her superiors. But she was equally as furious at being ordered about by her equals and wasn't going to stand for it, goddess or no. "I'm afraid it's official. There's nothing I can do about it, even if I wanted to."

"That isn't good enough." the woman snapped "I demand that something is done! You must be able to do something about it."

"There's nothing I can do. It's official now and everything." Sera shrugged.

"I *said* it's not good enough." she repeated and rolled her eyes "I shall speak to your superior." She swept off in the direction of the bar. Sera shrugged and turned her attention back to work. She felt bad about leaving it to Freya, but there was no dealing with people like that. They were the sort of customer that would have trouble viewing themselves as below royalty, so even Freya might have trouble putting her in her place. But Sera could always hope...

Sera sipped her wine and glanced furtively over at the snooty woman and Freya, who was annoying the woman even more by being infuriatingly reasonable and by making a big deal out of her business talk with Hermes and insisting she would be *delighted* to talk to her about it another time. After about a minute, Sera put down her glass and began to tidy the tables. It was then when a young man approached her.

"May I sit?" he asked her politely. Sera sighed inwardly at her sudden and unwanted popularity, but she smiled and said;

"Of course." Unlike the snooty woman, this one looked like he really was a customer. But it was strange, customers at this time of night were at least a little tipsy, but this man seemed to be perfectly in control. He seemed like he was carefully calculating everything he did. Although he had a youthful, handsome face, he wore an eye-patch over what seemed to be a terrible burn around his right eye and he had a thin, black moustache and scarred lips. Sera wondered what could have happened to him. But then again, the Norse pantheon got up to some surprising, stupid and above all *dangerous* things. She decided it was better not to ask. She'd probably be horrified. She seemed to recall seeing the youth before, but she couldn't remember where.

"You seem to have a knack for solving problems. For example, that inelegant lady-" he said, leaning across the table, and tilting his head to indicate the blonde woman, who was currently being politely but firmly – and cheerfully – ejected from the bar by Freya "- but I have heard other things as well."

"Well, I'm just trying to help everyone out. You've all been very kind, so it's the least I can do." she replied.

"I have... several problems." he confessed "Would you help me with my problems also?" Sera nodded.

"Of course." she replied "Just tell me what they are and I'll do my best, although I can't promise anything, I'm afraid." The youth looked a little taken aback.

"Tonight is..." he began and hesitated "It is too late tonight. I have many problems and I do not know where to begin. May I meet with you again tomorrow to discuss things when I have thought about them?"

"That's fine. I'm here almost every night." Sera told him.

"Very well." he replied "Then we shall meet again tomorrow. Good night to you then, lady." he finished and vanished into the bustle of the bar. Sera blinked. It was quite crowded, because several guests were unsteadily rising from their seats to totter back to their homes or hotel rooms, in the case of the increasingly frequent Off-Worlders. She had an uneasy feeling about the strange man. It seemed as though he'd been surprised when she'd said yes. But then, why would he bother to ask her at all? Sera mentally slapped herself.

'I have a lot of work to do.' she thought firmly, beginning to tidy up the various glasses and bottles from the night's custom 'I wonder who he was? I should have asked...I'm sure I've seen him before...' As Sera made her way to the sink behind the bar she noticed Freya and Hermes saying goodbye at the door.

Freya acknowledged her as she went past to collect more errant glasses.

"It sounds like you've had an eventful evening. Least of all that stupid woman." Freya said as she came to help Sera clean the tables "Hermes' plan sounds very interesting. I might even have to expand the bar." she said happily.

"What were you talking about?" Sera asked "If you don't mind me asking."

"Oh, just various ideas... brochures, flyers, special offers, that sort of thing. Widening the appeal of the hotel and the bar, you know. Lots of things." Freya clapped and rubbed her hands together "I think there's some fun to be had in all of this."

"You really like working, don't you Freya?" Sera said, smiling.

"I do." Freya smiled back "It's just nice... to have something that's all yours, you know? I mean, the Aesir gave me Sessrymnir and my own realm, but... this is all my own idea. It's all mine."

"I hope I can find something to be so passionate about

someday." replied Seralina wistfully. And there it was, the reason she admired Freya so much. She was so passionate and she was working really hard. She really knew what she wanted and she did something about it. Sera wanted to be like that. Of course, it would be a lot easier to follow her dreams when she knew what they were and when they weren't just dreams where she ate a whole bucket of chocolate before remembering she was allergic.

THE CASTLE AND THE FOX

The next day Sera came to the breakfast bar to find Hermes already there. She smiled at him and put her and Phin's breakfast on the table and went to find Freya. She quizzed one of the valkyries bustling about the kitchen and was pointed towards the pantry. Seralina thought she recognised most of the other valkyries by now, but she hadn't known that girl. Sera wondered how many valkyries there were. They needed quite a lot to serve everyone in Valhalla, which was huge, although they needed considerably less to serve in Freya's bar, the whole point of which was a small, regular set of customers who knew all the girls by name and thus had rather more respect for them.

The pantry of Sessrymnir was not the poky, cold, stone cupboard as found in many houses back on Midgard. It was *huge*, almost cavernous. Shelves upon shelves of meat, fish and poultry stretched away on one side, whereas the other was taken up with racks and racks of spices, wines and herbs. There were moveable ladders on wheels attached to a rail somewhere further up the shelves. Sera hadn't realised it, but there were three or four valkyries working in the pantry the whole time, their sole responsibility to fetch the ingredients required by the cooks. There were shouts from above and further down the hall on the lines of 'We're out of *cinnamon!* There was a whole bloody *bucket* up here yesterday and we're bloody well out of bloody *cinnamon!*'

and 'I'll never carry this stag on me own! 'Ere Hrist, give me an 'and!'.

"Freya?" Sera called uncertainly, her voice echoing away into the recesses of the pantry. After a few moments Freya appeared from around a corner Sera hadn't even realised was there. She suddenly appeared out of the gloom, hauling a huge sack of flour and a bucket-sized pot of honey. There were two more valkyries with her; one was struggling with a massive bag of sugar, one was holding a candle and some mercifully small pots of spices.

"Isn't that dangerous?" Sera pointed to the candle "If you dropped that bag of flour and it all went 'poof' the candle could cause it to explode." Freya put the bag of flour down. Carefully.

"Is something wrong, Sera?" Freya asked, pushing a few errant strands of hair out of her face. She had her hair tied up in a tight bun and was wearing an apron. She looked a little like the annoying woman from yesterday, only she didn't have a look of utter scorn on her face.

"Not really. I just need to talk to you." Sera looked around and peered into the gloom. She could make out the glow of another candle or two in the distance. "All this about moving with the times and you don't have any lights in here?" she asked.

"Well, you try getting a bloody electrician in here." Freya replied, a little crossly "What is it you need to talk to me about?"

"It's about your work with Hermes." Sera explained "I think we should all discuss it together, over breakfast if you can."

"Oh, right." Freya handed her pot of honey to the girl holding the candle, who Sera recognised as one of her fellow Ginza girls "Hildr, take this to the kitchen will you? I'll send one of the other girls for the flour, all right?" The girl addressed as Hildr nodded. She smiled at Sera, then nodded to the valkyrie carrying the sugar and they set off.

They found Hermes arguing with Phin. Hermes glanced up at the two approaching women and then glared at Phin, who was sat by the table staring up at him, before realising who they were and focusing on them properly. He waved a hand irritably at Phin.

"Sera, will you tell your familiar to *back off*." he said crossly. Sera gave Phin a suspicious, sideways look.

"It's *his* fault." Phin insisted "He won't give me his bacon."

"Get your own bacon!"

"I want *that* bacon!"

"Phin, shut up." Sera intervened "Here, have some of this pancake." Sera tore one of her pancakes in half and put it on Phin's nearly empty plate. She was continuing to enjoy eating the various things that really ought not to be on a breakfast menu as part of her 'pudding image' exercise. Phin sat by her plate and glared up at Hermes for a while until she thought no-one was looking and tucked into the pancake.

"You're joining us for breakfast today, Freya?" Hermes asked "Aren't you normally working at this time of the morning?"

"I *am* working." Freya replied cheerfully and helped herself to one of Sera's pancakes "This is a business breakfast."

"Oh?" Hermes was momentarily shocked, but then remembered what he was doing there "Ah, right! What we talked about yesterday."

"That's right." Freya nodded "So, I take it you two will be making this something of a joint venture?" She leant her chin on the back of one hand "I know you were talking about

110

it last night."

"We are?" said Sera.

"That's right." Hermes replied for her "We thought we'd make some brochures and flyers, that sort of thing."

"Er, right." Sera said a little uncertainly. She didn't remember agreeing to this, but she'd made it her business to help people after all. And she didn't dislike Hermes. She'd liked the trip she took with him to the other Afterlives. And it looked like there would be Art involved. At least, there would be if she had anything to say about it. "We need to know what sort of thing you'd like to put on your leaflets. And information for the brochures, what sort of image you're going for, that sort of thing." she finished.

"Hmm... image..." Freya mused.

Freya had thought for a while and then they had all tossed a few ideas around, Sera insisting on getting some paper and making some notes. She got Freya to scribble or sketch a few things so that they had a rough idea of what she wanted.

Sera had suggested either photography or cartoons for the pictures on the front of the brochure and leaflets, with photos of the rooms and nearby beauty spots in Asgard for the inside. That, or some nice artistic pictures of the bar and hotel scenery on the front. She was currently trying to explain graphic design to Hermes;

"You draw lots and lots of little pictures, lots of ideas and stuff. Then you pick one or two and work on those. And you try them in different colours and with different fonts and stuff and-"

"OK, I get it." Hermes complained "I am a patron God of the Arts, you know."

"Sorry." Sera apologised "I got a bit carried away. Plus, you never know with you gods. You don't even have light

111

bulbs."

"We don't need light bulbs, we're gods." Hermes replied, annoyed. He was absent-mindedly chewing the end of his pencil as he thought about what to draw.

"Well if you want to trip over things in the dark and then drop your candle and set the whole place on fire, I'm sure it's none of my business." Sera shrugged "I just think you could come up with some sort of safer alternative. You are gods, after all." she added mockingly.

"Ha ha." Hermes said sarcastically and glared intensely at his blank paper, as though willing ideas to spring to life on it. It was always worth a try, if you were a god. "When I've sorted this out, I'll think about it. Don't you have a castle-building to oversee? Dwarves to talk to?"

"Fine, fine." Sera stood up and made a show of brushing herself off. "I can take a hint. And I suppose the sooner I let the dwarves know I can hold up my end of the bargain, the better."

"Oh, that reminds me." Hermes snapped out of his not-so-creative daze and looked up "What am I getting out of this by the way? I'm helping you uphold your end of the bargain with the dwarves. So what do I get?" Sera stopped and opened her mouth, then shut it again. The sheer selfishness of the question had left her momentarily dumbstruck.

"You're getting customers out of it, of course." she said irritably "You get my services as an agent or something. For free, I might add." she added, hoping he would get the hint.

"Well it's not for free, is it?" insisted Hermes "You're getting payment for your castle sorted out."

"I suppose so, but I owe the *dwarves*, not you. I could have just done all the drawing and delivering of leaflets myself you know. So there."

"Well..." Hermes began doubtfully.

"Anyway, like you said, I have dwarves to talk to." Sera said, before he could argue "I must be going. See you later."

Seralina followed Freya's directions to the outskirts of Folkvang, Freya's realm, to the spot where they were building her castle. There were dwarves hurrying around everywhere. Sera looked around for any of the three from last night, but apart from the fact that she had a hard time recognising faces, the dwarves' faces were half- hidden behind their long, straggly beards. It didn't help that all the dwarves were wearing leather overalls and horned helmets. Add in the thick mist that hung over the place and it was almost impossible to recognise *anything*. Sera noticed though, that the horned helmets were, mercifully, all quite distinct. Whilst one may be a dull, silver colour with long, curved, bronze horns, another would be copper, with short, stubby, ivory horns. She tried hard to remember what the dwarves helmets had looked like. She remembered that they had been quite big horns, and one of them had definitely been silver... Had it been silver horns and an ivory helmet? Or was it the other way around?

Just as Sera was struggling with this question, she was found by Stan, the brown-haired dwarf from last night. His helmet was indeed ivory with long silver horns.

"Miss Sera!" he boomed, his voice ringing clear across the noisy building site "I'm glad y' could make it! We're just erecting the scaffoldin' an' such. We've got your foundations dug out and the metal skeleton is goin' up a treat." He gestured towards the castle.

It was as Stan had said. New iron struts gleamed in the pale sunlight that managed to penetrate the mist. Sera wondered why it was so misty. It had been so clear and warm on the way here.

"What's with all this mist?" she asked, making a half-hearted attempt to fan some of it away.

"Well, that'll be the barrier, Miss Sera." Stan replied.

"Barrier?" Sera asked, her forehead wrinkling.

"That's right." Stan nodded "Well for one thing, us dwarves turn to stone in the sunlight so it's partly for that. But the other thing is, you're not from our bunch, so... the land is setting up a sort of barrier. It's still in Folkvang, but it needs to make itself separate, y' see? Not that your worshippers need to know that."

"I don't think I have any worshippers." Sera replied uncertainly.

"Oh?" Stan seemed surprised "Don't gods need worshippers?"

"I don't think I'm the worshipping type." she stopped "I mean, I don't think I'm the type to be worshipped." she corrected herself "I think."

"Suit yourself." the dwarf shrugged "Goddesses can do what they like, I'm sure."

"Wait..." Sera said suddenly, stopping dead "You really just started building this morning? You've done all this already?"

"Of course." Stan replied proudly, his chest swelling a little "We haven't had much work lately, like I said, so the lads are really keen. Speakin' of which, do you have any ideas about your end o' the bargain?"

"Oh, that's right." Sera smacked herself in the forehead "That's what I came here to tell you. Hermes is going to promote your business for you. We're going to make flyers and leaflets and deliver them to prospective customers. Also, if it works, tell your friends. And I need to ask you what sort of images and info you want on your leaflets."

"You can really do all that?" Stan said, impressed.

"Sure." Sera shrugged "It's not too difficult. Oh, but we have to finish Freya's stuff first. We're working on it right now, but we're going to finish it as soon as we can."

"Right then. Problem solved." replied the dwarf, rubbing his hand together "I'll tell the lads to speed up, then."

"Speed up?" Sera said, surprised "You mean they're *not* working fast? So how long will it take to finish?" Stan looked at the ground and shuffled his feet a little.

"Well, y' see we were worried y' might not make good on your bargain, so we were going a bit slow, like." he explained sheepishly "I reckon it'll take about three days if we speed up. Woulda took us a week if we'd kept going slow."

"A *week*?" Sera exclaimed "To build a *castle*?"

"I know, I know." the dwarf replied hurriedly "But like I said, we was goin' slow because we were worried about not gettin' paid. I'll tell the lads to speed up right away." Sera just stood there, shocked as Stan unscrewed one of the long silver horns from his helmet and blew into it like a horn, causing a blast that attracted the attention of the nearby dwarves;

"We're gettin' paid all right!" he yelled at the listening dwarves "Get the job sped up! Pass it on, lads!" The dwarves nodded and carried on about their business, pausing to tell other workers to speed up. Stan screwed his horn back onto his helmet and put it on, beaming at Sera.

"Could I ask you a question?" Sera asked cautiously.

"You could." Stan replied, nodding.

"Well, dwarves all look the same to me... um... I know that sounds awful." she apologised.

"Does it?" Stan replied, rubbing his chin thoughtfully "I reckon it sounds about right. Especially when we're wearin' our daytime armour."

"Oh? Well..." Sera rubbed her nose, a little derailed and then continued nervously "Why do you all dress similar but have different helmets?"

"Ah, well." Stan nodded "That's it, you see. In the middle o' a battle or on a busy site like this, y' can't tell one person from another a lot o' the time. But y' can tell a helmet. Helmets are all unique to the dwarf that wears 'em, and they're passed from father to son and suchlike. The length o' the horns indicates skill and position in society." He looked smug "As y' can see, the horns on my helmet are rather long." Sera nodded.

"It's quite an unusual helmet. Why are the horns made of silver?" she asked "Won't they get dented easily? Silver's very soft, isn't it?"

"It is. You're a smart woman." Stan nodded approvingly "It's just a silver coating over some more ivory and some iron." he admitted "I'm rather proud of it. My father handed it down to me." Sera felt a pang of loneliness for her own family. She decided to go and phone them when she got the chance.

"Well, I'd better be off." Sera said sadly. Stan gave her a worried look.

"Everythin' all right Miss Sera?" he asked, concerned.

"Oh, it's nothing." Sera replied hurriedly "I'm fine. Keep up the good work." she said a little more brightly "I need to tell Hermes you're very interested in the flyers and things. You should drop in to see us in a day or so, OK?" The dwarf nodded and turned round to shout orders and tell off a small group of dwarves who'd stopped to watch.

"I said *speed up* y' bunch o' no-good *lollygaggers!*" Sera heard him yell as she walked away.

Sera arrived back in Asgard to see Hermes wandering thoughtfully and aimlessly out of Sessrymnir, as it turned out, herded by Freya.

"Shoo! I have things to set up." she complained, shooing him along the hall "I'm sure you can find somewhere else to pile paper and ink all over the tables. And if that purple ink stains my table..." she warned and trailed off "Sera!" she shouted as she saw Sera approaching and pointed straight at Hermes "Take this man somewhere he won't bother me! And remember, you're on rota for dinner." Freya disappeared back into Sessrymnir, muttering to herself. Sera escorted the still dazed Hermes out of the halls into the sunshine.

"How are you getting on?" Sera asked.

"Hmm?" he replied, as if only just noticing she was there "Oh, Sera. I'm doing fine. Why don't you have a look? How's your castle coming along?"

"They said it'll be finished in a few days." Sera replied, taking a bunch of paper from Hermes and rifling through them "It's just a metal skeleton at the moment, though. No gingerbread walls or anything, yet."

"Sounds good." Hermes peered nervously over the top of the sheets Sera was looking at and glancing up trying to read her expression "By the way, are you going to do anything about that dress?"

"What dress?" Sera said suspiciously, looking up from a rather good sketch of a valkyrie, leaning on a table with a whole tray of drinks in her hand. Most of the drawings were like that. The overall message basically boiled down to 'Look! Girls!! Girls *and* alcohol!'.

"*That* dress. The one you're wearing. You're wearing armour over it." Hermes pointed out helpfully.

"Yes?." Sera said crossly "What about it?"

"Well, it's a valkyrie's outfit." he said "You won't be a valkyrie any more when you have your own castle and so on.

Will you?"

"Oh. No, I suppose not." Sera replied sadly. She liked working with Freya and she actually really liked her valkyrie outfit. She didn't really *want* to do anything about it.

"You'll have to come up with something else." Hermes said.

"I guess so." she replied "These are very good, by the way. I like this one, this one and this one." she said, stabbing at various pictures on the sheets "I think you should go with *this* title though. That other one's a bit... corny."

"I don't know if you've noticed, but Freya seems to like corny. Have you seen her signs?" Hermes pointed out. Sera nodded knowingly. Freya did seem to like corny.

"Well, I'm going to go to Midgard." she announced "I want to check on my family and stuff. See you later." She turned to go and then stopped. "Hey, Hermes?"

"Yes?" he said looking up from his latest sketch.

"Do you think I should have followers?" she asked.

"I think so." he replied "And... some sort of magical artefact. One you can be famous for. Like my winged boots - " he said, waggling one at her "- only of course it should be pudding based. A magic spatula or something. Ask the dwarves about it. They made most of the Norse gods' stuff you know. Mjollnir, Gungnir, Freya's boar... all sorts."

"You can make a boar?" Sera said, mostly to herself. There was a thoughtful pause and then she said "I'll do that. Thanks."

Five minutes later, Hermes looked up at the sound of Sera's footsteps, pounding down the hall.

"Cloak!" Sera yelled as she passed him and disappeared into Sessrymnir. Hermes shrugged and settled back down to his designs. After another few minutes, Sera re-emerged. She held up a white, fuzzy bag and pointed to it.

"Cloak." she repeated and smiled. Hermes smiled back in a slightly bemused way, watched her walk triumphantly down the corridor, then shook his head and got back to work.

After going to retrieve Phin from her room, Sera set off for the edge of Folkvang where her castle was being built, riding on Phin. Phin had no problems manoeuvring in her cloaked form. Sera wondered how she knew to fly, but then again if she'd created a bird, she'd be perplexed if it couldn't fly, and she *had* given Phin wings after all. There was little point creating something that didn't know how to behave like itself. Maybe Phin really was picking up something like morphic memory from blue tits.

The dwarves had made progress already; the castle's framework was already complete and work had begun on dragging slabs of gingerbread up to make the walls and there was a huge slab of wood in the middle of the hall that one dwarf was carving to *look* like it was made of gingerbread and other sweets.

"Can I help you with something, Miss Sera?" Stan asked, suddenly appearing from the other side of the huge block.

"Yes, actually." Sera replied "Could you make something extra for me?" Stan rubbed his chin thoughtfully.

"I reckon so." he said "What did you have in mind?"

"Well, I want you to make me an artefact. A magical one." she replied.

"You mean apart from the one to make the food? I reckon we can do that, seein' as we're makin' y' one anyway." Stan nodded "It'll be no problem. We're thinking of makin' it an oven, by the way. Food generally comes out of ovens down on Midgard, I understand."

"That sounds great." replied Sera, who wasn't very good with ovens. They tended to somehow undercook or overcook her food regardless of what she did with them or how much attention she was paying them. "I think the other one should have something to do with puddings. Or cakes or something. Just not chocolate." she added hurriedly.

"Something pudding-based, eh?" Stan's eyes twinkled "I think it'll be a challenge, but we can do it. We normally work with weapons and things, though. And jewellery, o' course."

"Thank you very much." Sera said gratefully.

"I ought to charge you for it..." he began "But seeing as how you're going to be doing such a good job of spreading news of our skills -" he said meaningfully "- I'll let you off. What I'll do is, I'll turn it into a contest. Nothing the lads like more than a contest. You might even get more than one." he smiled. Sera thanked the dwarf again and set off for Bifrost.

Sera arrived at the rainbow bridge to find Heimdall arguing with the strange youth she had met in the bar the night before.

"You were late again, this morning!" crowed the youth gleefully "Wait until Odin finds out you've been sleeping late!"

"I *deserve* a lie in sometimes!" Heimdall shouted back "No-one else guards this bridge aside from me! And *you* never do any work! You should still be chained to that rock, by rights!"

"Ragnarok is over and my punishment is served!" the youth retorted "And I shall do as I please! I haven't forgotten what happened you know. I remember what you all did!"

"You *deserved* your punishment and you know it!" Heimdall began hotly. Then he caught sight of Sera. "Be off with you!" he shouted "Leave me to guard in peace!"

"You'll have your peace!" snarled the youth nastily "Oh

120

yes. You'll *all* have your peace soon enough!" With that, he transformed into a hare and fled.

Sera approached Heimdall with caution. She couldn't believe what she'd just seen. Heimdall was always so friendly and polite; whatever could have happened to make him so angry?

"Morning, Miss Sera." he said, giving her a respectful wave "Are you off to Midgard again?"

"Good morning, Heimdall." Sera replied "I am. Umm-" she hesitated. It wasn't really any of her business, but she had to know. "What was all that about, if you don't mind me asking?"

"Nothing to worry yourself about, Miss Sera." Heimdall reassured her "That was Loki. He's just picking fights as usual, Miss. It seems to be his hobby these days." he added darkly.

"Um." Sera could see that this was not a good line of questioning, especially since she had agreed to talk to Loki that night. She'd already agreed to help him. It wouldn't do any good to just turn around and say 'Sorry, but I heard you're a trouble-making git.' She tried to think of something else to talk about.

"Oh, is your water bed comfortable?" she asked "Did you try it out yet?"

"I did, Miss Sera." he replied happily "It's very comfortable." he looked around conspiratorially and leaned over "I've been having a few lie-ins." he whispered "That's what Loki was arguing with me about."

"I see." Sera nodded.

"It's none of his business, of course." he added in a more normal tone of voice "But he's right. If I left the bridge unattended..." he trailed off.

"Could someone watch it for you?" Sera asked.

"I suppose so..." Heimdall said thoughtfully, rubbing his chin.

"Why don't I watch it for you, one day?" Sera suggested "But not just yet" she added hurriedly "I still have a lot of things to sort out first."

"That would be very kind of you." Heimdall said gratefully "I could go and visit my mothers." he stared wistfully into the middle distance "Would you *really?* I... I'll look forward to it Miss Sera!" he finished and treated her to a salute and a grin. "Have a nice day, Miss!" Sera smiled and turned to leave, but he suddenly leaned forward and gently grasped her wrist. "You mustn't tell anyone, Miss Sera." he warned "If anyone found out... there could be trouble." Sera nodded solemnly.

"I understand." she replied "I won't tell anyone."

Seralina walked down the street towards her house. Someone was in, so the door was unlocked. Sera opened it very carefully, so as not to make any noise. Phin slid in after her. She wanted to see her family really, but it was bound to cause trouble and she thought it was about time to pick up some of her things. She checked cautiously around every doorway. She found her father relaxing on the couch, watching television. He seemed to be watching some sort of documentary on some students who were backpacking through Poland, Bulgaria and Russia. Sera guessed that she was supposed to be in Poland or Bulgaria right now - with no mobile phone signal, of course. Oh well. She'd find out later when she phoned them.

'One day I'll have to tell them what's really happened.' she thought to herself as she climbed the stairs to her room. A door creaked. Sera jumped.

"Nyaow?" said the door. Sera peered at the door "Nyaaaaow?" it said again. Sera opened the door and her cat

Bella shot out.

"Bella!" Sera cried, scooping her up and squeezing her "Oooh, I have missed you! Yes, I have!" Bella tried half-heartedly to wriggle free as she was mercilessly cuddled. When she was finally put down, she and Phin cautiously sniffed each other, then Bella backed away slowly and settled for watching warily from several feet away. She was black and fluffy, with a little patch of white under her chin and was one of those cats who is always nervous and ready to flee.

Sera rummaged through the things in her room, trying to remember what she'd come for exactly, but ended up picking up a million other things in the process; a cuddly toy, some hair clips, her best markers... By the time she'd finished, Sera had a whole rucksack full of stuff, mostly stuff that was quite useless but that she couldn't bear to be without, now that she had come back home.

She made a final stop in the kitchen. She packed some snacks and took her stash of money from the tin on top of the medicine cabinet. She'd missed snacks and she'd certainly missed money; it wasn't that she needed any as such, rather that she wanted to pay for things when she should.

Sera gave the nervous Bella one last cuddle before setting off for Bifrost again, but as soon as she got there she headed straight back to Earth.

Sera arrived in the woodland park for the third time. She still had no idea where it actually was, even though she'd said the name when she phoned the police. For the second time, a red squirrel shot off up a tree, surprised at her sudden appearance. Sera headed first for the old oak tree, where she had planted the two saplings.

The children were playing together and looked up as she approached. They laughed and clapped and ran over to the Old Dryad to alert her. The Old Dryad smiled at Sera;

"So, you came back to check, like I asked." the dryad said, beaming "The little ones are fine, I shall look after them as best I can. You needn't worry. Not that I'm not grateful." she reassured Sera "I shall tell everyone I know about you. Those who do a favour for spirits are owed a favour in return." she finished solemnly.

"Oh, you don't need to do that!" Sera protested "I just wanted to help, really." The dryad smiled again.

"Have you found what you're looking for yet, young lady?" she asked.

"No, not yet." Sera admitted "But I'm getting there."

"That's good. Life is a journey." the Dryad replied "Not so much if you're a tree, I'll admit." she added after a momentary pause. Sera stifled a laugh. "You have things to do, I expect. I'll not keep you. Please check on the other little ones for me. I'll be seeing you." Sera nodded and set off.

She arrived at the garden centre and attempted to find the section with the saplings. Just as she thought she would have to ask an assistant for help, she saw them. She then spent an instructive ten minutes looking at the various trees until she found the ones she was looking for.

"Right... £6.50 each..." she muttered to herself as she made her way to the counter. She made sure she had the exact change before addressing the man on the counter;

"Excuse me." she said loudly, making him jump. He could have sworn there was no-one there a moment ago.

"I'm sorry, I didn't see you there. I do apologise!" he said quickly.

"That's all right." Sera replied "Look, this is going to sound odd, but I took four trees last week and I didn't pay for them." she explained "So I'm paying now. There was some sort of problem with my debit card or something."

"Oh, er... right then." said the assistant bemusedly.

"This is the exact amount." she reassured him, whilst handing him the money. Then she just left, before the assistant had the chance to actually check anything.

"Phew." she gasped as they turned the corner "I was so worried they were going to do something..."

"Oh, don't be silly." Phin complained "They don't punish you for *paying* for things."

"Well, yeah, but still-"

"Oh shut up." Phin cut her off "Let's just go and get the other thing paid for and we can go home."

"*Fine.*"

Sera did much the same at the department store, although she had a lot further to briskly walk to reach the door.

"Now what?" Phin asked as Sera leant on a wall and wheezed.

"Now we go home, obviously."

"Excuse me." a voice said from somewhere around Sera's ankle, making her jump "Excuse me!" said the voice again, a little louder. Sera looked round to see where the voice was coming from and was surprised to see a fox, sat right there in broad daylight, next to her foot. She would have expected a fox to be bigger. That, and for them not to talk.

"Do you have a moment, lady? Only my friend really needs some help and the tree lady said-"

"The Old Oak spirit sent you?" Sera cut off the fox in mid-babble "Did something happen?"

"No, no, not to the tree lady! To my friend, she's stuck and she can't get out! She can't get out, kind lady!"

"All right, all right." Sera held up her hands in what to a

human would have been a 'calm down' gesture. The fox lay flat on the floor, as if he'd been hit.

"Please, kind lady!" he pleaded desperately.

"Take me to this friend of yours." Sera replied, as kindly as she could.

"Oh bugger 'em." Phin piped up "They attack cats, you know." she pointed out.

"Oh shut up. I'll help whoever I damn well please." Sera retorted, following the fox as it darted away.

"I was just saying..." replied Phin sulkily, trailing after them.

They were led past the playground, and quite a way into the wood. The sunlight filtered down through the leaves, causing a beautiful dappled effect across the whole floor. There was a clear, well trodden, dirt track through the forest; it branched off in all directions. The fox led them nervously down the path, dashing on ahead and then waiting for them to catch up, always ducking his head or lying flat, as though he was afraid of attack.

"Over here, kind lady!" he called at last "Over here!" Sera and Phin ran towards the fox; as they came around the corner they saw the problem. A second fox was caught in a steel trap. It was whining and trying to pull itself free. It struggled even harder when it saw Sera and even tried to gnaw its own leg off.

"No, no!" the first fox reassured it "The kind lady, friend to the trees, came to help!"

"You have to stay still!" Sera commanded, feeling a lot less confident than she sounded. The fox's leg was in bad shape and there was quite a lot of blood. Sera tried to lever the trap open with her hands, but it was no use. It moved a little, but then it snapped back and the fox yelped in pain. Sera had never felt so awful in her life. "I need a stick or something-" she said, trying to stay calm "Over there!" She spotted a fairly thick, fallen branch and ran to get it. She handed it to Phin.

"Here, you put this in when I lever it open-"

"I think this would be easier if I had hands-" Phin began.

"Well, I can't lever it open AND stick the branch in, it's too strong!" Sera replied crossly. She wasn't in the mood for arguments.

"No, I just meant I should do this." Phin said, changing to human form and grasping the stick "Ready."

"I... I completely forgot you could do that." Sera stuttered, tearing her gaze away from a now human-shaped Phin and back to the trap.

"Ready then?" Sera asked. Phin nodded. "One, two, three, -now!" Phin thrust the stick into the trap, but it snapped. Sera swore. "All right, try a thicker bit, make sure it isn't brittle or anything, we have to hurry!" Sera commanded rather shakily, her panic starting to show. "Ready? One, two, three, -NOW!" This time the branch stuck, but the trap sunk into it. Sera quickly helped the fox's leg out of the trap, just before it crushed the branch.

"That was close." Sera wiped her forehead; she was even more relieved than when she got out of the department store after paying. "Are you OK?" she asked the fox, who was licking its wounds.

"I am." said the fox in a female voice "Thanks, missus. A favour to a spirit is a favour to all and it has to be paid back." explained the vixen in a firm tone. It was exactly what the Old Dryad had said. Sera wondered what it meant, exactly.

"You don't need to do anything for me." Sera replied, slightly stunned. The trapped fox seemed to have a completely different personality to its rescuer's. "I just wanted to help."

"It has to be paid back." the vixen repeated in the same firm tone "See ya around, missus." And with that, she hobbled off into the undergrowth. Sera finally noticed that the other fox didn't so much walk as flow; she even saw it flow over a fallen tree. Phin, now back to her usual cat self and watching Sera's expression, explained;

"It was a fox spirit. Probably the spirit of all the foxes in the wood. You don't think a real fox would come out in the day, do you? Well, one that isn't caught in a trap, anyway."

"Oh." Sera replied. 'A spirit?' she thought to herself 'Are they some kind of god?' she wondered. Out loud she said;

"I can't believe I forgot you could turn into a human." Phin shrugged.

"It's not a big deal. I bet that fox spirit can do it, too. Familiars can usually do something like that. We're supposed to be clever and resourceful." she explained "If I wasn't, I'd probably be the stupid kind that gets dragged underwater by nymphs at the first opportunity. Quite frankly, I'm amazed you managed it. Some goddess. You don't even know anything about your own creation. You'll be telling me I was an accident next or something."

"Sorry." Sera apologised "I was just upset. And panicking. You weren't an accident, OK? Let's go home...I'm tired."

"Didn't you have something else to do? Something about a dress?" Phin asked "I mean, not like I care or anything." she added quickly, pretending to still be huffed.

"What?" Sera asked, surprised. She'd expected an argument.

"When you came to get me before you said something about a dress. And followers. I'm pretty sure it was something to do with that -" Phin took a deep breath "- *and* you still haven't phoned your parents."

"Oh my god, you're right!" Sera shouted, slapping her forehead.

"See?" Phin said smugly "I shape-shift, I remember things... What would you do without me?"

IMPLEMENTS OF DESTRUCTION

The first thing Sera did was to phone her parents. Luckily, there was a payphone right on the edge of the playground. It was like the ones you always see in train stations; a huge box-shaped phone attached to metal pole, with a half-hearted attempt at a roof over the top and down the back of the phone. Sera was amazed it still worked, with how much it must get rained on. Bits of the pole and roof were rusty, as was the lock to the coin compartment. Sera tried her trick of glaring at the payphone again. It worked.

Her parents did indeed believe she was currently backpacking through Poland - with no mobile phone reception, of course. Sera thought briefly about telling them she was in fact living in Asgard, but decided against it. It was too soon.

Then she went to find a fabric shop. There didn't seem to be any around, so she headed for the town market instead. There she found two stalls selling material and thread and other sewing supplies. She'd never been very good at sewing, but she reasoned that she was a goddess now and if she wanted to be good at sewing, then she would be good at sewing.

Sera bought plenty of thick, white material similar to the material her valkyrie dress was made from. She bought plenty of thread, a selection of interesting buttons and sew-on decorations and an odd square metre or two of various other materials that caught her eye. Satisfied that she must be able to make *something* decent out of it all, she followed the signposts to the community centre.

Once there, she sat outside for about ten minutes and drew her poster. It had a rather nice drawing of a sponge pudding on it, and it proclaimed thus;

'The Goddess of Puddings Welcomes You!

Meeting of the Sacred Pudding Community
this Thursday at 6:00pm
at the Community Centre.

Please bring a pudding or similar to share,
custard and other sauces will be provided.

NO CHOCOLATE PLEASE!'

Happy enough with her handiwork, Sera went into the community centre to find the reception.

The man at the counter looked up as she approached.

"Right." she started, in a business-like manner "First, I'd like you to photocopy these for me. About... twenty copies I'd say. Then I'd like to book a room."

"All right." the man said, taking the poster and heading into the back room. There was a whirring noise as the photocopier started up, then he returned to the counter. "It'll just be a few minutes. Oh, you did want them in colour didn't you?" he asked nervously.

"Yes." Sera confirmed "Thank you."

"You wanted to book a room?" he asked.

"I want to book a room for one and a half to two hours

on Thursday from 6:00pm." Sera told him in the same firm, business-like tone. It seemed to be working quite well. He hadn't looked at her funny or mentioned her costume or anything.

"I'll just check that for you-" the man replied, taking out a folder and rifling through it. "I'm afraid Thursday is all booked up."

"Then you will move someone else to another day." Sera told him "You will tell them there has been a mistake."

"Very well." the man replied vaguely "I can move the dance classes to Tuesday..." He crossed out and rewrote things in the folder, closed it and put it away. The racket from the back room stopped. "I'll just get your copies for you." he said and disappeared into the back room again.

He handed Sera her posters and asked;

"Is there anything else?"

"Yes." Sera replied "It will be every Thursday from 6:00. It must not be booked over. That's very important."

"Very well." replied the man dreamily "Have a nice day..."

Sera repeated her little stunt several times in a few other places. She also made sure to post a few posters around the towns, so that even people who didn't go near the community centre would see them. Luckily, she didn't have to meddle with any more dance classes.

"It was a bit mean, really." Phin piped up suddenly on the way back to Asgard "I mean, you didn't have to have it exactly then, did you?"

"Yes I did. It has to be the same time, all over the country, else there's no point." Sera replied "Besides, I'd already put the time on the posters." Sera and Phin walked along in silence for a little while. "I suppose it was a bit mean." Sera admitted "But you have to be a little bit mean, if you're a goddess. You have to be a little bit mean if you're human, really. Or else people will walk all over you, won't they? That was one of my problems, you know. I wasn't very assertive. Goddesses can't be like that, though..." There was another interlude of silence. "I can't believe it actually worked." Sera continued "I mean, I just told them stuff and they just said 'Yes ma'am.' I wish I could have done that when I lived on Earth. It seemed like no-one listened to me at all."

'That's the thing about gods and goddesses...' Sera thought as they set foot on Bifrost 'People listen to them... '

Heimdall greeted them as they reached him;

"Welcome back, Miss Sera. You're on rota duty today, aren't you? Miss Freya told me." he explained "Oh, about that 'thing' -" he lowered his voice and motioned for her to come nearer "Do you think next Thursday would be okay?" Sera shook her head.

"Thursday is no good." she whispered "How about Friday?" Heimdall thought for moment.

"Friday is fine." he nodded "Thank you very much, Miss Sera." Then he waved her away and said in a slightly louder than normal voice "You'd best be getting off to work, Miss Sera. Miss Freya has been worried about you."

"She has?" Sera said and scratched her head, which was suddenly itchy "I'd better go, then."

Heimdall looked around, as if he'd heard something. He listened for a moment, but all that could be heard were Sera and Phin's retreating footsteps.

Sera wondered why Freya was worried. She hurried to Sessrymnir and into the kitchen. Freya wasn't there, but as it was almost time for the valkyrie-only evening meal, she would almost certainly be in the pantry.

Sera gingerly pushed open the door and called out;

"Freya?" Her voice echoed away into the gloom.

"Sera!" came a shout back almost immediately "Where have you *been*?" There were hurrying footsteps and Sera could make out the light of a candle, bobbing up and down and getting bigger as it got closer.

"I've been in Midgard all day!" Sera called back, just as Freya appeared out of the darkness.

"I was so worried." Freya said, panting. It looked like she'd run all the way from the other end of the pantry. "Heimdall told me he had a fight with Loki this morning. He said you turned up right after."

"I see. Um, Freya..." Sera began cautiously "Is Loki... well, is he *bad*?" Freya pulled a face.

"Good or bad are usually a matter of one's point of view and the situation at hand, but as definitions of people go, I'd say *yes*." Freya answered "He isn't called the Wizard of Lies for nothing."

"I see. Well, the thing is..."

Sera explained the encounter she'd had with Loki at the bar and what she'd overheard of his argument with Heimdall that morning.

"Well, it's not wise to refuse to help him, in your current position." Freya advised "But I would be very careful about what you do for him. *Very* careful."

"I understand." Sera nodded.

"Good." Freya gave a firm nod "Now I need you to get all this stuff put out on the tables." Freya gestured at the plates and plates of food carefully stacked together on the inadequately sized kitchen tables. The other tables were full of knives, chopping boards and spices. There was clutter everywhere. Useful clutter, but clutter nonetheless.

134

After dinner had been served, the valkyries working in the Ginza bar went to change into their evening armour. By the time they were all ready, there were already a few customers loitering about outside Sessrymnir's doors. Freya threw them open dramatically and trilled;

"Come in, everyone!" The guests strolled in happily after her.

One of them was Hermes. He had managed to bind all the sheets of paper together into a makeshift folder using a sharp pencil and some string.

"Are you back again?" Freya asked him, grinning "Can't keep you away, can I?"

"Nope." Hermes replied happily "But I've got to show you this stuff anyway. It's the final designs for your leaflets and things."

"Ah, I see." Freya sat down on the table nearest the kitchen and indicated that he should sit down "That was fast! Let's have a look then-"

The evening was fairly uneventful; Sera served drinks, chatted with several of the customers and talked at length with Hermes about their promotion plans for the dwarves. A few gods Sera didn't know approached Hermes and asked if they might talk to him about business when he wasn't busy. Sera was happy to see that her advice had worked, although the amount of work he was doing made her feel a little lonely. Freya was always busy too, and the valkyries were all out in the daytime collecting einherjar. She felt a swell of affection for Phin. They might argue a lot, but she was always there. And it wasn't like they argued about anything serious.

'I wonder if he's still coming?' Sera thought as she tidied up some of the recently vacated tables. The guests were starting to thin out as they came closer to closing time and Loki still hadn't shown his face. Almost as soon as she'd thought it, Loki appeared in the doorway. He acknowledged her with a nod and went to sit on one of the empty tables near the back of the room, where there were fewer guests.

Sera made her way to the bar to get them some drinks and then went to join him.

"So, how can I help you?" she asked, pouring him a glass of brandy "You said you have a lot of problems."

"Indeed I do, lady." Loki took his time, swirling his drink and looking at it thoughtfully. Sera just waited, saying nothing. "I think the most important thing I need done is-" he produced a piece of paper, sealed with red wax from a pocket of the elaborately patterned silk waistcoat he was currently wearing "-to deliver this letter. I am not allowed out of Asgard, so I cannot deliver it myself." he took a leisurely sip of his brandy before asking "Will you deliver it, lady?"

"I will." Sera nodded. Delivering a letter didn't seem too bad. However... "May I ask what is in the letter?" Sera asked politely, whilst very carefully *not* asking why he wasn't allowed out of Asgard.

"I may not leave Asgard, but my friends are free to come and go as they please." he answered "It is merely a request for a meeting, lady." He took another slow sip of his drink "Do you trust the gods, lady?" he asked suddenly.

"Yes." Sera replied "The ones I know."

"Do you trust *me*, lady?" he asked watching her face.

"I don't know you yet." Sera replied carefully.

"A wise answer indeed. But do you *really* know the gods as you say you do, lady? Do you know what they did?" he asked, studying his swirling drink again "They killed my children, lady. They killed two of my children and they imprisoned another. My *other* two children they have bribed to stay where they are, so they are as good as imprisoned. These are the feats of the gods you know, lady." Sera said nothing. "I expect you are thinking 'What of his feats?' I have helped the gods many times. I have performed callous acts under the instruction of Odin himself! On pain of death if I did not comply! Do not judge me so harshly, lady." He handed over the letter. "You have promised to deliver it." he said finally. "It is for my friend Thrym. He lives in a great hall in the land of Jotunheim. You can get there through Asgard or Midgard." Sera nodded.

"It's for Thrym of Jotunheim. I understand." she replied.

"Farewell then, lady. I shall see you tomorrow." Loki replied, suddenly up-ending his glass and leaving. It was closing time, so he was followed by all but a few extremely tipsy guests who had to be escorted out by some of the girls.

Freya sidled over to Sera;

"What did he want?" she whispered.

"He wants me to deliver a letter." Sera whispered back.

"Let me know if it's suspicious." Freya whispered again as she started to head towards the kitchen. Sera nodded. Tomorrow was going to be a long day.

Sera got up early and headed to Sessrymnir for breakfast. Freya was nowhere in sight; she was presumably somewhere in the depths of the pantry. Hermes was there already, poring over his designs again.

Hermes was wrapped up in his work, so Sera sat at a different table. Besides that, she wanted to sneak a look at the letter. She turned it over and peered at the wax seal.

"You'd better not break it." Phin said quietly from under the table "Or they'll know we looked. Try to peel off the paper... really carefully." Sera tentatively tried the peel it off. To her surprise, it peeled right off without damage.

"It says.. 'Let's meet up next Friday'." Sera turned the paper around and held it up to the light. There didn't seem to be a hidden message. "It looks like he was telling the truth, after all."

"How are we going to seal it back up?" Phin asked "Do you think heating it up at the bottom would work?"

"It should, but where can we... oh wait, I know!" Sera said suddenly, earning her a curious glance from a nearby breakfaster "The candles for the pantry!"

"Well it won't catch any harm until after breakfast will it?" Phin complained, tucking back into her tuna.

"I guess not..." Sera shrugged and started on her egg and bacon. She'd chosen a non-pudding based breakfast this morning, but it still wasn't too healthy.

When they finished eating they let themselves into the kitchen and looked for the candles. Their search of the kitchen proved fruitless, so they pushed open the door of the pantry. There were a few lights bobbing about in the distance, but there was a single candle left burning on the table.

"Careful you don't burn the paper." Phin warned as Sera held the wax over the flame.

"Shh! You'll distract me!" Sera complained, wiggling it about so that it was evenly melted.

"I'm just saying, if you mess up-"

"Argh!" A drop of wax fell onto the flame, making it splutter. "See, I *told* you." Sera quickly pressed the paper against the wax before it cooled. "There!" she said blowing on the wax to cool it further "No thumbprint. This Thrym guy *should* be none the wiser... hopefully."

The two of them asked for directions to Jotunheim from Heimdall. He said that Thor often went through Asgard, so they should probably go that way, but if they had business in Midgard they would be as well to go through there; Jotunheim was behind a barrier of snowy mountains in Norway. He explained that mortals couldn't get past it without help, but Sera should have no problems as she was a goddess.

Seralina and Phin arrived in Jotunheim to find that even though they had been given good directions to both Jotunheim and Thrym's hall, no-one had bothered to tell them to wrap up. Jotunheim, Land of the Giants, was in fact, one giant freezer. Thick ice and snow covered everything; Sera could barely walk. They had to literally wade through the snow - that is, Sera waded whilst Phin rode on her shoulder. The biting wind felt like a thousand knives slicing through the air.

"Should we fly?" Sera asked doubtfully.

"In *this* blizzard?" Phin retorted "We'd go *backwards*. And that's if you could even get the cloak out without it blowing away!" The two of them struggled onwards until they saw a gleam in the distance.

"Do you think that's it?" Sera asked, shouting above the noise of the wind.

"I *don't care*, I just want to get out of this *bloody* snow!" Phin yelled in her ear.

Finally, in the shelter of the hall, Sera rubbed some life back into her arms. She was chilled to the bone.

"I don't know if I can make it out again, you know..." she said through chattering teeth. It was almost worse in the warmth of the hall, where she could feel how warm she was *supposed* to be...

"I have guests, it seems." a voice boomed from above

them "My servants told me there was a valkyrie approaching. I thought they were seeing things, naturally." Sera and Phin looked up - and up - into the face of a giant. He wasn't as big as Sera had been expecting... he was at least twice the size of a normal man and built like a brick outhouse, but she had been expecting him to be, well, *bigger*. She was relieved that he wasn't. "Why did you come here alone? What could you possibly hope to gain? It was foolish of you, to say the least-" he moved forward threateningly-

"Wait, wait!" Sera held up her hands "We're just here to deliver a letter from Loki to a giant called Thrym! Then we'll go home!"

"I am Thrym, Lord of the Giants." Thrym said "A letter from Loki - whatever does he want?"

"He wants - I mean, er... I'm sure it's explained in the letter, sir." Sera stopped herself just in time. She dug out the letter and handed it to him. He read the single sentence and then stood there thinking.

"Right. Next Friday... *that* Loki. I see." he waved dismissively at Sera "Thank you, you may go."

Seralina stayed in the hall for a few minutes to warm up, despite her discomfort around the giants. She pulled a face at the door.

"I really don't want to go back out there." she said, mostly to herself.

"Did you see his face when he first saw us? I really don't want to stay *in here*." Phin hissed in reply. Sera took a deep breath and they battled their way back out through the snow. Before long a shadow fell over them – a massive giant had strode over to pick them up.

Sera screamed.

"We just came to deliver a letter, I swear!" she yelled above the roar of the blizzard.

"I just thought you would like a lift to the edge of Jotunheim, madam." said the giant "But I can leave you here if you wish."

"No! I mean, yes please! Thank you, that would be very kind!" Sera replied quickly. The giant that had picked them up looked rather old, although he was still well-built and had no problem with the snow storm whatsoever. He was much, much bigger than Thrym; Sera fit in the palm of his hand. She wondered if giants simply didn't stop growing at all.

You picked a rather inhospitable bunch of Jotunns to visit, madam." he said as he strode easily through the snow "I presume you're new?"

"Th-that's right." Sera replied "But we had to go there to deliver a letter, s-sorry." They were clear of the bitter weather in no time. The giant put them down and introduced himself;

"My name is Utgard-Loki. Please remember it. You should visit my lot next time, we're much more welcoming. Might I ask your name, madam?" he asked.

"My name is Seralina." Sera answered, dropping a curtsey. She figured it was a good idea to be polite to someone many times her size. "I'm a part-time valkyrie and the Patron Goddess of Puddings and Similar Confections. This is my familiar, Phin." she added.

"Wotcha." said Phin, giving the giant a nod. Phin couldn't care less how big anyone was, on account of being mostly a cat.

"I see." the old giant nodded "I shall remember your names also. I'm sure I'll need to." He gave them a smile and turned round and set off back into the blizzard "Well go on, be off with you, madam. You don't want to be hanging around here all day." Sera nodded. Then she shouted after him. "I'll try to remember! Thank you very much!"

Relieved to be back in the warmth of Asgard, Sera headed straight back for Sessrymnir. She found Hermes outside, sitting cross-legged on the floor, humming to himself and sketching. It seemed that without her to drag him outside he'd just plonked himself down where Freya had pushed him to.

"How's it going?" she asked him, peering over to see what he was working on. A rustling noise made her look up "Hermes... did you know there's a bird on your shoulder?"

"Hmm?" he said looking up "Oh? It appears there is. Good."

"Good?"

"It's my new familiar. I call it a Lightning Hawk. Because it's as fast as lightning." he rifled through a few sheets of paper and found the one he was looking for "See, it's white, and it's got yellow bits on the tips of its wings and yellow plumes on its head-"Hermes explained excitedly, forgetting that Sera was looking at his creation "-with blue bits round the edges." It looked like a cross between a cockatiel and a peregrine falcon. Phin's ears pricked up and she slunk round to the other side of Hermes, flat on her belly and watched the bird, rather ironically, like a hawk. It turned on her a stare that said 'Make my day, punk.' Phin thought better of it and slunk back round to the other side and hid behind Sera, peering out to give the hawk dirty looks occasionally.

"Very nice." Sera said approvingly, taking the Lightning Hawk sketches and looking at them properly "What do you need that for?"

"It's a messenger hawk and I'm going to make lots of them." Hermes explained "They can go as fast as lightning, so they can go anywhere in just a few minutes, even a few seconds. Isn't that great? I'm really proud of myself."

"Wow." Sera exclaimed "You just invented the Afterlife version of e-mail."

"E-mail?" Hermes said uncertainly.

"Yeah, you know. Electronic mail? Like paper mail, only, well, electronic. So you can send it down a phone line and it's super fast."

"Oh." Hermes looked crestfallen "So mortals already did it, huh?"

"You mean you didn't know?" Sera asked him, trying her best not to sound amazed so she wouldn't hurt his feelings "Well... gods don't have computers, do they? They're not very godlike. So... you invented, um, D-mail. D for deity."

"You think so?"

"Well no-one else invented it, did they?" Sera reassured him. Hermes brightened up.

"Yeah, you're right." he said proudly, his chest swelling a little "I'm a genius. No-one else thought of it, right?" Sera thought to herself that 'genius' was a bit strong, but the Hermes she met on her first day had certainly deserved a moment or two in the sun, so she let it slip.

"Well then, Mr. Genius-" she began "-what have you got for the dwarves? I'm going to go and see them in a minute. I wanted to show them *our* progress." she added pointedly.

"Oh, right." Hermes rifled through his drawings again "Here you go. I'm still working on Freya's stuff and I didn't know what they wanted, so I just did a lot of rough sketches and slogans and stuff. Think that'll be okay?"

"Yeah, I think so." Sera replied, nodding "I'll ask them to give us a proper brief when I see them." Sera stood up and brushed herself off "Right then. I'll be off."

Despite Phin's protests that Sera should walk and she should ride on Sera's shoulder, Sera pointed out that it wasn't a blizzard, that she was in a hurry and if Phin wanted fish to feature in her near future then she'd better do as she was told. It made absolutely no difference, because threatening a cat usually has the same effect as threatening, say, a rhinoceros. Only it's a lot less likely to end in death. Nevertheless, after walking for about ten minutes Phin got fed up and made it perfectly clear that she was flying because *she* wanted to and owed Sera nothing, blizzard or no.

They arrived at the castle a short time later. It was now much, much easier to find, especially by air, because the dwarves had indeed sped up. The castle walls were half finished and seemed to grow even as Sera watched.

"They weren't kidding when they said they'd only be a few days, were they?" Sera exclaimed, staring in wonder at the glowing, white walls.

As usual, Stan saw them before they saw him and he strolled up as they landed with a big smile on his face.

"Afternoon, Miss Sera!" he said brightly "You're late today. Had a busy mornin', have y'?"

"Yes, actually." Sera replied, dismounting "I had to deliver a letter to Jotunheim."

"Ooh, that's a nasty place for a young goddess like yourself to go, an' no mistake." he shook his head "So what have y' come to tell me this mornin', Miss Sera?"

"Well, I came to show you what Hermes has got so far and to ask you to give us a more concrete idea of what you want." she explained "And I wanted to check on progress." she shrugged.

"Right then, let's have a gander -" he took the carefully bundled drawings from Sera and unrolled them. He studied them for a while and then said "What are all these little pictures, then?"

"They're just rough ideas for the design of the flyer. Hermes thought he should include pictures of some of your earlier work as well. He also thought featuring the castle would be a good idea, when it's done. And I'll put a quote on there saying how good I think it is and recommending you." she explained.

"Oh." the dwarf seemed a little taken aback "That'd be very good of y', Miss Sera. You'd really do that for us?" he thought for a few moments "Could y' get other customers to say what they think o' our engineering? We made a hammer for Thor and Odin's spear and all sorts. Freya has at least two of our treasures. Could y' ask them to put in a good word f'r us?"

"That's a great idea!" Sera exclaimed "I didn't think of that. And Hermes has just made some lightning-fast messenger hawks! It should be easy."

"Well, that's grand!" Stan laughed "And now I have something to show *you*, Miss Sera!" he winked "The lads have been very busy and they're in the process o' competing to make you the best pudding-based artefact!" he beamed again "Would y' like to see?"

"Yes please!" Sera nodded eagerly. No-one had ever made her anything special before, except for the odd full English breakfast, so she was quite excited.

"Well then, we'll have to take a short trip to Nidavellir." Stan replied, rubbing his hands together.

The journey to Nidavellir wasn't particularly long, but it was spectacular. They rode there in a chariot, pulled by two of the most enormous horses Sera had ever seen. They seemed to travel over two or three realms, which zipped along below them. One seemed to be Jotunheim, it was very cold, although mercifully they were travelling above the clouds and didn't get pelted by snow. The frozen landscape abruptly turned into a burning, red land covered in volcanoes and flames. Sera was informed that it was Muspelheim, the land of the Fire Giants. She was also told that the Fire Giants were supposed to have invaded Asgard at Ragnarok, but had gotten half way there, wondered why they were bothering and had turned right back round again. A few of them had gone on to Asgard to mess about and caused a bit of a ruckus and some damage, but it was nothing major.

They also travelled over a lush, green and bright landscape, dotted with what looked like small castles and groups of stone houses with thatched roofs. Stan told her it was the land of Alfheim, home of the light elves. All of this information was rather muffled. This was due to the dwarf travelling with a rather large sack over his head, right down to the top of his boots, so that he would not be turned to stone.

Sera didn't need telling that they had arrived in Nidavellir. They moved suddenly from the bright light of Alfheim into a land of perpetual twilight. A full moon hung in the sky.

They landed next to what Sera had thought were rows of houses from the air, but now they were on the ground the sounds of hammering and the red glow spilling out onto the streets gave them away as forges.

'I wonder if a forge and a home are the same thing to a dwarf?' Sera thought as she stepped down from the chariot. She didn't risk asking; it would probably be very rude and Sera was one of life's rudeness avoiders, sometimes to the point of acute, embarrassing but polite silence.

"Well Miss Sera, this is where we've been workin' on y' pudding-based artefacts!" Stan announced, gesturing at the surrounding forges "I don't think all the lads have finished yet, but they won't mind you askin'. Y' might even be able to give 'em some hints." he added, winking.

"I doubt it." Sera replied, and smiled back "I'm sure they're doing a great job by themselves."

"That's very kind of y', Miss Sera, but if you suddenly think 'That'd be better if it spat fire' or 'I wish that had a secret compartment wi' a knife in it' you just say so."

"Er, right." Sera replied brightly. All of a sudden this didn't seem like such a good idea; she simply couldn't imagine anything pudding-based that would have a secret compartment for a knife, nor did she want to. Thanks to the dwarves though, she wouldn't have to waste her energy *imagining* it.

Stan showed her from forge to forge, where the dwarves proudly showed her their finished artefacts or explained the various glowing bits of metal lying around their workshop that would soon become some sort of magical spatula with decapitating capabilities.

"Show the lady your work, lads." Stan said kindly to a group of young dwarves working in the same forge. "They're very keen." he said to Sera "They've been working very hard to make their artefacts. They're very promisin'." He nodded approvingly as he spoke. None of the dwarves in the line-up had beards. Not great, bushy, long ones like the builders at the castle had at least. Sera presumed it was because welding and smithing weren't great things to do if you had something large and flammable on your face.

The first dwarf in the line-up showed Sera a set of three metal fountains. One small one was bronze, one slightly larger one was silver and a big one was gold. They were all the same shape; a smooth slightly curved base, with a perfect half sphere forming the bottom of the bowl and another two smaller half spheres held above those on two progressively slimmer poles.

"This one-" he indicated the large gold fountain "-makes custard that makes the person who eats it happy, just for an hour or so. Don't eat too much of it." he warned "This one-" he indicated the silver fountain "-makes white sauce that makes the person who eats it very generous for a few hours.   Again, don't eat too much." he indicated the last fountain "This one makes butterscotch that makes the person who eats it tell the truth for a few hours." he paused for a moment "You might not want to eat that at all, Miss." he said "I know I wouldn't."

"Are you sure there isn't just alcohol in everything?" Sera asked suspiciously.

"Oh no, Miss. You'll have to add that yourself." he replied, a little taken aback.

Sera couldn't help noticing that there were thick rims attached to the outside of the spheres. They were metal rectangles, stuck all the way round, in the same colour as the fountain they were attached to.   They looked quite decorative, but at the same time they looked like they didn't really belong there. In fact, they looked like they were out the other side, as if special effort had been made to make them look as if they belonged, like a middle aged lady wearing far too much make-up, so that she wouldn't look out of place amongst younger women.

"Is this a decoration?" she asked the dwarf. He looked round and nudged the dwarf next to him.

"You see, the three of us built these..." said the nudgee, nudging a third dwarf in turn;

"Well, what they do is... if someone who isn't a guest tries to get at the sauces, well-" the third dwarf waved a hand very quickly over the rim of the nearest fountain. There was a nasty 'shing' noise and two-inch long knives shot up from the rectangles. "-that happens." the dwarf finished proudly.

"Oh. Er... very good." Sera said weakly, turning rather pale. They moved onto the next dwarf.

"And what have you got for Miss Sera, lad?" Stan asked the fourth dwarf, who was nervously clutching a fork. "Well, lad?" Stan raised an eyebrow. The nervous dwarf held out the fork.

"This is the Fork of Infinite Strength." he said "It can pierce anything and you can lift anything with it. And you can stab people with it." he went on "Um.. you can also use it to eat things..." he added shyly, as if this was an embarrassing by-function he hadn't counted on.

"That sounds very useful." Sera reassured him. He smiled happily and stepped back into the line of dwarves. The fifth dwarf had hold of a hand whisk. Stan gave him a nod.

"This is the Whisk of Destruction." the dwarf explained "It will whisk *anything* to a light, fluffy consistency. And-" he tapped the handle on the table. A blade sprang out. "-it has a knife hidden in the handle." he thought for a moment "I don't recommend usin' it to cook things, Miss." Sera merely nodded. She was beginning to turn green.

The last dwarf was holding something that didn't look like it was used for cooking at all. It seemed to be a machine of some kind; it was a small metal box, about the size of a old-style piggy bank. It had a circle of metal stuck out from a matching hole in the top of the box. It also had a small hole in one of the sides.

"Show Miss Sera your contraption, miss." Stan encouraged the last and youngest looking dwarf.

"And what might this be?" Sera asked, as kindly as she could.

"It's a badge maker, Miss." the dwarf replied quietly "Would you like a demonstration, Miss?"

"Yes please." Sera replied.   She was pleasantly surprised. The last dwarf was a girl and didn't seem to have made anything dangerous at all. But she wasn't out of the woods yet. There was always the possibility that the badges were explosive or something. The machine didn't look like it could make anything big enough to hide a knife, but Sera was willing to bet it didn't matter.

"You put in some metal, it doesn't matter what sort... just a penny or something will do, even a lump of ore-" the dwarf popped a lump of metal into the hole on the side "-then you just press this button down for a few seconds-" she pressed the button and held it down "-and out comes a badge." she finished, releasing the button and tipping it on its side until a small, coppery badge fell out.

It was a small pudding. With an arrow through it.

"Why an arrow?" Sera asked.

"Well, I thought I should put a weapon in it *somewhere*." the dwarf explained, shuffling her feet nervously "Plus now you can see the gooey centre of the pudding. It probably symbolises something." she shrugged "You need things that symbolise things, when it comes to gods. So I invented you one. I hope that was all right."

"It's not a chocolate pudding, is it?" Sera asked sternly.

"Oh no, Miss. It's toffee." the dwarf replied.

"Excellent." Sera smiled and nodded approvingly.

"Thank you, Miss." the dwarf replied handing her the badge maker "Please use it wisely. Oh and... actually, I thought you might like something else..." she trotted over to what Sera assumed was her workbench and rummaged around on it. She came back holding a set of three pans. She looked a bit embarrassed. "Um, I hope you don't take offence, miss... but these pans are for cooking with." she explained, holding them out to Sera and looking at her feet.

"For cooking with?" Sera took the pans gingerly and inspected them for hidden flamethrowers.

"Yes. Um. They'll cook anything perfectly. I invented them a while back, because I'm not very good at cooking. I sort of forget that food isn't the same as metal." she scuffed the dust with her toe .

"That's really useful. Thank you." Sera replied, relieved to get something almost normal.

"Oh, but don't worry miss!" the dwarf said hurriedly "You can hit people with them, if you like!"

BORED GAMES

They made their way back the same way they had come, riding on the massive chariot with Stan hidden under the huge sack. By the time they reached Sera's castle, it had already grown some more. Sera had been offered a magical sack with which to carry her Cooking Implements of Doom and her badge maker but had politely declined, saying she would put them in her backpack. She headed back to Sessrymnir in a thoughtful mood.

As soon as she arrived back, she went straight to Hermes who was still sitting outside on the floor and stole some of his paper. Then she went to her room and started to draw.

"What are you drawing now?" Phin asked, peering over the table "It better not be another cat." she added warningly.

"It's a dress." Sera replied "I have my artefacts and my castle... now I need an outfit. Preferably one that says 'pudding'." There was a thoughtful pause.

"You could put a walkie talkie on it and get someone else to say 'pudding' into the other one all the time. Then it'd say pudding."

"That's not what I had in mind." Sera replied, scribbling away.

"Then what did you have in mind?" Phin asked, having a good stretch and then curling up on the rug.

"I'm not sure... something like... custard..." Sera half-mumbled as she industriously rubbed out whatever she had just drawn, frowning.

"Suit yourself." Phin shrugged.

"Mmm." Sera replied distractedly, re-drawing her design.

When she'd finally rendered the paper a grey, unusable smudge, she decided to finally do the right thing and do it the graphic design way. She drew a lot of little dress templates and added various bits to them and tried out different colours until she was happy.

A little later Phin opened a lazy eye to see what all the rustling was. Sera had laid out in piles all the materials she had bought back in Midgard. She selected the thick white material and lay on it. Then, having had a better idea, she took off her armour and her dress and put on some of her old jeans and a t-shirt that she had picked up from her house. She examined her valkyrie dress and laid it out on the floor. She lay on it. Then she lay on the white material again. Then she said;

"A little help?"

"I'm sure you can get up by yourself." Phin answered.

"I don't want to get up. I want you to draw round me in pencil. Carefully." Sera explained patiently.

"What do you want me to do? I'm a *cat*."

"Just *do it*."

"*Fine*." Phin changed into her human form and drew carefully around Sera.

"Not in the middle of my legs!" Sera warned "I don't want pencil marks there."

"Right."

When the marks had been drawn and Phin had taken up her place on the rug again, Sera began to cut out the shape of the dress. She'd need to pad it out with something, probably and there was a lot more to sew onto it, but Sera had never even made anything dress-shaped before, so she thought it wise to start with that. She could worry about everything else later.

Sometime later, and quite unexpectedly, there was a knock at the door.

"Seralina?" came a familiar voice "It's Hildr. Freya wants to know where you've got to. You've not forgotten you're working tonight, have you?"

"What?" Sera replied, looking up from her sewing "Is it time for work already?" Sera looked up at the darkening sky through the window and swore. "Argh! Tell Freya I'm really sorry and I'm coming right away! I was just busy and I didn't realise what the time was! Sorry Hildr!"

"All right then. Hurry up, okay?" Hildr called, her footsteps echoing and she walked back down the hallway.

Sera struggled into her evening wear and half-ran, half-stumbled down to Sessrymnir.

"Sorry, sorry!" Sera apologised as she tried to make a nonchalant entrance and failed miserably.

"It's fine. You're not *that* late." Freya told her in an effort to calm her down; several customers were watching with raised eyebrows.

"What in Nifelheim were you doing?" Freya asked Sera as she got her breath back "You're not usually late."

"I was making a dress." Sera explained, grabbing a tray and some wine to serve to some nearby customers who were waving their glasses at her and shouting "Wa-hey!" in what they probably thought was a friendly manner.

"A dress?" Freya asked, surprised "Why?"

"Well, I'm going to have to have my own clothes for when I'm the Goddess of Puddings, aren't I? So I thought I'd make a dress." Sera explained.

"I see." Freya replied "You'll have to tell me about it later, when it's not so busy." Sera nodded and went to serve the cheerful drinkers; they would undoubtedly be wanting a lot more wine.

Osiris came to the bar for the first time, and specifically requested for Sera to serve him, but pointed to two other random girls as well.

"How are you enjoying you stay, Sire?" Sera asked him as he sat down amongst them looking extremely pleased. "I know you've been here a few days, but I haven't seen you in Freya's bar yet."

"I've been going to Valhalla since I came here." Osiris beamed "I wanted to experience the traditional Viking Afterlife, after all. And the other day I went to visit Odin and he gave me a tour of all the nine worlds. It was most exciting." Sera smiled;

"I'm glad you've been having such a good time, Sire." she said.

"Now, why don't you girls tell me all about this lovely bar and what you get up to in the daytime?" Osiris asked, clapping his hands together enthusiastically.

Osiris and the three valkyries - that is, two valkyries and one part-time valkyrie, part-time Goddess of Puddings and Similar Confections - talked together for almost the whole night. They were just as interested in his stories about the Egyptian Afterlife - which he delighted in telling them - as he was in their stories about the Norse one.

As the three of them waved him goodbye at the doors of Sessrymnir, Sera caught sight of Loki. He waited until she was by herself and then approached.

"Did you deliver my letter, lady?" he asked her.

"Yes." Sera replied "I delivered it this morning."

"Was there any response, lady?" Loki asked cautiously.

"He just said 'I see, *that* Loki' and told me I could go." Sera replied "He didn't give me a letter or a message or anything."

"I see." Loki nodded thoughtfully "Thank you, lady. I will see you again."

When she was sure he had gone, Sera allowed herself to shudder. She never wanted to deal with Loki again.

When she had finished tidying up the bar and had said good night to Freya, Sera headed straight back to her room so she could work on her dress for a little while before going to bed.

Sera found Phin curled up asleep by the fire, where she had left her. Sera sat down and stroked her absent-mindedly while she surveyed her room.

Soon, she wouldn't need it any more. She was a little sad. It was a fairly basic room, but it was nice and it was her own space.

The walls were mostly wooden and decorated with various tapestries and wall hangings, although the fireplace and the area around it was made of stone. The floor was also wooden and covered with a selection of rugs. There was a real fire. At least, presumably it was real - Sera never had to throw any fuel on it. Her rucksack lay open on the bed, which was a mattress stuffed with goose feathers covered with a few animal skin blankets. She sighed and returned to her sewing.

There was a knock at the door. She blinked. Surely Freya didn't need her at this hour?

"Come in!" she called. No answer. "I *said* come in!" Sera repeated, walking over and opening the door. She blinked in surprise. Standing on her doorstep, and looking rather put out, was the snooty woman from the bar. Sera stared. The Domestic Goddess coughed.

"So... you should come to game night." the blonde woman practically forced an envelope into Sera's hand "You will come, won't you?"

"Er.. sure?" Sera hesitated "Well.. maybe not. I mean, I might be busy. Probably. What sort of games?" she asked suspiciously.

"Board games." the Domestic Goddess answered shortly "You'll like them, I'm sure. You *are* coming?"

"Umm... sure. I *do* like board games." Sera replied, scratching her head "I wasn't going to go if it was sports though, I'm rubbish at sports."

"It's not. It's board games." the woman repeated "You have to come. I'm going. Bye." She turned and strode away down the hall as fast as she could. There was a snort from Phin, who'd appeared at the door.

"What was that all about?" she scoffed.

"Maybe it's her way of an apology." Sera shrugged and looked at the now slightly battered envelope.

"I wouldn't open that, it's probably got anthrax in it or something." Phin warned.

"Oh don't be silly, it's not even sealed." Sera chided, taking out the slightly crumpled paper inside and wandering back over to her bed.

It was a flyer, similar to Freya's flyers about the Ginza bar.

'The Bored Game of the Gods!' it proclaimed in large, ornate writing. There was a picture of what Sera assumed to be the game board underneath, but it just looked like a big, badly carved, wooden box to her. It was rectangular shaped, but the inside edge wasn't even, as though the carpenter had only bothered to smooth down the outside edges and had chipped out the inside with a chisel. Underneath the drawing, in smaller writing it said;

'Join us for Bored Game night!

Everyone welcome, competition encouraged!

Ask Osiris for details.'

"First she accuses you of nicking her stuff or whatever, now she's inviting you to go play games? Sounds fishy to *me*. I wouldn't go." Phin said, sniffing the paper and pulling her face.

"But Osiris is the one organising it, look." Sera pointed to the 'for details' bit "It's a bit odd really, I wouldn't have thought he was the type to spell things wrong... but then again, Ancient Egyptians wrote in little pictures, I suppose."

"There's some reason she wants you to go." Phin warned, ignoring the issue of spelling "She was unusually insistent for someone who doesn't like you."

"Maybe." Sera shrugged "But maybe not. Maybe she really is sorry. If I'd upset someone, I'd invite them somewhere fun to say sorry. And... It sounds like fun." Phin gave up and went back to curl up by the fire.

"Suit yourself." she replied and went to sleep.

Sera stayed up late to finish sewing the base of the dress. She tried it on and stood on the bed, so that she could see into the mirror above the fireplace. She wondered who had put it in such an awkward place; you clearly couldn't see into it without having to stand on something.

'Perhaps the last girl who lived in here was really tall.' Sera thought to herself 'Or didn't like mirrors...'

"You should probably leave it like that." Phin piped up all of a sudden, making Sera jump.

"But it's just plain." Sera argued "And it's no good on its own. There are bits I didn't stitch neatly because they'll be covered up by other bits."

"I just feel like you shouldn't ruin any more material by

trying to make something out of it." Phin replied matter-of-factly "That was perfectly good material before you got at it."

"Thanks." Sera replied sarcastically "I don't know what I'd do if you weren't so supportive." She peered at herself critically, turning this way and that, then jumped down and twirled. The dress flared out nicely. Despite what Phin had said, she'd made a decent job of it for having barely picked up a needle in her life.

'Now I need to pad it out and add sashes and stuff.' she thought to herself 'And buttons.' She definitely wanted to add buttons to it. She'd bought a whole bag of interesting buttons and she was determined to use them. But for now, what she needed was some sleep.

Sera worked non-stop on the dress for the next two days. She had an evening off on the first day, so she didn't even leave her room except to go for meals. It was also partially so she could avoid Loki. He'd said he had 'many problems' after all, and all she'd done was deliver one letter. She suspected he would turn up again.

Having once again spent all day working on her dress, Sera made her way to Sessrymnir for the evening meal at Phin's insistence.

"Honestly, just because *you* don't want to eat doesn't mean *I* don't." Phin complained as they walked down the corridor.

"I didn't want to get distracted! You could have gone by yourself." Sera replied sulkily. She hated being interrupted when she was working on projects.

"Oh well excuse *me*, I didn't know I had opposable thumbs all of a sudden." Phin carried on.

"You bloody do!" Sera retorted "You can shape shift! And anyway, you could have asked someone else to get it for you!"

"Oh yeah, right 'cause I'm going to do *that* -" Phin started.

"Sera, my dear girl!" Osiris appeared abruptly from round the corner, startling them both, his voice booming down the hallway "I'm so pleased to see you, I did hope to see you outside Sessrymnir before I left!"

"Hello, Sire." Sera replied politely "How have you been since the other night?   Still having a nice stay at our Afterlife?"

"Oh, It's been wonderful, just wonderful!" he beamed and clapped his hands together "And it's not over yet, my dear! I trust you've seen one of my flyers? I had that Hermes fellow write it up for me. He asked me if I wanted more pictures, but alas, there wasn't time. Pity, really."

"Flyers, Sire?" Sera asked, puzzled. She was a little bothered that she hadn't, since she usually looked over Hermes' work for him, but she *had* been working on the dress for two whole days now. "I must have missed them. I've been making a dress. What sort of flyers?"

"My goodness, how odd." Osiris folded his arms and frowned, matching her expression "A young lady asked me specifically for one. She said she was going to deliver it personally. She was most insistent. I was getting rather worried, you know."

"Young lady...?" Sera's frown deepened.

"It wasn't the Domestic Goddess, was it?" Phin piped up "Blonde lady, looks like a Victorian, looks down her nose at everybody?"

"I believe the young lady's name was Ellis, not Victoria. But she was certainly blonde, yes. Wore an apron. A frilly one.   Looks down her nose, you say?" he paused and considered this description "I should imagine she'd go

160

terribly cross-eyed, wouldn't you say?"

"Yes, that'll be her." Phin confirmed "She didn't say *why* she wanted to invite Sera, did she?"

"Oh, general friendliness I should think." Osiris mused "Definitely. Said something about burying the hatchet, If I remember correctly..." he sounded unsure.

"She didn't say *where* she was going to bury it by any chance?" Phin continued "You know, like in Sera's fa-" Phin was cut off by a kick from Sera.

"I'm sure she just didn't want me to miss out." Sera said and smiled. Osiris really did remind her of her jolly uncle. The kind to whom even the most hideous and possibly violent teasing would be dismissed as 'just high spirits, I'm sure'. Sera never could stand upsetting her uncle, and she wasn't about to upset Osiris either. "So, about these board games-"

Osiris explained at great length the Great Egyptian Tradition of Board Games - 'We invented them, don't you know!' - and that he had been most anxious that she had not been to see him yet, as the games were in fact, that very night. Sera listened politely for as long as she could and then excused herself to go and get some dinner. She was rather annoyed that she wouldn't be able to carry on working on her dress as she'd planned, but she'd now told Osiris she was going and in any case, she hadn't seen much of her friends outside of work lately.

"I still think this is a bad idea." Phin grumbled. They were making their way to Valhalla, which Osiris had commandeered as the game room, and where Sera hadn't been since she'd found out about the 'extra service' valkyries were supposed to provide.

"Oh, shush. Osiris will be there, and he likes me. If she

tries anything funny, I'm sure he'll help." Sera grumbled back "And there'll be others there, too. It's not like it's just me and her."

"Osiris won't notice if she does something. And I don't even know if anyone else will even care." Phin argued "Gods are a nasty, spiteful bunch. Ha, she fits right in. Anyway, someone like her will do it sneakily. So it's like she hasn't even done anything. You just watch."

"I still think you're overreacting..." Sera replied, a little doubtfully. She'd been brought up to give people the benefit of the doubt. The problem was that people often took it and ran. She suspected that Phin was right and also that Phin might be the bit of her that secretly wanted to be rude to people she didn't like and her repressed urge to scratch their eyes out.

Valhalla seemed a lot, *lot* bigger without the long tables cluttering it up. And it had been pretty huge to start with. Only two of the long tables remained, one down each side of the hall. They were laden with food and drink, and a few bored-looking valkyries were on duty at each end. Sera didn't envy them. Their tired eyes and grim expressions said 'We've been serving einherjar all night and now *this*'. Sera nodded at them and made apologetic expressions as she went past. They shrugged non-committally back.

In the middle of the room there had been several small tables set up. Many of them had some kind of rectangular wooden box on top, but some of them seemed to have piles of cards or dice. Sera wandered over and looked at a few of them, but they were all completely unfamiliar. Sera looked around to see if there was anyone she knew. Freya had been discussing business with Hermes again, so she probably wasn't coming. Sera weaved her way through a small crowd that had gathered, having to apologise to a rather tall

Egyptian god after he turned around rather suddenly and she bumped into him. He had some sort of wading bird's head.

"I'm terribly sorry!" Sera apologised, readjusting her headband that had come askew after colliding with his beak "I really am-" she continued, but the bird-headed god merely patted her on the head and then made his way over to the drinks table. As he moved out of the way, Sera spotted Hildr, another of Freya's Ginza girls.

"Oh, Sera you came too!" Hildr shouted, hurrying over "I'm actually really glad -" she continued, much more quietly "I really wanted to come, but none of the other girls were interested and I felt really self conscious. I mean, look at this lot -" she indicated the assembled gods and goddesses "I feel like a peasant at the king's table. And have you seen how they all look at us? One of them asked me to get him a drink!" she finished hotly.

"Well... I suppose this *is* Valhalla and there *are* some of the girls on duty -" Sera mused, always ready to excuse someone else's bad behaviour. She was a little disappointed that none of the other girls had come, though.

"I told him I was off duty and I was here for the games and, you should have seen his face." Hildr pulled her own face "Like I'd just given him cheek or something. It's not like I wasn't polite. They think we're servants or something!"

"Well we *do* serve wine and stuff-" Sera began.

"Yeah, but only because that's our *job*." Hildr scoffed "Like it's their job to look after rivers or hinges or whatever. I'd like to see him pulling his face if it was the daytime, when I'm at the other end of a bloody spear!"

"Well, he *is* from another pantheon-" Sera continued in vain.

"That's not the point!" Hildr paused and mentally backtracked "Well, OK it *is*. I mean, this is *our* pantheon. I

163

take orders from Freya and Odin and stuff, but their *ours* and I'm a *warrior* and -" she sighed and threw her hands up at the impossibility of describing how annoying it is to women that men expect them to drop everything and make them a sandwich or something "I'm just glad there's no einherjar here. They weren't allowed, because they aren't gods."

"Oh? Would it be bad if there were non-gods here?" Sera asked, a little shocked.

"Well, it's the Bored Game of the Gods, isn't it?" Hildr explained "It's what gods play when they get bored. We can't have mortals playing it, it'd mess it all up." Sera took a good look at Hildr. She was fairly tall, with long, dark hair. She was much slimmer than Sera. Her dress seemed to be less expansive than Sera's, too. She was wearing her battle armour, not the gilt stuff they had to wear in the evenings. Sera guessed that she hadn't been on serving duty today. If Sera didn't know better, she would have thought that Hildr had *never* been on serving duty. Although, she looked like she was more suited to being a waitress than a warrior. She was like the classical painting version of a valkyrie to Sera's classical opera valkyrie. All slim and delicate - not like a woman who would run screaming at the enemy.

'Maybe if they'd asked her to get them a drink...' Sera thought to herself. Out loud she said "Were you always a valkyrie, Hildr?" The comment about 'mortals messing it up' had been quite jarring. There were quite a few bits of Sera that could swear she was still mortal. Her fingers, for one thing. She'd turned out not to be very good at sewing and wasn't getting any better, particularly in the not-stabbing-your-fingers department. She'd always wondered what thimbles were for and now she knew.

"I think so." Hildr replied "I'm not quite sure."

"You *aren't sure?*" Sera blinked.

"No. It's been a couple of hundred years at least and I feel like I've been doing this for ever." Hildr just shrugged, as if her origins were of no more interest than say, a new type of trousers.   They may have an interesting cut or be an interesting shape, perhaps. But at the end of the day, they're still two tubes of fabric to put your legs through, like all the other kinds. Life was pretty much the same; you got born, then stuff happened. "Mortals become valkyries, valkyries become mortals. It happens. It doesn't really matter, so long as I'm a valkyrie *now*, does it?"

"I suppose not." Sera conceded, slightly begrudgingly "I was just interested, that's all. You know. With me being new and everything."   To herself she thought 'I wonder if I'll be like that in a hundred years or so? When everyone I know on Earth has died, will *I* care if I was ever human...?'

Sera suddenly felt very alone. She was painfully aware of what Hildr had meant when she said it was like being a peasant at the king's table. What right did she have to be here? She was no-one special. She couldn't do anything remotely magical or goddess-like and she certainly couldn't think of people as 'mortals'. It made humans sound like something you found living at the bottom of a pond. She had friends and family back on Midgard. And a cat. And she couldn't even imagine *Bella* as being beneath her. And there probably *were* things living on the bottom of ponds that were more intelligent than Bella.

"I think I'm going to go back to my room." she announced suddenly "I'm really tired."   Hildr looked disappointed.

"Oh, don't go!" she cried "I'll be all alone and they'll be starting any minute! You'll be all right once it starts."

"I don't know, I really am tired -" Sera started. She turned to leave. She got half way to the door when Osiris walked through it.

"There you are, my dear!" trilled Osiris, beaming "You simply must come and play at my table!"

"Actually, I was-" Sera was steered towards a table with one of the strange wooden boxes on "I was going to go and -" she tried again.

"To go and get a drink?" Osiris enquired, beaming "Don't worry my dear, there'll be plenty left when we take a break, you needn't rush!"

"Oh, well, OK, then." Sera smiled weakly and gave up. There was something reassuring about Osiris. She couldn't imagine him thinking badly of anybody. He'd met the Domestic Goddess and seen her as a charming young lady, after all. *He'd* stick up for mortals, surely.

Up close, the box was a lot more complicated. It wasn't anything like the rough hewn slabs of wood it had looked like on the flyer. It was smooth and varnished on the outside. What had seemed to be a splintery, chiselled out interior on the flyer was actually an incredibly delicate looking landscape. It was intricately carved, and looked like a map of some kind. There was a river, with a city built around it. Around that there was also some green, and on one side the map seemed to reach the ocean. It looked worryingly familiar. Sera frowned. Surely it couldn't be London? What was London doing on an Egyptian game board? Even if it turned out to be a Norse game, it still didn't make much sense. Unless the game was 'Let's All Raid London And Burn It Down' of course, which Sera hoped it wasn't. Not that Sera blamed the Vikings for invading Britain, and indeed, burning quite a bit of it down, because then she'd have to be annoyed at *everyone else* who'd invaded Britain. And *then*, she'd have to be annoyed at *Britain* for invading everyone else, which was hardly surprising, because by then the population was presumably mostly made up of invaders.

"Well then, let's choose our pieces and get started, shall we?" suggested Osiris, reaching into the big box and pulling out a smaller, darker box with a lid on.

"Wait a minute, please!" came a voice from behind Sera "May we join you?" Sera turned to see the Domestic Goddess and another woman push some spectators out of the way.

"The other tables are rather full." said the other woman, pushing her thick, blonde hair out of her eyes and accidentally elbowing Sera in the face.

"Ow." Sera moved to one side and rubbed her cheek.

"Oh, sorry." said the newcomer, turning to Sera "Oh... you're that girl. The new one, from a while ago." Sera had been paying more attention to the Domestic Goddess in case she was going to try something, but when someone elbows you in the face, there is a tendency for them to become the centre of your attention, just in case they do it again.

"Oh, you're...Er..." Sera hesitated for a moment "Idunn. Hello." Sera hadn't thought very much of Idunn when they'd met before, but she was also aware that she'd only met her for about a minute and that she had been dazed and confused at the time, which is not a great situation in which to form balanced opinions of people. The overwhelming impression she'd been left with was of pink. Sera had never liked pink very much, except when she was five, which is an age when it is impossible for girls *not* to like pink.

"Oh, you remember my name." Idunn replied "What was yours again?"

"Seralina. But you can call me Sera. Everyone else does." Sera answered.

"Yes, I'm sure they do." Idunn pushed her hair out of her eyes again, making her jewellery tinkle. She was wearing

167

rather a lot of it, today. She had gold bangles and bracelets up the length of both arms, and several gold necklaces to boot. However, she wasn't wearing pink like Sera remembered; she had on a long, black, evening dress and a black feather boa. She had on the same ruby red lipstick as before, though. She put her hands on her hips.

"Are we getting started then?" she asked, moving away from Sera. Sera decided she probably didn't like Idunn after all, pink or no pink. She'd pretty much just been blanked, and in her book that was just about the rudest thing someone could do. She'd been brought up to put up with things she didn't like, and that included people. If you didn't like someone, you didn't *blank* them. You put up with them and treated them like anyone else. You might come to like them later. Sera didn't see any point in burning bridges. It was a waste of a good bridge.

"Right then, let's hurry up and choose our pieces!" Osiris clapped and rubbed his hands together in a business-like fashion. He took the lid off the box and took out a little figure and a card. Then he passed it to the next person. They did the same. The Domestic Goddess took longer choosing than everyone else, and Sera could have sworn she kept taking sidelong glances towards her.

Finally it was Sera's turn. There weren't many left. Sera took out one of the pieces and examined it. It was a tiny replica of a person. They were amazingly detailed, and seemed to be made of something like pewter. Some of them were brightly painted, others had only the merest hint of colour. She picked up another one. She could even make out the freckles on its face. And humans weren't the only playing pieces. There was a dog, a little terrier. And a curious, yellow butterfly. There was also, for some unexplained reason, a boot.

Next, Sera looked at the cards. They seemed to correspond to the figures, but in the way of board games everywhere, it seemed that a few of the pieces had gotten lost somewhere. At least she was pretty sure that 'Clive the Ninja' was *not* in the box. On the other hand, perhaps he was a *really good* ninja.

Finally, she chose the one she felt she could relate to; a Chinese student who had come to study in London in the hopes of getting a good job and being able to send lots of money back home to her family. She had actually wanted someone she *couldn't* relate to, like a sorceress who could turn people into toads or a fairy princess or something like that. She didn't see much point in playing a game to pretend you were something that you *are*.

'I guess that really is London...' she mused, re-reading the card 'Maybe this is like all that dungeon-raiding game business, only for gods...? After all, they go around *really* doing all that stuff. Maybe they think it'd be kind of fun being human?'

"Right, is that everybody?" Osiris shouted. A few people hurriedly squeezed themselves into the circle, having returned from the drinks table, and scavenged what they could from the remaining pieces. One of them was the bird-headed god Sera had bumped into before. Osiris sighed and waited for the latecomers to finish squabbling over who had to be the dog. Finally, the loser of the argument fished her terrier card out of the box. "Very good then, let's begin!" Osiris announced, clapping.

"Wait. Umm..." Sera hesitated, feeling like a fool for holding everything up even more "What are the rules? How do we play? I've never done this before, sorry."

"Rules?" scoffed a short, blonde haired god across the table from Sera "What *rules*? What do we want *rules* for?

Rules are for *mortals*."

"Oh *do* excuse her." the Domestic Goddess chipped in "She's *new*, you see."

"Oh, I see." the blonde god nodded, as if this was all he needed to know. He grinned unpleasantly.

'Yes, I see, too.' Sera thought to herself 'This is like all that old money, new money business with rich people. I use the wrong kind of salad fork, and you all laugh patronisingly.' she narrowed her eyes 'Well, let's see how funny it is when I *stab* you with it.'

"Sorry, sorry." Sera smiled as brightly as she could "No rules, eh? How exciting. This is going to be so much fun!" Sera was a perfectly nice person in the real world, but the point of a game is to be as nasty as possible. In a game, she could be as nasty to jerks as she liked and not feel bad, because that was the *point*. She had no idea how, but she was going to *win,* or at least beat these three. No-one was going to push her around in a *game*. She *liked* games.

"Well then. Now that's settled, I'll go first, if no-one minds." the Domestic Goddess announced "Oh, and *do* call me Ellis. If you all stand around calling me the Domestic Goddess, well, we'll be here all night!" she laughed "Right -" she started, reading her card "I'm playing *Amanda*, who is a recent graduate and looking for work in London, because she wants - *and deserves* - a high flying job there." Ellis placed her figure on the board, at which point it started to move. Sera stared. The box's surface seemed to ripple, and sort of zoomed in on the map. The green disappeared and the bottom of the box was now more like a series of tiny cubes. It was rather grey, aside from the area where the river ran through it, which was now less blue and more brown coloured. Sera could feel Ellis looking at her. She kept her mouth shut. She wasn't going to react. She wasn't going to be laughed at again.

"Right then." announced the bird-headed god who had come and stood next to Sera "Please call me Thoth. I'm... Er-" he squinted at his card "I'm Mr. Bun the Baker, apparently. I don't think that's quite right-"

Everyone went around the table, announcing their names and their characters. Whenever one was placed on the board, it would zoom in or out until they were at what must have been the correct locations on the map. When everyone placed their pieces, the pieces themselves began to move. Sera, determined to ask as few questions as possible, just looked on with interest. She could feel Ellis watching her to see if she'd react. She wasn't going to give her the satisfaction.

Sera paid careful attention to the other players as they took their turns. They didn't seem to be going in any particular order, and one goddess, who appeared to be Greek, went twice. They had all announced fairly standard things, like 'my character will go to the shops' or 'my character decides to go on a diet'. Then Hildr announced her turn.

"My character is going to have her hair styled, and then have a manicure. She's going to go and put on her new make-up, too." Hildr's character was a college girl, doing her A-levels. She wanted to be a model, according to the card. Was the point to role-play what you thought the character would do? Sera decided to give it a shot.

"My turn!" she cut in, just as the blonde-haired god from before had opened his mouth "My character is going to hand her CV in to as many companies as possible and keep studying hard." she announced. She waited to see if there was any sniggering. There wasn't.

"Nice move. Done? Right. My turn." said an Egyptian

woman next to Osiris. She was one of the latecomers, and had ended up with the dog. "My character is going to… let's see…" she looked hard at the game board "Yes, he's going to head to *here*-" she pointed to the map "-and rummage through some bins and beg for scraps and other doggy things." she finished. Sera wondered why she'd bothered to consider her move so carefully when she was playing a dog. The area she'd pointed to didn't seem to be special in any way. Sera couldn't quite remember the woman's name. It had sounded more like a sneeze.

"*My* character-" announced the blonde haired god loudly, before he could be cut off again "-is going to put an ad in the lonely hearts section of the newspaper. And he's going to go to the pub."

This went on for some turns. Sera wasn't sure what her character should be doing, so she hadn't moved. She'd felt stupid at first, but then she'd noticed that the Egyptian lady from before hadn't moved again either. She'd just kept watching the other pieces movements and humming to herself. Sera looked more carefully at the board. She wondered what the woman was watching for exactly. The only thing she could see was that the pieces seemed to be closer together than they were before. Sera decided to wait another turn or two. The other players had done what seemed to be random, ordinary things. The blonde haired god had gone on a few dates - they had been successful and as far as she could tell, he was dating several women at once. Thoth had had to stick with Mr. Bun the Baker, whatever his real name was, and had been quietly baking away in a corner and apparently nothing else. Hildr's piece had been looking around for modelling opportunities and had started her own website as a sort of online portfolio. Sera felt it was time to move again.

"Having studied hard, and got really good, my character will apply for a few translator-slash-interpreter jobs at some big companies." Sera announced.

"My piece will move *here*-" the Egyptian woman announced suddenly, pointing to a place near the river "- and forage for scraps. And hunt rats. And chase foxes." And Sera saw it. With that move, the dog was now in the centre of all the other pieces, that had gradually been getting closer and closer together. Sera wondered what it meant.

"I think we should take a break." Osiris said, looking at the board thoughtfully "I for one, would like a glass of wine." There was an murmur of agreement and the group dispersed. "Sera, my dear?" he called. Sera jumped.

"Yes?" she said, looking up from the board. She been staring at it trying to figure out what the point was.

"You wouldn't fetch me a glass of red wine from the table, would you?" he asked "I'm the game master you see, so I'm not allowed to leave the board." he paused "Well I *am*. It's just not a very good idea." he gave her an apologetic look. Hildr was trying to glare at him without actually looking, so Sera grabbed her hand.

"You'll come with me, right?" Sera asked "I might need *help*." she added meaningfully. Hildr shrugged.

"Oh all right." she replied, sighing "Since it's you." When they were about halfway to the table, suitably far enough away from all the other players, Sera grabbed Hildr's arm.

"Why can't Osiris leave the table?" she asked "The game doesn't have any rules, right?" Hildr sighed.

"Trust me, even in a game with no rules, gods will find a way to cheat." she explained "Anything else? While that woman can't hear us. She's the one from a few weeks ago, isn't she? Freya had a right time getting her to leave. *She* thinks we're just waitresses, too. The *nerve*. I mean, you expect that from the male gods, but-"

"Yeah, that's her." Sera cut her off "I don't know, she doesn't seem to be actually doing anything. But Phin thinks she invited me here to show me up or something."

"Probably." Hildr paused and looked puzzled "Didn't your familiar come here with you? Where did she go?" Sera looked around, suddenly worried that the Domestic Goddess had kidnapped her while she wasn't looking. She relaxed. Having been unable to see over the table, Phin had apparently got bored and was asleep under it.

"Phew." Sera fanned herself "Don't worry me like that! We'd better hurry up with that wine."

Sera and Hildr got the wine for Osiris and their own drinks and snacks and made their way back to the gaming table. The other groups had hung about around the other tables, chatting or discussing strategies. There were other games going on too, but Sera was surprised to see that they seemed to be perfectly ordinary, like poker and chess.

"Your wine, Sire." said Sera cheerfully as she handed it over "Are you doing well, do you think?" she asked, indicating the game board.

"Oh, not too bad, not too bad." Osiris replied, taking a sip of his wine "We'll find out soon enough." Osiris' character was a lawyer. He'd been making such bold moves as 'sorting out the executor of Mrs. Norris' will with all the right paperwork' and 'looking over various case files'. Sera looked around to check that none of the other players were in earshot.

"How exactly do you win, then?" she asked. It had been puzzling her for quite some time. She got the idea that in the ones with dungeons and monsters and things it was to do with how much gold you had or who died the least.

"We-ell..." Osiris began, taking another sip of his wine "It's a bit tricky. It's to do with who has the best character at the end, I suppose." Hildr chipped in;

"It's not so much about winning as it is about not losing." she explained "You see how everyone has bunched up close together?" she frowned at the board "Except for Thoth and his baker, anyway. He might well win actually, if he's lucky."

"Why? What exactly do you have to do?" Sera peered at the layout again.

"You get close to the players, preferably while staying a reasonable distance from as many of the others as possible." Hildr explained "So that you can trip them up. While trying not to get tripped up yourself, obviously."

"So you mess up the other players?" Sera replied, horrified "The point is just to be horrible to everyone else, for no reason? Like, get them to lose their job or, or, I don't know, catch smallpox or something?"

"Oh it's all right." Osiris reassured her "Humans get over these things." Sera froze.

"*Humans*?" she stared at the two of them "I thought you said they couldn't play?"

"Oh no, they can't. Of course not. They're the pieces." Osiris explained "Except the dog, of course. It's a dog." he added helpfully. Sera was in shock.

"You can't do that! You can't just-" she put her hands over her face and tried to will the situation away for a minute. Her determination to win drained right away. She couldn't possibly carry on playing if it meant messing up someone else's life.

"Look, we do this all the time, it's fine, really -" Hildr started, but Sera shook her head. Hildr frowned and continued "Come to think of it, humans do it all the time, too. All those ones that have the task of deciding who gets what job and who needs firing and who gets their art exhibited and all that stuff. Humans control other humans all the time. I don't see why you should get so upset just because gods are doing it."

"But, but it's not *right*!" Sera shouted "Those people have got to do those things! Someone has to make those choices! But they aren't playing a game! They aren't trying to mess other people up!"

"Oh *yes* they are!" Hildr snapped "People work in businesses and businesses are always trying to trip each other up! They have to, to survive! No matter how far humans think they've gotten away from nature, it's still survival of the fittest out there! And what about all the damage humans do to other species? You can't tell me you aren't being hypocritical, Sera." Sera bit her lip. She knew Hildr was making some kind of sense and that she was making a scene, precisely where she hadn't wanted to make one. But the thought of her parents or Meena as just some god's pawn was terrifying. "Besides, you haven't done anything nasty, have you?" Hildr pointed out "You can win without being nasty. Thoth just has to sit there out of everyone's way and he could win. It depends on whether or not Osiris wants to just sit there or whether he wants to start causing trouble."

"Is it all happening right now?" Sera demanded "Do these poor people just have to do as we say, right now?"

"No, no, it doesn't work like that." Hildr explained, trying to calm Sera down "We're sort of making their destiny, *but-*"

"But?" said Sera suspiciously.

"Humans have a tendency to muck about with destiny. We can't say for sure it'll happen. Maybe someone will get in

176

trouble like someone said, and maybe someone will try to fire them, but *maybe*-" she continued, holding up a hand when Sera opened her mouth to protest "Someone else will say 'no, you can't do that'. We don't have control over the pieces that *aren't* on the board. So we can't say for sure. You're blowing it out of all proportion, honestly." she put her hands on her hips and waited.

"So, say someone said they stole something, like, like, a water bed or something-" Sera said, suddenly appalled at her own previous behaviour "-and the staff got in trouble for it going missing, because-"

"How in *Nifelheim* do you steal a *water bed*?" Hildr asked.

"Exactly. So say they got in trouble, well... if they did, a god could fix it right? If it was their fault, they should, right?" Sera asked "But it might not, because of destiny being made by humans themselves, is what you're saying? Because they might just have said 'oh, well it was a stock checking error, never mind.'"

"Yes. Exactly." Hildr answered, giving Sera a calculating look "This isn't about the game anymore, is it?"

"Well -" Sera began.

"Is everything all right?" It was Ellis. "We heard shouting, so we came back. I do hope you weren't playing without us."

"Oh, no we were just-" Hildr started.

"I was just saying how I went and took some trees and a water bed once. It must have got the humans in trouble." Sera explained, smiling "I went back and paid later, which probably got them in even more trouble. I was just wondering if anyone else did that sort of thing? It sounds like a good game tactic, for one thing." she finished brightly. There was a snigger from somewhere.

"You did what?" Ellis snorted, forgetting that she was pretending to be charming "What did you do that for?"

"Well, I needed them and I couldn't not pay for them..." Sera trailed off.

"Stupid. Why didn't you use your card?"

"...card?" Sera replied, bemused.

"The one you get when you become a goddess, you idiot." Ellis pulled a shiny, black card out of her apron pocket "This, here. You use it like a credit card or like paper money. I can't believe you went and just *took* things, and then went back and actually *paid*!" There was a chorus of laughter from the rest of the players.

"Well, I didn't know..." Sera mumbled "No-one said..." she trailed off.

"Look this is all hilarious, but I'd like to get back to kicking your butts, if it's not too much trouble." It was the blonde god.

"Yes, yes. I'm sure we'd all like to go home at some point." Ellis shrugged and took up her position next to Idunn.

"My move." said the blonde god "I'm going to move here-" he pointed right next to the Domestic Goddess' piece "-and ask your girl out. And she says yes."

"We'll see about that." Eliis drew herself up "I say she says no. She might not know about all those women you've got, Sataere, but I do."

"Well then, you shall have to roll for it." Osiris announced, producing a dice from somewhere "Ellis will go first, then Sataere, you must roll higher than her."

"Right then." Ellis took the dice and rolled. "There. A five. Tough to beat." Sataere gave a lop-sided smile.

"We'll see about that." he said and took the dice. With his other hand, he grabbed the hilt of his sword.

"Oh no, you don't." Osiris announced suddenly,

grabbing his hand "*No-one* is to go cutting the die in half. I'm not made of dice, you know."

"Wasn't going to-" Sataere began sullenly, but Osiris waved his finger at him.

"Oh yes you were. There's not a bugger that doesn't try it!" he replied crossly. Sera had never seen Osiris cross before. It looked like this Sataere had hit a nerve. Maybe *he* was perfectly nice until it came to gaming, too.

"Sorry. Anyway, I'll roll shall I?" the blonde god rolled the dice and the eyes of every player watched as it spun to a halt.

"There, see?" Osiris said in a 'told you so' manner "It's a six. You rolled higher and more importantly, my die is still intact."

"Oh dear." said Ellis, smiling a waxy smile.

"So your girl is going out with my piece, here." stated Sataere smugly "Isn't that nice."

"We'll see." replied Ellis sweetly "My turn, then. My character will go for a job interview at... where was it?" she looked at Sera "Oh yes, Gaijin Corp. For the secretary position."

"That's what my character is doing, I believe." Sera matched the Domestic Goddess, smile for smile.

"Oh my, so it is." Ellis continued "Incidentally, she completely accidentally spills mascara on your character's nice, white blouse in the waiting room."

"I think that must be quite difficult." Sera replied "I think my character avoids having mascara spilled on her, completely accidentally."

"Roll the dice, ladies. I think this calls for two." Osiris produced a second die. Sera grabbed the dice and rolled. Just as the dice bounced, the Domestic Goddess seemed to trip, while she was craning to see the result. She grabbed the table for support rather violently and one of the dice fell off the table. The other dice showed a six.

"Where did it go?" Sera asked "What does it say? Anyone?" Osiris stood up with the errant die in his hand.

"I'm sorry dear, if it falls off the table, it doesn't count." he explained "Six then. Your turn, Ellis my dear. Do try not to trip up like that, I do so hate losing my dice." he added pointedly.

"I'm so sorry, I shall try to have more patience next time!" the Domestic Goddess laughed, and took the dice. She rolled. One was a three, the other a five. "Too bad, Sera. Looks like your character will have to sit this one out. Better luck next time."

"Indeed." Sera replied. 'But Osiris won't let you pull that again. He's the game master and it looks like he's touchy about his stuff, plus I happen to know he's one of the judges of the dead in the Underworld... I can't believe Phin thought he wouldn't notice anything-'

Sera watched and waited as all hell let loose. Suddenly, everyone was out to cause as much trouble as seemingly innocently as possible. It ranged from standing on people's feet in the street at the most inconvenient moment, such as when it would cause someone to get knocked over and then miss their bus and be late for work, to Sataere extorting money out of his player girlfriends 'to help him out', right up to Osiris suddenly suing Thoth's Mr. Bun the Baker for copyright infringement.

"But, it would be your client suing my bakery!" Thoth protested as he took the dice to roll - it required a LOT of dice that Osiris had somehow produced from about his person "I think I deserve some extra dice."

"Ah, but who do you think tipped off my client to the copyright infringement, eh?" Osiris remarked back "We can't have you sitting there quietly, hogging all the good karma now, can we, Thoth?"

"Fair point, fair point!" Thoth nodded. It was hard to tell because wading birds don't have a great range of facial expressions, but Thoth actually seemed pleased at the challenge.

"Ha! Out-rolled you, you old devil!" Thoth shouted triumphantly, after they'd retrieved all the dice, a considerable few of which had gone bouncing across the floor.

"Oh dear me, that was my big plan for beating you." Osiris tutted and shook his head "You might just win, old boy!" Several of the players looked from Osiris to Thoth and then eyed each other. Poor Mr. Bun's bakery then had to put up with a string of thefts, a mysteriously infected batch of bread rolls resulting in another failed suing attempt and an 'accidentally' broken window.

Meanwhile, the quiet, Egyptian lady with a name like a sneeze had put her dog to shockingly good use, which they couldn't avoid because she was in the midst of them and couldn't counter attack, because the dog was a dog and therefore couldn't easily be caught or sued. She'd given one player's pet fleas, resulting in a large vet's bill and shook herself out over the nice, new dress of Ellis' character that she was about to wear to an interview. She even had a crack at Thoth and his baker, stealing a loaf and getting several others muddy and disgusting the long line of customers that were present in the process.

Ellis seemed to have an annoyingly one track mind, and basically concentrated her efforts on blocking Sera's character whenever she could, since they were aiming for the same kind of jobs. Sera had given up all hope of winning and was just desperately trying to keep her character out of trouble. Like Osiris had said though, she might actually be able to win if she kept out of it the most, so she clung on to the strategy with grim determination. She wasn't entirely sure if the Egyptian lady was trying to help her, she seemed to be trying to place her dog between Sera's and Ellis' pieces whenever possible, although she always seemed to be splashing and biting her way through the other competitors at the same time, so maybe it was just coincidental.

Then Sera got an opening. The Domestic Goddess, trying to avoid the little dog, was quite far away from Sera's piece when she tried another interview. But Ellis declared that there was a mistake and the interview was in the wrong place, it being the company's old location, and that Sera's character must hurry to a building practically next to Thoth's bakery. Sera had to wait a turn. Then, just as the Domestic Goddess was about to declare her move-

"Sorry, sorry!" Hermes shoved his way through the crowd, followed by Freya "Can we join in? Oh, there's only one piece left." Hermes picked up the boot and offered it to Freya, who waved it away.

"No, no. You take it." she insisted "You worked far harder than me today. Besides, I'm not that keen on this one." Freya gave the board a disdainful look "I *like* humans, thank you very much." The Domestic Goddess tried again, but was silenced by Osiris.

"There's only one piece left, I do apologise." he explained.

"I don't think you can join in so late." tried Ellis, desperate to make her decisive move against Sera "There's hardly any game left really, I mean... it's not fair, you'll be better off than the rest of us."

"You know what, I could *swear* I heard someone say there's no rules to this game." came a voice from what sounded like under the table.

"Yes, well." Hermes started "I also think I'm a boot, so I shouldn't think I've got much karma anyway."

"Oh, yes." said the Domestic Goddess, visibly relaxing "I suppose not. It's just a boot, after all. My mistake, go ahead, do."

"Right then." Hermes said picking up the boot and looking at its card "Who's what then?" Players dutifully explained their characters and what they'd been up to as best they could. Hermes gave the board a calculating stare and then met the gaze of Thoth. He pointedly put the boot down right on the bakery. The board shifted so it was in the right place. Ellis looked from one to the other, to the position of her and the other characters, who happened to be passing by on a date and possibly, on their way to the interview to mess with Sera's Chinese student. Too late, the Domestic Goddess tried to declare her turn-

"My turn!" Thoth announced cheerfully "I'm going to open the upstairs window in my bakery, because it's awfully hot, but I shall have to hurry, because there's no-one downstairs to look after the shop and my goodness, what a string of thefts there's been lately-"

"My turn then!" announced Hermes equally as cheerfully, cutting off both Ellis and Sataere, who had also seen trouble looming "I do believe that Mr. Bun has opened his window far too quickly, and his lovely potted plant, planted in fact, not in a pot, but in this here boot, has been knocked rather badly and is going to fall off the shelf."

"I say it doesn't!" shouted Ellis and Sataere together.

"Oh my, you can't roll for that. I'm afraid it was Thoth's man who set it off, so it would have to be him who objects." Osiris put in.

"What?" Thoth looked offended, insofar as a wading

bird can "Go back upstairs to check on my plant so that you lot can come and nick all my stuff again? Not likely!"

"And I do believe that Mr. Sataere's character is walking right underneath it, too." Hermes said with mock concern "I do believe it's going to hit him on the head."

"I roll for a dodge-" Sataere began, but the Egyptian lady interrupted him.

"Oh, he'll be too distracted to dodge, because my little doggie is about to bite him in the unmentionables." she said, smiling serenely.

"But, you can't-"

"What was that about rules, again?" piped up the voice from under the table.

"So, the boot hits this guy on the head." Hermes began in a conversational tone "Which he is unable to dodge, because he's being bitten on the nadgers by Lady Hatshepsut's doggie, there. Incidentally, if I have everything right, he's dating this lady here, and this lady here...oh, and this one." he pointed to Ellis' Amanda, Idunn's character, who had actually been fairly inoffensive, much to Sera's surprise and a third girl "I think they'd come running, wouldn't they, hearing their boyfriend yell out like that, goodness, look how close you all are together."

"Oh dear." Osiris chimed in "These three ladies do not appreciate the sight of one another, because this is clearly their boyfriend, wooing another lady." he explained, fulfilling his role as game master "And I'm sure Mr. Thoth doesn't want a fight breaking out like that in front of his bakery, my goodness, no."

"And I do believe that my baker here recognises the miscreants he has been trying to catch who keep stealing his stuff. From the security camera footage. And I do believe that he is wise enough to ask them all to come in and calm down... and then lock the little buggers in, while he phones the police."

"Meanwhile, I'm sure us three ladies will have realised who we should be angry at and treat Mr. Saratere's man to his own private hell while we wait for them to arrive." claimed the Greek goddess who was playing the third girlfriend.

"Well now." Osiris hushed everyone while he stared at the board with a faraway look in his eyes "Causing irreparable damage to four other players, while restoring a great deal of karma to one, with an uncounterable move, whilst not actually being accountable for any of it, in only one turn." Osiris nodded at Hermes "Also, it is unlikely that any counter-attack could be made on the boot, because it is an item of footwear, and accumulates bad karma at an incredibly slow speed, because it is in fact inanimate and thus, not subject to karma hardly at all. I do believe you win, Mr. Hermes." he began to clap "A round of applause, ladies and gentlemen!" The other gods began to clap, the losers somewhat reluctantly, but applause led by Freya was destined never to be lonely, and in fact half of the rest of the hall joined in on principle.

THE SACRED PUDDING COMMUNITY

For the rest of her time off, Sera went back to finishing her dress. It had been an eventful evening, and had eventually wrapped up with Sera talking by the buffet table with the other gods and goddesses who'd helped take out Ellis and Sataere. Apparently, they'd been annoyed by her sneakiness. It was all well and good being nasty, they'd said, but she could at least have the decency to be nasty upfront. They'd noticed how Ellis had been blocking Sera earlier on and had wondered what they could do about it, but hadn't really had a good plan until Hermes had come along. Hermes had blushed and said it was all luck and the nature of everyone being close together at the end of the game and easier targets, but the other gods were impressed nevertheless. Sera had also demanded the names and addresses of all the players' pieces, so that she could go and check up on them later. Phin had argued that she had enough to do on her 'To-Do List of Happiness' as it was, but it seemed to be more for the sake of arguing with someone than anything else, because she'd been so bored all night.

The next day was mercifully uneventful, and finally, the dress was finished. It was a mix of brown and white at the top, with the white mostly spattered over her shoulders. Then there was a dark yellow waistband and the skirt became completely brown. But over that was another, shorter skirt, slightly ruffled, of a silky, toffee coloured material. The same material went in broad strips over her shoulders, overlaid with the same yellow material as the waistband. Finally, there was a white, patterned, net-like material that overlaid the toffee-coloured skirt, down to the knees. There were two white sashes overlaid onto that. The left sash had a loose, expanding cluster of brightly coloured, differently shaped flowers sewn onto it. The same buttons were sewn sparsely onto the white net material as well.

Sera had also made herself a sort of hat, although to call it a hat would be an insult to hats and hat-like things everywhere; the most accurate way to describe it would be as a head decoration, despite the fact that it wasn't particularly decorative. Sera had decided to call it a head decoration anyway and have done with it.

"It doesn't look very decorative to *me*." Phin remarked.

"Well tough. I'm the goddess around here and if *I* say it's a head decoration, it's a head decoration!" Sera argued. She was tired and frazzled from the several times when thread had managed to knot horribly by itself and material had almost ripped right off. But it was finally done.

The 'head decoration' was a train of the yellow material, attached to a circle of the toffee-coloured material which was covered by more of the white patterned material, which also made a shorter train than the yellow material. It also had the colourful buttons sewn onto it, in the same loose cluster pattern as on the sash of the dress.

Sera stood on the bed in the completed dress and admired - or at least took a good look at - her handiwork.

"You look like a badly iced chocolate cake." Phin told her as she jumped down from the bed.

"Good." Sera replied "At least it reminds you of cake. It's supposed to."

"Is it supposed to look terrible?" Phin asked sceptically

"Because it does."

"Oh, it's not *that* bad." Sera replied, doing a twirl before adding "And yes, it is."

"Congratulations, then." Phin said, getting up and stretching "Just in time for dinner." she paused for a moment "I *dare* you to wear it to dinner."

"I was going to wear it *anyway*." Sera replied haughtily.

"I should think so, too." Phin replied, in much the same tone "Let's go then." she finished and stalked through the door.

"Ooooh, Sera, that looks *awful!*" Freya remarked and giggled "Wherever did you get it?"

"I didn't. I made it." Sera replied coolly.

"Oh." Freya's face fell for a moment and then she burst out laughing again. "What *for?*"

"It's my goddess costume." Sera replied, grinning "It's supposed to remind you of pudding." Freya stopped laughing long enough to have a decent look at it.

"It does actually." she admitted before bursting into giggles again "Did it have to look so awful? Couldn't it look *nice* and remind people of pudding?" she asked.

"Apparently not." Sera replied, still smiling "I must admit, it looked a lot better on paper."

Sera ate dinner in her new dress, earning her a lot of funny looks from the other diners, apart from Hermes for some reason, who had been allowed in for the valkyrie-only dinner because he wouldn't go away and he looked like one anyway.

He only noticed her when he was finally hungry enough to get up for some food.

"What *are* you wearing?" he asked sceptically, raising an eyebrow.

"It's my new dress. I made it." Sera replied, in the tone

of someone who has had to answer the same question more times than they can count in the last half hour.

"Is that why I haven't seen you much the last few days?" he asked, sounding relieved "I see. I mean I saw you at the games, but then you vanished again..." Sera found that she was pleased Hermes had noticed her absence. It was nice to be missed.

They spent dinner catching up on work and sharing ideas about what to do about delivering the posters and where to send them. Hermes was adamant that he should use his new hawk familiars to send them, whereas Sera thought it would be better for one of them to go, so as to explain what the leaflets were and answer any questions. They compromised by agreeing to send the hawks with a short letter and a form that they could send back if they had any questions, that Hermes, Sera or the dwarves would answer. Hermes had already sent his hawks to various people asking for positive comments about Freya's Ginza bar and the dwarves handiwork and had received plenty of replies. He had a few more clients on a waiting list but had informed them that he must finish his other projects first. Sera suggested he send them hawks too, to ask what they wanted, so that he had a better starting point for them.

Sera spent most of the evening discussing business with Hermes and Freya, despite the fact that she was working.

The next day, Sera got up early and went to the bar to get breakfast. As always, Hermes was already there. She was surprised he didn't sleep in Sessrymnir, the amount of time he spent there. She watched him for a minute as he tried to study his drawings and eat his toast at the same time. He dropped jam on one of his sketches and swore. Seralina had to bustle off to get her breakfast after her snigger made him

189

look up. He'd taken to eating non-meat food at breakfast, to stop Phin from bothering him. It didn't really work, because she tried to bully him into letting her try whatever it was he was eating. When Sera returned, having chosen cereal and fruit for once, Phin was sitting on a chair, trying to get at his toast.

"I just want to try it!" Phin whined, trying to reach it with her paw, which Hermes held absentmindedly out of her reach while he shuffled through his sketches with the other hand. "C'*mon*! I just want a little bit! Don't be mean!"

"You won't like it." he told her, taking a bite and spilling more jam on his papers. He swore and reached for a napkin to wipe it up. "Do something about this cat." he demanded as he wiped the jam off his sketchbook.

"Fancy some cereal?" Sera asked, pushing Phin off the chair and sitting on it herself.

"Do you expect a civil answer to that question?" Phin replied bluntly.

After breakfast, Phin and Sera went to see how the dwarves were doing. To her amazement and delight, Stan informed her that the castle was almost finished and would be completed by the end of the day.

"Y' should bring your things over later." Stan advised "It's not good t' leave a buildin' uninhabited. Would y' like a tour, Miss Sera?"

"Yes please." Sera answered eagerly "I have to go to Midgard soon, but I've got some time." Sera was excited. She'd never had her own castle before. She'd never even had so much as her own tree house before. She couldn't wait to see what it was like.

From the outside, the castle looked like a fairytale castle. It was white and shiny. Unless you came right up to it and possibly broke a bit off, you wouldn't know it was made of gingerbread, marzipan and icing. The inside of the castle was the same. Shining, white walls reflected light from a huge chandelier hanging right over the huge wooden table, which was in the middle of the main hall. She was a little disappointed that the castle didn't *look* like it was made of gingerbread, which had been the original plan, but it was really pretty, so Sera decided to leave it be. Besides, she could always ask them to redecorate later.

"The chandelier is made of metal, Miss Sera." Stan explained "Only if we made everythin' of sweets, you wouldn't be able to have any light or heat or anythin'." Sera nodded. It made sense. She was glad the dwarves were sensible.

Nothing was furnished yet, so most of the rooms were actually quite dull; they were just blank, white rooms reminiscent of an insane asylum without the padding.

When they returned from the roof - Stan wanted to show Sera the view, but the mist made it rather pointless - the three dwarves from the forge Sera had visited were setting up her fountains. One gave her a cheery wave as she went past. She smiled and waved back.

'Right.' she thought to herself 'Time for *me* to go to work.' To Stan she said "I can't wait to see it when it's finished!" she gave him a smile "Right, I'm off back to Sessrymnir. By the way, Hermes should have finished your flyers today or tomorrow. He's going to send you one by hawk."

"Won't that take days?" Stan asked, puzzled, rubbing his chin "Why doesn't he deliver it himself? It'd be faster."

"Ah, not with D-mail!" Sera replied happily and smiled again "Hermes' hawks travel at the speed of light."

"That's fast, is it?" Stan asked suspiciously.

"They're   Lightning   Hawks."   Sera   explained,

191

remembering she was dealing with creatures akin to gods.

"Oh, *lightning*." understanding dawned on Stan's face "That's *bloody* fast, isn't it?" he exclaimed.

"Don't we need to get ready for the meetings?" Phin asked, as they reached the door to Sessrymnir. Sera gave the door an experimental push, but it was closed. It wasn't yet close enough to dinner for Freya to have opened it, after all.

"We are." Sera replied "The poster says bring a pudding or similar to share, so... I should bring one, right?"

"I don't think you get how religion works." Phin retorted "They give *you* stuff. It's a sacrifice or whatever. Isn't it?" Sera knocked on the doors.

"Well the point is, you give the god or gods or spirits or whatever stuff because you're grateful for what they do for you. They can hardly be grateful for something I haven't done."

"I thought the idea was that if you haven't, it's sort of an advance payment for something later? Or like, if you haven't done anything, you just say 'ah, but I have, but I'm all subtle and you didn't notice, now fork over the goods'." And if they don't, you get a lawyer and say 'prove I didn't do anything, go on, I dare you' or something."

"I don't think that's-" Sera started, then mentally backtracked "What the hell do you get a lawyer for?"

"Well people'll say anything, won't they." Phin shrugged "But you get a lawyer or Mr. Nice Policeman involved and they'll soon shut up."

"I don't think they have lawyers in religion. You leave that sort of thing up to gods or... or priests, I suppose." Sera replied, tapping her foot.

"Well there you go, then. You just say 'you can't prove I didn't do it' and you're good."

"Phin, the point in religion is not for the god or

whatever to get free stuff. It's... it's to set down a bunch of rules for people to live by, so they can live peacefully." Sera explained, irritated "In theory, anyway. I wonder if she heard me? I hope we don't run out of time-" As she raised her hand to knock again, the door opened.

"*What?*" said Freya crossly, yanking open the door "Oh, it's you Sera. Didn't you have that thing today?"

"Sorry, am I bothering you?" Sera answered apologetically "I just wanted to use the kitchen, if that's okay."

"The kitchen? It's a bit of a mess, but sure." Freya replied, pushing some errant strands of hair out of her face. It looked like she'd been cleaning. She had her hair tied back under a white cloth and was wearing an apron over what must have been an old dress.

"I wanted to try making a pudding for my meeting. I'll only be able to make one this time, but if it works out, then I can make more next time. And um..." Sera hesitated "I'm a pretty useless Goddess of Puddings if I can't even make puddings."

"If you say so." Freya shrugged "I take it you'll be needing to go into the pantry then? I'd best show you the map."

"Map?" Sera asked warily.

"Well, yes. You'll get lost if I don't show you the map." Freya explained.

Sera had thought that the pantry was merely huge. It turned out it was labyrinthine. Freya stabbed at a copy of the map she'd obtained for Sera with a pencil.

"So if you want sweet things, you need to head *here-*" Freya circled an area quite far into the maze of shelves and corridors and marked it with a number one. "Sugar should be on the lower shelves, but that other thing you wanted, what was it?"

"Golden Syrup." Sera replied.

"Golden Syrup, that will be higher up, because it's a sugar derivative and we don't use it much." Freya explained "Got that?" Sera nodded "Right, so wheat derivatives are *here*, quite close to the entrance, because we use that a lot, if you don't want much you should take a bucket or something, 'cause the bags are pretty big. Eggs are a bit further down, round about *here*-" Freya circled another place a little further on "-but you'll have to go all the way over *here*-" she circled a blue coloured area at the end of a twisty looking passage to the west "-for the milk because that's where we keep all the iced stuff."

After a few more pointers from Freya on how not to get lost and what to do if she did - "Don't worry, there's maps posted in there with 'you are here' painted on them, just wander around and you'll find one eventually" - Sera took up a candle and headed into the pantry.

"Doesn't seem like such a good idea all of a sudden, does it?" Phin piped up after they'd been walking for a few minutes.

"Oh, shut up." Sera replied, squinting at her map in the candlelight "We'd best get the cold stuff last, else it'll go warm or melt or something."

"Considering that it's going in the oven and is in fact, going to get very hot, does that matter?" Phin argued.

"Yes. I don't know about you, but carrying around melted butter isn't my idea of fun." Sera squinted at the map again. It looked like the sugar was furthest away, so she decided to head for that first. The pantry was eerily dark and quiet. There was the occasional gleam of a candle in the distance, but it wasn't anywhere near dinner time yet, so there was no-one running around and fetching ingredients.

Sera's footsteps echoed and the light gleamed off rows of oddly coloured, oddly shaped bottles. She was actually incredibly glad of Phin's company, although she'd rather not admit it to Phin. She would probably take advantage of it, somehow. As they proceeded through the endless corridors of vegetables, grains and dried meats, Sera reflected on Phin's view of religion. It had seemed odd to her at first, but then she realised Phin was mostly a cat, after all. In ancient Egypt, cats were revered as gods. To a cat, the main uses for a human are to bring them food and open doors. It was hardly surprising that Phin thought gods were there to be catered to.

"The Old Dryad and the fox said the same thing." Sera announced suddenly.

"What?" Phin replied "What's this all of a sudden?"

"It's got to be paid back, they said." Sera continued "I think... I think that's how it works with spirits. If you do one a favour, they have to pay it back. I think that's how it should work. Something like that."

"Oh?" Phin replied "Not 'Can't we all just get along?'. I thought that'd be your first thingy, revelation or whatever. Or 'Thou shalt not put bloody chocolate on everything'."

"Well-" Sera started "Wait, that's a good one actually."

"Paying favours back is all very well, but if you don't want to or you can't, then what? Won't people just avoid doing each other favours?" Phin asked. They turned down a corridor and finally reached the sugar and derivatives section. Sera had brought a few buckets and boxes that the girls used to carry ingredients about. She fished around in the big bucket for a suitably small one to put the sugar in.

"Do you reckon this is caster sugar?" Sera asked peering into a huge, open sack of sugar "This looks granulated to me."

"How would I know?" Phin complained, sniffing at the next bag "And don't avoid my question."

"I'm not, it's just I'd like to hurry up. We won't have time to make anything at this rate!" Sera complained back. She scooped up some sugar into the little box and put it back in the big bucket. Then she dug out a few little bottles and tins.

"Here, can you hold this candle?" Phin obligingly turned into her human form and took the candle, while Sera began to climb up a nearby ladder, peering at the various sacks and jars on the shelves. "I was just thinking about something... I did a homestay once. It was a with a family on a little island. It was only for a week, but it was really nice. It was one of the best things I ever did. I helped the host mother teach English and I got to learn about her culture and we went out on lovely walks and things. One day the host mother got a phone call from a lady she knows." Sera opened a likely looking jar, put the top on again and put it aside. "The lady had left some homemade pickles and things in the back of my host mother's car. With it being a little island, I suppose people don't worry too much about their cars being stolen..." Sera mused, prying the lid off another jar. She nodded to herself and filled up a bottle she'd brought up, then passed it down to Phin. "She told me that this lady often did things like that for her. She was really grateful, because my host mother had shown her how to use a particular machine... at the post office, I think it was. Anyway -" Sera found another promising jar, and tipped the contents into her own small tin "-she said that people weren't really like that in the city. She'd lived abroad in New York for two years. She said she was amazed how grateful people could be and how nice it was. I was thinking more along those lines. No-one says you have to do favours, but wouldn't it be nice if it turned out like that?" Sera climbed down the ladders and took the candle from Phin, who changed back.

They got the eggs and the flour and a few other bits, made a brief stop back at the kitchen to ditch it all on the table, and finally headed for what Freya had called the 'iced area'. The two of them navigated their way around a few groups of shelves and then headed into a tunnel. It was small and it seemed to wind its way around and downwards.

"I wonder why this bit is so different to the rest?" Sera mused as they continued down the little tunnel.

"It's probably to keep the cold in." Phin guessed, shuddering and ruffling her wings up. It was indeed getting colder and colder the further they went. Finally, they emerged into another cavern. This one however, was lined with huge blocks of ice, with further bags and buckets of ice everywhere. Huge fish and whole carcasses of what were presumably deer and oxen wallowed in vats of the stuff. As Sera wandered along looking for the eggs, something else came back to her;

"My host mother said something else, too." she mused.

"Oh?" Phin responded, sniffing the air, vainly trying to detect the scent of eggs over the permeating stench of fish.

"She said that she spent a lot of time when she was younger worrying about her purpose in life." Sera replied, finally locating the butter and cutting out a block "Do you think this is 115 grams? I've no idea how much that is."

"...Probably." answered Phin reluctantly "Maybe you should overestimate it. I mean, you don't want to come back here for the sake of a few grams of butter, do you?"

"But then it'll be wasted." Sera pulled a face.

"Well just tell the girls who are making dinner that there's some butter going. I'm sure they can use it for *something*." Phin supplied. Then she continued "So what about it then? Did she find out her life's purpose or what?"

"Well a bunch of stuff happened." Sera continued "And she said... she said that she realised it was enough just to live."

"Yeah?"

"Yeah. Well, don't you think that makes sense? I mean if everyone went around being all... all purposeful all the time, no-one would get anything done, right?"

"I suppose. Wait, what?" Phin stopped, confused. Sera tripped over her and the candle went flying and landed in some ice. There was a faint sizzle, and the room went black. "It would be nice if you would go around being a *little* purposeful, sometimes. Like with the purpose of not getting us lost in the dark in a giant, underground freezer for example." she continued crossly.

"Um. I just meant if everyone went round having a grand purpose, then no ordinary jobs would get done... like... cooking and cleaning and laundry and everyday stuff...." Sera's voice seemed to echo around the cavern. It was strange, the effects darkness had. She could have sworn it wasn't doing that before.

"That's nice, but it doesn't get us out of this cavern." came Phin's reply. Sera tried to move forward and tripped right over Phin.

"Ow." Sera rubbed her knee. "Can't you smell your way out of here or something? And can't cats see in the dark?"

"I can't smell anything over all this blasted fish and I need *some* light to see by." Phin answered "Don't you remember which way the entrance was?"

"I think it was this way..." Sera replied doubtfully.

The two of them groped around until they found a wall

and followed it. That led them to another wall and an even worse stench of fish. By the time they got to a third wall, they were freezing.

"This is no good!" Sera wailed "I d-don't even know if we're heading towards the d-door! What are we going to do?"

"I don't know what you're asking me for, you're the one who dropped the candle!" Phin complained from somewhere nearby.

"Maybe we should sh-shout for help?" Sera suggested "Wh-while we can still shout. We should have brought an extra c-candle or something..."

"But no-one will hear us down here!" Phin protested "It's not near enough to dinnertime. Maybe in a few hours..."

"We don't have a f-few hours! I wish we were on Midgard..." Sera said wistfully.

"I can think of better places than Midgard." Phin retorted "Like your room. There's a lovely *fire* in your room."

"No, I mean whenever I go to Midgard, Heimdall c-can always hear what's happening to m-me." Sera paused "Hey! What if it's not just Midgard?"

"You mean we should shout to Heimdall for help?" Phin asked sceptically "But he's not allowed to leave the bridge!"

"I don't care. I'm trying it anyway." Sera took a deep breath "HEIMDALL! HEIIMDAAAALLL! WE'RE STUCK IN THE FREEZER AND WE CAN'T GET OUT!! SEND HELP!!" she yelled, as loud as she possibly could.

"Do you think it'll work?" Phin asked. Sera could hear her pacing about in the dark.

"I don't know. We'll just have to hope." Sera replied "I wonder if we should move? When you're lost you're supposed to stay still..." she added doubtfully.

Time passed. Sera and Phin huddled together on the floor, as far away from the ice as they could get.

"I hope it worked." Sera said after a while.

"Me too." Phin replied. Then she yelled "HEIMDALL IF YOU CAN HEAR US, YOU'D BETTER HAVE SENT HELP BECAUSE IF WE FREEZE TO DEATH I'M GOING TO HAUNT YOU SOMETHING AWFUL!!"

More time passed.

"Bugger." Sera exclaimed all of a sudden.

"What now?" Phin complained.

"We forgot the milk."

"How much was in the recipe?" Phin asked.

"Umm... two tablespoons I think." Sera replied.

"Well I should think we'll manage without it, don't you?" Phin replied bitterly "Considering."

"I know." Sera hugged her knees and tried to wrap her dress more tightly around her "It's funny the things you think of at times like these though, isn't it?"

"Not 'ha ha' funny, it isn't." Phin complained. After a while she piped up again with "You know what one of your rules should be?"

"Go on, what?"

"'Never, under any circumstances, get lost in a giant freezer'."

"That was 'ha ha' funny, right?"

"I hope so. Maybe 'always bring an extra candle'. How about that one?"

"Maybe you were right after all, Phin."

"Mm?"

"Maybe 'get someone else to get it for you' is a good one after all... I think cats might be onto something."

"Damn right we-" Phin stopped "Did you hear something?" The two of them listened. "I'm not crazy ri-"

"Shh!" Sera cupped her hands round her ears. She didn't know if that actually ever worked, but right now she'd try anything. There was a faint noise in the distance. There was also an echo of some kind. "Should we head that way? What if we're crazy?"

"I don't think two people can be the exact same kind of crazy." Phin replied, ruffling her wings "I hear it, too. Let's go!"

"Hey!" Sera called, feeling her way along the shelves "Hey, is anyone there? We got lost! Hello?"

They continued to feel their way along, yelling and calling, until they saw a faint glow.

"Light!" yelled Phin "I can see well enough to lead now! This way, come on!"

"I still can't see a darn thing, hang on!" Sera yelled after her.

"This way, just follow my voice!"

"You haven't forgotten we're in a freezer, right? It's bloody slippy! Hang on a minute!" Sera shouted, and tried to run. She immediately stepped on an errant ice cube and slipped, banging her wrists as she flung them out grab the shelves and missed. "Ow!" Sera sat in the dark and hissed, trying to rub some life back into her wrists.

"-era!" came an echo. There were running footsteps and she thought she heard Phin yelling at someone.

"Hello?" she called "Phin?"

"-iss Sera!" came the echo again, and now she could see light coming much, much closer, and Phin and-

"*Heimdall?*" Sera gasped, as the god bounded round the corner and swept her up into a hug.

"Miss Sera!" Heimdall boomed, his voice made even louder by the freezing cavern "Miss Sera, I was so worried! You should have called me sooner, Miss Sera!"

"Ut I ort oo cudn't lea' th' 'ainbow 'ridge?" Sera tried to mumble through Heimdall's tunic.

"Well, I'm not supposed to, Miss, but I heard you calling and yelled at a valkyrie who was going past could she please mind it for me a minute." he explained "And she looked at me funny and said okay, but just for a minute and she wasn't going to be responsible if we all got invaded and then I rushed over here and Miss Freya let us in. This way Miss Sera!" he grabbed Sera's hand and pulled, causing her to slip on some more loose ice cubes. "Sorry about that Miss Sera." he apologised and then looked at her critically for a moment. Then he set down his candle.

"It's okay, I just slipped. I slipped before t-" Sera began, before Heimdall literally swept her off her feet. He bounded back towards the exit of the freezer room and yelled "Mr. Hermes! I found her, Mr. Hermes!" he leaned down by what was presumably the entrance and said "Get on then, Miss Cat!" Phin jumped onto Sera's chest. "Off we go then! Don't worry, Miss Sera, I'll have you out of here in a jiffy!" Heimdall strode through the darkness at what felt like a terrifying speed. Sera wondered how he wasn't taking any shelves out.

"You..um.. you can let me down now..." Sera mumbled, as she spotted the entrance. Phin was still sat on her chest and looking extremely smug at Sera's complete loss of dignity. Sera stumbled upright and staggered over to the door, where Freya was waiting.

"When I said you might get lost, I meant you wouldn't know where the eggs were kept or something." Freya chided "For goodness sake, you've not even been gone an hour. I didn't think we needed to send out a search and rescue!"

"I'm afraid I lost my candle in the freezer." Sera replied sullenly "I tripped over Phin and it went flying. If someone

202

gets a lump of really suspect butter, that'll be it."

"Well, I'm just glad you're safe. Thank you, Heimdall." she said and smiled.

"Right you are, Miss Freya! It was no trouble!" Heimdall replied, practically standing to attention "I, um, I'm very grateful to Miss Sera, after all!"

"I think you're on to something with that 'being grateful' and 'doing favours' business after all, Sera." Phin said as Sera put her down on the table. Just then, Hermes appeared from the entrance to the pantry. He was out of puff and red in the face.

"Sera!" he wheezed "You're okay!"

"Hermes?" Sera blinked in surprise "What are you doing here?"

"Well, I was outside Sessrymnir working on some designs and suddenly Heimdall came running down the corridor. And he yells at me that you and Phin are freezing to death, so I grabbed a candle and took off into the pantry. But I forgot to take a map, so I had to keep finding the ones on the walls. What on Olympus where you *doing* in there?"

"We were going to make a pudding for my meeting and- Oh nooo-" Sera groaned "I left my butter in the freezer!"

"It was where I found you, right Miss Sera?" Heimdall asked "I'll get it for you! I left my candle in there anyway!" and off he went. Almost before Sera had recovered, he was back, holding Sera's bucket and his candle.

"How did you do that?" Sera asked, bemused "How could you see in there without the candle?" Heimdall wrinkled his forehead.

"I didn't need to see, Miss Sera." he answered "I could hear where everything was."

"You could... hear...?" Sera trailed off.

"Heimdall can hear even the grass growing." Freya explained.

"Oh, so that's how you could tell what was going on in Midgard." Sera heaved a sigh of relief. Heimdall mustn't have been spying on her as such, after all. He'd probably just heard when she was in trouble and listened in. "But... that doesn't explain why you could see in the dark."

"I told you, Miss. I could hear where everything was. My footsteps and other noises... they... they bounce off the shelves and things, Miss." he said hesitantly.

"Oh. Like echolocation?"

"What's echolocation, Miss?" Heimdall asked politely.

"Um. It's that thing you just said, Heimdall." Sera replied.

"Oh. Well, that's how I did it, Miss." he beamed "Well, I'll see you at Bifrost then, Miss Sera! Miss Freya, Mr. Hermes, Miss Cat." he nodded to each of them and then took off.

"I'll leave you to it, then Sera." Freya said, laying a hand on Sera's shoulder "You *are* OK?" Sera nodded. "Right then." Freya left the kitchen to carry on with her cleaning.

"All this for pudding." Hermes shook his head and collapsed at the kitchen table. He looked like he'd been really worried. "What sort is it, then?"

"It was going to be syrup sponge, but I don't know if I feel like making it, now." Sera sighed, sitting down next to Hermes and prodding the bucket of flour.

"I think we still should." Phin chipped in "There's still time and anyway, after all that trouble, how could you *not* make it? And if that doesn't work, just think how lovely and *warm* the oven will be."

"Sold." Sera nodded "Let's do it. Oh and, thank you Hermes."

"What for?" he lifted his head up off the table, where he'd been slumped over.

"For coming to find me. I really appreciate it."

"I didn't find you though, in the end."

"It's the thought that counts." Sera smiled at him. Then a book was plonked in front of her. "What's this?"

"The recipe. You can be grateful while you're cooking." Phin was now human formed again and had managed to find a mixing bowl or two.

"Right, right." Sera read the first instruction. "Grease a pudding bowl or basin. Okay." Sera walked over to the sink and washed her hands. Then she walked back and grabbed some butter, and smeared it all around the smaller bowl.

"What are you doing that for?" asked Hermes, transfixed.

"You have to grease it, or it gets stuck to the sides." Sera explained.

"Can I help?" Hermes asked, leaning over and trying to read the book upside down.

"Sure." Sera shrugged and turned the book round, so he could see "First, you need to cream the butter and sugar together. You can do that, or beat the eggs." Hermes nodded and dragged the butter, sugar and mixing bowl towards him. Phin found him a wooden spoon from somewhere. Meanwhile, Sera beat the two eggs and looked for some tinfoil and tried in vain to figure out how to preheat the oven. It was black and ancient and huge.

"I think it just has one setting: On fire." remarked Phin, as she poked about in another cupboard, looking for a roasting tin.

"Now what do I do?" shouted Hermes. Then "Never mind. Says here 'add the flour, eggs and vanilla extract a little at a time'. ...what's vanilla extract?"

"It's that little bottle of yellow liquid. You only need about four or five drops." Sera shouted back "Shall I light it, then?" she said to Phin, who nodded.

"Says here 'quarter of a tsp'... what's a tsp and how do I quarter it?"

"It means 'teaspoon', it's the same as four or five drops, like I said."

"Okay!" Hermes gave her a thumbs up. As Sera made her way back to Hermes, there was a 'ha!' of triumph from Phin as she found both a large tin and a tea towel. "What do I need to add it bit by bit for?" Hermes asked as she came up behind him "Wouldn't it be faster to just dump the whole lot in?"

"Yes, but then it goes lumpy or there isn't enough air in it, or something. Oh, don't forget the baking powder!" Sera grabbed a tin and prised it open "At least.. I think this is baking powder. It said it was, but then why don't they have any self-raising flour? I could only find plain. ...unless it's all self-raising..." she mused.

"How many tsps do I need of that then? It doesn't say in the book-" Hermes squinted at the page.

"Two, I think." Sera read the next step. "Ha, fold in milk. You'll be lucky."

"You don't have any?" Hermes asked, mixing away.

"No. The candle went out!" Sera yelled in answer as she went to help Phin boil the kettle. They lined the tin with the towel and wet it. "Looks like the oven's doing nicely... we need boiling water, don't we?" Phin nodded and grabbed one of the huge copper kettles to fill up.

"What next... ah, syrup..." she muttered to herself. She poured the syrup into the bottom of the greased bowl.

"I'm done." Hermes announced "Doesn't that go in the mixture?"

"No, you tip the pudding out and it runs down the side and... is syrupy." Sera shrugged "It's nice. Right, pour the batter on top of it.... Right, now we just have to put tin foil over the top and leave it to steam for an hour or so."

"Sera, it says in the recipe to tie some kind of baking sheet thingy over it." chided Phin, hauling over the roasting tin.

"Well, we don't have any, so tough." Sera replied. She covered the bowl with foil and put in the roasting tin. Then they poured in boiling water and shoved it in the oven.

"Right!" Sera sighed and collapsed at the table again. "Thanks, guys."

They all rested at the table in silence. It was blissfully warm after the cold of the pantry. After a while, Sera announced;

"I was going to take the pudding to one of my meetings, but I think you should have it, Hermes. You and Freya and Heimdall. To say thanks for rescuing me today."

"Oh, you don't have to do that, Sera-" Hermes began, but Sera waved him into silence.

"No, no. I want you guys to have it. I can always make more for next week, right?"

"If you insist, then." Hermes gave her a thumbs up again "Understood. Do you want me to sort it out while you go get ready for your thing? It must be nearly time now, right?"

"Would you?" Sera nodded gratefully "Thanks, Hermes. Will you tell Freya for me? I'll tell Heimdall on my way out."

"No problem!"

"Right then." she nodded "Let's go Spread some Happiness."

Sera went to her room to pick up the cloak and the

dwarfish badge maker. She knocked out a whole pile of badges using pennies from her purse that she'd put in her rucksack. They weren't pudding, but at least they were something. Finally, she put on her new dress and set off for Midgard.

When she reached Bifrost, Heimdall greeted her and leaned closer as she walked past;

"Glad you're safe now, Miss Sera!" he looked around surreptitiously before whispering eagerly "Are we still okay for tomorrow, Miss Sera?" Sera just smiled and nodded, before vanishing into the mist. Heimdall watched her go. He smiled and began to dream of tomorrow.

Another person dreaming of tomorrow was Felicia Potts. Tomorrow would be the day she started her diet. It always was. Sera wouldn't have known this if Felicia hadn't been mumbling it to herself as she waited apparently alone in the community centre for the others - if indeed, there were any - to arrive. She'd brought a Victoria Sponge Pudding. Sera stopped eavesdropping on Felicia and returned to setting up the table in a panic. She'd brought the badges but had forgotten that she'd said sauce would be provided; she'd planned on taking sauce from the fountains she knew would be in the castle, but as nothing had been properly set up as of yet, it had been a no-go. Thus, Sera had got to Midgard and her first stop to find that she was sauce-less and panicked. She'd rushed off to the nearest supermarket, bought several tins of custard powder and about six huge jugs using her goddess card and commandeered a school kitchen. Then she panicked because she couldn't actually remember where half of the community centres were and had to be bitten on the ankle by Phin before she lost her composure completely and became visible to the assembled mortals. Phin of course, as she pointed out, could remember where they were, being a cat. Cats have good memories because they bear a grudge and can remember everything you did to them that they didn't like and will get you back one day and make it look like an accident.

Thus, they came to the final stop; the community centre in the town where the old oak tree was.

Sera carefully laid out her last batch of badges on the table, trying not to make any noise, in case it drew attention. She placed her last jug of custard on the table and stepped back into the corner where she wouldn't be in the way. Phin decided to sit on the table; it wasn't very high, but it was the highest point in the room nonetheless, and thus the best place to lord over everyone from. Besides, she knew she wasn't supposed to.

One by one, more people trickled into the meeting. They were a mixed bunch. Felicia, who Sera would have guessed was a few stones heavier than she was, was dressed in an expansive skirt and a gypsy top; she looked like she was wearing a pink tent. In direct contrast, there was a rather thin, pale girl sitting on the next chair, dressed in a t-shirt that was too big for her and some faded, baggy jeans. There was also a twenty-something man who looked like he was a student; he was also wearing jeans and a t-shirt, only his were well-fitted. There was another young man who looked rather tatty and needed a shave. Finally, there was an old man and an old lady. The old lady had brought something she'd presumably made herself; it was in an old, square biscuit tin, which is what cakes made by little old ladies are traditionally transported in. Seralina had thought the old man and woman were a couple at first, since he hadn't brought anything, but he was sitting in the corner, away from her and he made no effort to acknowledge anyone. Sera wondered if they'd had a fight. Everyone looked rather nervous and confused; Sera was afraid that a loud noise would scatter them like birds. Suddenly Felicia stood up and announced;

"My name is Felicia Potts and I eat too much pudding. So I have come here today to *not* eat any of the pudding we all brought and really, *really* start my diet and hopefully with all your support, I can lose some weight. I put it on when I moved away from home and I'm having trouble getting it off again." she finished. She looked around expectantly. The thin girl said;

"Oh, is this some sort of Weight Watchers meeting?" she asked "I thought it was a group to help with-" she hesitated and continued more quietly "-with anorexia."

"Is it?" Felicia asked.

"I thought it was an informal cooking contest." said the old lady.

"I thought it was some sort of party." said the student.

"Me too. I thought it was one of those 'keep young people out of trouble' things." said the scruffy young man. Only the old man didn't offer an opinion. The others looked at him expectantly, but as nothing seemed to be forthcoming they turned their attention back onto each other.

"So, did you organise this meeting, then?" the old lady asked Felicia.

"No, I didn't." Felicia answered "I don't think the person who organised it is here..." she added uncertainly.

"Why is that?" asked the old lady.

"Well, I just decided to speak on my own because I was getting really nervous and no-one seemed to want to go first... but if the person who organised it was here, wouldn't they be stood at the front, waiting?"

"How do you know they would?" asked the old lady.

"Well, I would if *I* organised something. I wouldn't just sit there and keep everyone waiting. Anyway, *did* anyone in this room organise the meeting?" Everyone shook their heads, except for the old man who didn't seem to be listening. He was just sat staring at nothing with a happy smile on his face.

"There's a jug of custard on the table." the student observed "So someone must have come before we got here and put it there."

"That's funny." Felicia said thoughtfully "I was here first and I don't remember seeing it then. But I haven't seen anyone."

"That's odd." the scruffy man mused "Wasn't it the old man?"

"No." Felicia replied "He came in about ten minutes after me and just sat there." she shrugged.

"It's a bit stupid really." the scruffy man continued "They've given us a jug of custard, right? But there's no plates or spoons or anything. What do they expect us to eat off?" Sera went pale. Phin rolled her eyes.

Sera crept quietly around them and dashed off to the nearest row of shops. She went in about three before she found one that sold paper plates. She picked up a few packs as well as a few packets of cheap plastic spoons and ran as fast as she could back to the meeting. There was nothing she could do about the other meetings; hopefully the people there would have had the sense to do the same as her. *If* there were any people in the other meetings. She'd have to go and check back later. She huffed and puffed her way back and caught the tail end of the conversation they'd been having;

"I know it's no good, but I can't help feeling like this.

It's a big problem. I came because I thought there'd be other people like me and we'd all egg each other on... you know, to have a bit of pudding." it was the thin girl talking "To say to each other 'it's all right, we're worth it, we deserve it'."

"Well you *do* deserve it." Felicia reassured her "You said that you just feel ugly all the time, that you don't feel like you deserve it, but if you don't eat anything then you probably will look terrible. And you *do* deserve it. I mean, look at me-" Felicia gestured at her own knees "*I'm* the one who doesn't deserve it. I've clearly had too much already."

"Um, don't take this the wrong way, but you make me feel a bit better. I mean, you're, um, you know-" the thin girl hesitated.

"Fat." Felicia finished.

"Um, yeah-" the thin girl spoke quietly "And um, well I think you look all right. I think you're quite pretty, really."

"So you think *I'm* pretty and you think *you're* ugly?" Felicia replied, shocked. Wherever women gather, this kind of conversation is likely to happen. If humans evolved into sentient beanpoles with the ability to float and burn things using only their minds, there would still be women who worried that they were too fat or unattractive. That's why the make-up section is so big. One of the boys decided to cut in before the conversation got any worse;

"It seems to me that people are always better at giving out advice than taking it, yeah?" said the scruffy youth "Like, you both have the same kind of problem-" the girls made a brief protest "-you both think you're too fat, which is like, associated with being overweight, right? But you're coping with it in different ways. One's trying to ignore it and one's trying too hard and can't turn back. But you're both saying the same advice to each other, but not taking it yourself, right?" The girls nodded slowly "But what I think you should be worried about is the health side of it. I mean, it's not healthy being too fat, but it's not healthy being too thin either, right? I think that's a better way to look at it, rather than thinking 'oh my god, I'm so ugly' or 'I'll never get a boyfriend'. I think it's more important you don't kill yourself, right?" The girls looked unhappy, like they felt they should argue, but before they could say anything the student cut in;

"I think..." he said slowly "That it's very hard, even though you know it's good advice, to take advice if you don't want to." he took a deep breath "'Cause I had a girlfriend and I was having problems with her, because she expected me to pay for everything, you see. And I kept paying for everything. And my friends kept saying 'look Steve, you have to just tell her no and say she needs to pay for stuff sometimes' and even though I knew they were right I kept saying 'no, she's my girlfriend, I should pay for our dates and stuff' and I thought she'd leave me if I said that and so on."

His audience waited.

"And no matter how much my friends said it, I just ignored them, so they gave up. But one day, I really needed something and I couldn't afford it that day and I thought 'I need to ask Stacy to pay for more things' and I asked her and she did leave me."

"So what did you do?" asked Felicia.

"I decided that it was probably for the best, because if she was just using me like a bank, like my friends kept saying, then she wasn't worth it."

"So what you're saying is...?"

"You won't take other people's advice until you get it into your head that you want to. So you girls can sit around saying 'I'm fat, you're pretty' and 'no, *I'm* fat, *you're* pretty' all day and it won't get you anywhere." he shrugged.

"I see what you're saying..." the thin girl said "I mean, I

think I already knew."

"Yeah." Felicia nodded "It's like my dad. He used to smoke, and we used to tell him 'you should stop smoking' and he never did until one day he decided himself that he would. I mean, usually when someone tells me I've not to do something, it just makes me want to do it more." There was a general chorus of agreement and nodding of heads.

"Right, now that's sorted out, shall we have some cake and pudding before that custard goes cold?" said the scruffy man rubbing his hands together.

"But there's no plates." the old lady said "Shall I just pop out and get some? We could all chip in 50p."

"Er..." Felicia had frozen halfway through standing up to check if the custard was in fact still warm. She nearly fell over. "There *are* some plates. *And* some spoons." Everyone turned round to look and indeed, there were both plates and spoons on the table.

"No-one left, right?" asked the student. Everyone shook their heads.

"And no-one saw anyone come in?" the old lady asked. Again, a chorus of silent 'no's'. They all looked at the old man. He was still just sat there, he waved dreamily at them, smiling faintly.

"Oh well." the scruffy youth concluded, shrugging "Let's have some pudding then."

They all produced their various cakes and puddings and finally bothered to introduce themselves, now that they had decided the point of the meeting was what pretty much what it said on the poster - 'bring a pudding or similar to share, no chocolate please'. The old lady was called Doris and the thing she was hiding in the box turned out to be a rather delicious apple pie. The student was called Steve and being a student, he had brought some cheap cup cakes from the nearest discount supermarket. The scruffy student had brought a big fruit tart from a nearby bakery and was called Adam. Finally, the thin girl was called Amanda, earning her suspicious looks from Sera until Phin pointed out that Ellis' piece had lived in London, miles and miles away. She'd brought a homemade sticky toffee pudding.

"I don't think it will be very good." she admitted to the rest of the group "But I thought if I tried to make it myself, it might encourage me to eat it."

When everyone had had a good look and decided what they were going to have, Felicia suddenly remembered the old man.

"Excuse me?" she said approaching him and offering him a plate "We're all going to have some pie and some cake now. Would you like some?" The old man smiled and nodded and started to get up. He shook like a shutter in a gale, so Felicia said quickly;

"Shall I get it for you?" the old man nodded gratefully "What would you like? There's some sticky toffee pudding, some cup cakes, some fruit tart, some Victoria sponge and some apple pie." The old man's face lit up.

"Apples!" he said happily, in a voice like freeze dried sandpaper "That's what I need! Apples! Golden apples!"

"Er, it's made from Bramley apples." Doris explained to him "I don't think you're supposed to use Golden Delicious ones for cooking."

"Would you like some custard?" Felicia asked him kindly. He nodded. The others arranged their chairs so that they included the old man, now that he had actually responded to them. They seemed to be wondering why he was even there; he hadn't brought anything.

"Are you in the right room, mister?" asked Steve, biting into one of his cupcakes "Only, the poster said to bring pudding or something. Why did you come to this meeting?" he chewed his cake thoughtfully. For having cost about 6p it wasn't that bad. "Did you organise it?" The old man shook his head.

"I was looking for something... been looking for something for years and years..." he wheezed and then took a bite of his apple pie "I saw a lady, lady I recognized... and I followed her here. Can't remember... can't remember why, though." He continued to eat his pie in silence while the others waited to see if he was going to say something else. Just when they'd turned their attention back to their own puddings he spoke again; "Looking for something, but can't remember what. But I think that lady can help me." They waited again. After considerably more of his pie was demolished, he spoke again, making a few of them jump. "I think that lady can help me." he repeated "I need to ask her."

"So you followed a woman here, who you recognised, and you need to find her to ask her something? About what you were looking for?" Felicia summarised "Would you like us to help you find her? What does she look like? She might work at the centre." The old man laughed like a blocked drain.

"Don't need to find her!" he cackled "She's right over there, in the corner!" he pointed directly at Sera, who froze "You look a bit like my wife. I think." he added. Slowly, all five heads turned round to look at the corner of the room.

Sera looked around shiftily and then waved at them, sheepishly.

"Er, hi." she said brightly "I'm the Goddess of Puddings." Amanda screamed.

"It's a ghost! We're all going to die!" she shrieked and bolted out the door. The others froze and then followed suit, Sera's protests were drowned out in the crazed screams

216

along the lines of 'The centre is haunted!' and 'The crazy old man's crazy wife is going to get us!'.

Sera stood amongst the forlorn plastic-spoon-and-custard debris and sighed.

"That went well." Phin said brightly, getting up and stretching from where she'd been curled up on the table "Can we do it again? That was funny."

"No." Sera said sadly. She was rather disappointed. It had been going so well. She sighed again. "You wanted to ask me something?" she asked the old man dejectedly.

"Looking for..." the old man began "...looking for... a rainbow!" he said suddenly, stabbing the air with his finger "A rainbow! Need to find the rainbow and get apples. Golden apples. Been looking for the rainbow all this time, can't find it, so can't get any apples." he finished with relief, collapsing back into his chair.

"A rainbow?" Sera asked slowly "Do you mean Bifrost?"

"Bifrost!" the old man cried again "That's right! Bifrost! Asgard! Supposed to be in Asgard!"

"Are you an einherjar?" Sera asked sceptically. She doubted that this old man qualified as an einherjar; for a start, he wasn't dead, which was a major qualification. He looked rather odd, his clothes, a simple brown tunic and a short, thick, brown cape, were faded and threadbare; it looked like he'd been wearing them for *years*.

"No, no." he shook his head "I'm Od."

"No kidding." Sera replied, raising her eyebrows "Right, well... I'm probably going to get into trouble, but you can come to Asgard with me if you like."

"Knew you were a valkyrie!" he wheezed happily "Costume doesn't look like I remember, but then again maybe it does. Don't remember anything, you see. No

217

apples." he finished sadly.

Sera walked out through the mist to be welcomed back by Heimdall, as usual.

"Welcome back Miss Sera. The dwarves told me you've to go and see them straight away. Oh, and the pudding you sent me was very nice!" he told her. Suddenly noticing the old man he added "Who's this?"

"He said he'd been looking for Bifrost for years. He said he needs some apples." Sera explained.

"I'd go and see Idunn if I were you, Miss." Heimdall replied "I think he must be a god."

"Oh, is that what he said?" Sera exclaimed "He said something that sounded like 'god' but I thought he was just being senile." she sighed "I don't have time to find Idunn right now. I've got to go and see the dwarves, then I'll have to go straight to work. Let's go, Phin." she ordered.

For the first time since she'd starting visiting the building site, it was completely silent. The only dwarves left were Stan and the other two dwarves she had spoken to in Freya's bar. They were waiting in a chariot that was parked outside the castle. The two huge horses tethered to it were grazing peacefully. The dwarves were playing a card game of some kind. They looked up as she approached.

"Miss Sera!" Stan greeted her, arms open as she approached the chariot "We've finished your castle! Would y' like another tour, or shall we leave y' to it?"

"I'd love a tour, but I haven't got long, so I'll pass, thank you." Sera replied.

"Right y' are, Miss Sera." Stan gave a firm nod "We'll call in on y' in Miss Freya's bar in a day or two, see how you're getting along."

Sera waved them off and, despite not having long before she had to leave for work, couldn't resist having a look inside the castle.

"Hey, this guy is *not* hitching a ride back on me, just so you know." Phin complained "You're heavy enough on your own."

"*Thanks.*" Sera replied sarcastically "Anyway, I think he should just stay here for now. I don't think it would be a good idea to let him wander around Asgard. He seems to be a bit confused." she turned around and motioned to the old man to follow her "You can stay here for now." she told him "We'll go and see Idunn tomorrow, okay?" The old man nodded. "Right... let's find you a room."

Sera had a busy half an hour as she dumped her rucksack, complete with a few new Cooking Implements of Doom the dwarves had left her, in her new room so she wouldn't have to carry it back. She'd kept forgetting to take them out when she brought her rucksack with her to Midgard. Then, having finally found the old man a room, worked out how the magic oven worked, warned the old man not to eat the castle and told all three fountains sternly that the old man was a guest, Sera set off to work.

It was an uneventful night; Osiris turned up again, but he sat down with Hera, who was paying them a rare visit, and asked her all about the Greek Afterlife, enquiring if he might visit them sometime.

RAGNAROK

The next day Sera had breakfast as usual and then headed straight for Bifrost. Heimdall was eagerly awaiting her arrival.

"Good morning, Miss Sera!" he said brightly "Thank you so much for this!" Sera smiled back at him.

"That's okay." she replied "I've made it my job, after all. Have a good day. I'm sure your mothers will be pleased to see you."

Heimdall thanked her one more time and walked off into the mist. Sera thought it would be a fairly boring job, but there were people coming and going all the time. They mostly looked rather puzzled to see her instead of Heimdall, but they smiled or stopped to make polite conversation. She seldom had time to speak to her co-workers at the Ginza bar, but she saw them coming to and fro with einherjar all day and spoke to them more than she had in her whole life as a goddess so far.

It became quiet around what must have been lunchtime. Sera didn't have a watch or anything; she just told the time from the sun and whatever clocks happened to be around for her to glance at. Sera was staring into the middle distance, wondering what Heimdall was up to and how long he would be when something made her look up. Phin hissed.

"Something's wrong." she growled, her fur standing on end. Then it happened again and Sera registered it as a dull thumping in the distance. She looked down and felt at the same time that the bridge had started to vibrate. Sera had been over the bridge enough times to know that it wasn't normal. The vibration got worse and worse until finally, the source of it came trudging through the mists at the end of the bridge.

It was an army of giants. They marched unstoppably closer.

Bifrost began to crack. Cracks appeared and spread, racing across the soft colours, splitting and spilling the light as if it were the hatching of the Egg of Creation. They stared in horror at the approaching giants. Phin took a deep breath;

"Remember when I said you could be responsible for whatever you liked?" she said "Well, I take it back. I think you shouldn't be responsible for *anything*, ever."

"Let's get out of here." Sera breathed "We've got to warn everyone." She turned and ran as fast as she could towards Asgard.

"And what are they going to do?" Phin yelled, running after her "Ask them politely to go home?"

"I don't know!" Sera yelled back "But they're *gods* aren't they? They must be able to do *something!*"

"Well, *you're* a goddess! Why don't *you* do something?"

"I *am* doing something!"

"Like what?"

"Running away, what does it look like?"

"Well you aren't doing a very good job of it! Get out the cloak, for goodness sake!" Phin yelled, catching up. Sera practically ripped open the cow-skin bag and threw the cloak over Phin, who blurred as it took effect. "I take it we're running away to rally the troops?"

"You're *damn right* we are." Sera said determinedly as

she climbed aboard "I have a horrible feeling this is all my fault."

"What's with you all of a sudden? You're all gung-ho."

"It's probably adrenalin. Let's hurry before it wears off."

They flew right down the great halls to Sessrymnir, without bothering to land, surprising many a wandering einherjar or valkyrie. Sera had screamed 'The giants are coming!' at every single one of them, although she wasn't sure if it was having an effect. All she saw was a glimpse of their shocked or confused faces as they sped away. Phin landed right outside Sessrymnir and changed immediately back into her cat form, causing Sera to fall off and fall flat on her face. Phin struggled out from under the cloak and then shot into Sessrymnir to find Freya, but Sera lunged straight at Hermes who had once again been ejected from the hall after breakfast and was sitting there amongst his drawings. He'd seen them land, having looked up at the commotion.

"Where's the fire?" he asked, giving her an extremely worried look before she nearly gave him concussion after trying to merely grab his shoulders, but instead bowled him into the wall.

"HAWKS!" she screamed into his face "WE NEED HAWKS!"

"Sera, what are you doing?!" Phin yelled emerging out of Sessrymnir.

"Ow, ow, ow!" Hermes rubbed his head "What for?"

"The giants are coming!" Sera shouted "We have to warn Odin and we have to get help!"

"Giants?" he replied bemusedly "What?"

"Stop asking stupid questions and get me some hawks and some paper *right now!*" Sera froze "Didn't you feel that?"

The ground was rumbling and the halls were shaking.

Freya emerged from Sessrymnir looking pale.

"Ragnarok." she said in a strangled voice "This rumbling... it's Ragnarok." Hermes looked from one woman to the other and made up his mind. He put his fingers in his mouth and gave a sharp whistle. There was a change in the air and several Lightning Hawks materialised, landing one after the other, and waited patiently for their orders.

"Tell them where you want them to go and your message." he said. Sera panicked.

"I don't even know where I want some of them to go! I don't even know the names of some of the people I need to send them to!" she chewed on her knuckle.

"It's OK! Calm down." he commanded "Just tell them who they're for. They'll know where to go even if you don't."

"R-right." Sera took a deep breath and addressed the nearest hawk "I want you to tell the Old Dryad that I need her help. Tell her the giants are invading Asgard and I want her to help, if she can." The hawk bowed its head low, then turned round, launched itself into the air and vanished. Sera then stood up and spoke to all the hawks at once. "I want to send the same message to the fox spirit from the forest near the Old Dryad, Osiris, the dwarves, Queen Hera, Odin and whoever is the leader of the light elves, just in case they're on our side. And Heimdall! And-" Sera knew she was forgetting someone, but she couldn't think for the life of her who it was.

"And Thor!" Freya shouted suddenly "Slaying giants is about all he's good for." She was still rather pale, but she had drawn herself up to her full height; her shoulders were squared and her eyes were ablaze. She turned round and addressed the few valkyries who had been drawn by the noise. "You heard Sera! We're being invaded! Go!" she commanded "Summon my einherjar!"

"But Mama-" began one of the them, rather unwisely "They're out fighting, as always-"

"Well they'll not be short of practice then, will they?" Freya snapped "And make sure you've got your good armour on, not that bloody gilt tin can stuff!" As the valkyries hurried off to do her bidding Freya declared "We'll show them what happens when they mess with the Goddess of War and Death!" She gave Sera a sharp look "Sera, get that bloody dress off, *right now!*" Sera sprinted to her room and got changed as fast as she could. She really, really wished she had weapons.

She skidded back into Sessrymnir to find Hermes and Freya pushing the doors shut to seal the hall.

"What are you doing?!" Sera exclaimed as she scurried up to them. Some of the einherjar had already arrived.

"Shut up and help me close the doors!" Freya commanded. Sera did as she was told.

"Why did you shut us in?" she asked as Freya moved around the hall, lighting all the candles. The assembled valkyries and einherjar all watched her nervously. Sera thought she recognised Mr. Turner and a few of the other einherjar she'd picked up. Most of them had never been in a real battle before, and they were acting like nervous cattle, only with a lot more edged steel, which made things worse.

"Sessrymnir is impenetrable unless the doors are opened by me." Freya replied confidently "We must wait for reinforcements. It's no good closing the doors when we see the giants coming. Even if the rest of Asgard falls, we'll be safe in here."

"I see." Sera replied doubtfully "But what will we do then? We won't be able to go anywhere."

"Well, there's always the pantry." Freya shrugged "We can hold out for a long time." They waited in silence for a while and the rumbling grew louder and louder. Dust drifted down from the rafters with every thump. The tables shook, making the candles flicker. All of sudden there was a hammering on the door.

"Who is it?" Freya demanded.

"It's me, Loki!" came Loki's oily voice through the rock-hard timbers "The giants are attacking, Freya! Let me in or I'll be killed!" Freya hesitated and then reached for the handle. Something screamed in Sera's head and she shouted;

"Wait, *stop!*" Freya froze and her head snapped round "Don't let him in!" Sera warned in desperate tones "I think he did - I mean, I think this is my fault!" she blurted out.

"*What?*" Freya fixed her with a megawatt stare.

"I delivered a letter for Loki! To a giant in Jotunheim. I read it first and it seemed harmless!" she half-shouted, half-spluttered, chewing on her knuckles.

"What did it say?" Freya asked sharply.

"It just said 'Let's meet up next Friday'." Sera explained, biting her lip "I thought it was nothing! But I didn't realise..." she trailed off, extremely unwilling to finish her sentence.

"What didn't you realise, Sera?" Freya said slowly and sternly.

"Well, that it was the same day... the same day I agreed to watch the bridge for Heimdall, so he could go and visit Midgard..."

"So that's why he hasn't sounded the alarm yet. I wondered why you'd sent him a hawk..." she gave Sera a Look "The road to Hel is paved with good intentions." she said darkly. Sera hung her head. It was utterly, utterly useless to say sorry. But she said it anyway. It didn't make her feel any better.

"Don't be sorry, lady." came Loki's oily tones from

across the hall. Freya's eyes widened and she whipped round to face him. "*I* want to thank you." Sera, whose nerves had once again temporarily overridden her brain, stepped forward. Freya stopped her.

"How did you get in?" she demanded "My hall is impenetrable! It's *impossible* for you to get in here!"

"You know it isn't, Freya." he replied nastily, and leered and her "I got in once before. Do you remember? I stole your precious necklace!" he laughed "It's a great pity you didn't find and block up that crack! A tiny crack it is, too. But a flea can squeeze through. Isn't it a *shame* you won't have the opportunity to correct your mistake!" he hissed.

The rumbling, which now made it hard to stand up, suddenly stopped. There was a great pounding on the door;

"Loki!" boomed a voice Sera recognised as Thrym "Let us in!" Loki strode forwards to the door, but found his way blocked by Freya.

"Stand aside, *wench*." he sneered "You and your band of dogs won't stop me!" The assembled einherjar and valkyries gripped their weapons. There was a general rustling of steel.

"Stop!" she commanded as both sides made towards each other. The soldiers paused. "It is well known that my hall is impenetrable unless I, myself open the doors. *I* will open the door. I won't have my remaining einherjar and loyal valkyries slain in my own hall." she hammered on the door "*Do you hear me,* Thrym? *I* am going to open the doors, and we will be *civil. Is that understood?*"

"Very well." replied the giant on the other side of the door "Open them, then." Freya moved to open the doors. She motioned to Sera and Hermes.

"Give me a hand, you two." they positioned themselves ready to haul on the great iron door handles.

Then she looked sidelong at Sera and mouthed 'Run for it. Take Hermes with you.' Sera gave an almost imperceptible nod.

They hauled on the doors and Thrym and the first few of his entourage were through them before the scraping had finished echoing through the hall. He strode right up to Freya and leered at her;

"You should have consented to be my wife all those years ago, goddess." Freya merely smiled.

"I thought you were dead." she replied sweetly "It's a pity I'm wrong, isn't it." Thrym merely laughed.

"It is a pity indeed. Pour me a drink, wench." he said, lounging on the nearest bench making it creak. "I'm sure Odin will be coming. While we wait, we shall be, as you declared, *civil*." He waved his followers into the room. They followed his example. In making room to sit down, they tore down the sunny backdrops of the breakfast bar, laughing, using them as mats and using the shards to play-fight with one another. Within a minute, the bar was destroyed.

"You call this civil?" Freya asked him bitterly. Her beloved bar was in ruins. Sera wondered if she would try to strike back on her own out of rage.

"I'm afraid I cannot be responsible for the actions of my men." Thrym answered smugly. He shrugged. "What does it matter? This hall is mine now. And when I deal with Odin so shall all of Asgard fall before me." Freya turned away from him, her face in her hands. From between her fingers she gave Sera a look that said 'Why are you still here?'. Her eyes still smouldered.

Sera groped for Hermes' hand and pulled him backwards, giving Phin a gentle kick and a meaningful glance as she did so. When the giants in front of her gave her suspicious looks, she pretended to be pressing herself against the wall to get out of their way. They lost interest and moved on. Slowly they inched their way out of the hall.

As they reached the door, giants still crowding into the hall, Loki, who had been watching Freya's distress with malicious glee, caught the movement out of the corner of his eye. His finger flew up and he screamed;

"They're trying to *escape! Get them!*" He transformed into a leopard and launched himself after them. But Phin was ready; she had dived under the cloak that was still lying in the hall. She caught Loki across the jaw, knocking him across the room and screamed "*Get on!*" before he even hit the floor. She took off, leaping straight up, narrowly avoiding a few giants who tried to seize them, causing them to blunder into each other. They flew straight along as close to the roof as they dared, avoiding the grasping hands of the giants that filled the corridors; Sera was hanging on to Phin's neck for dear life, likewise, Hermes was hanging onto her and he kept banging and scraping his head along the roof as they flew.

After what seemed like an eternity, they shot out into the sunlight.

"Get to the castle!" Sera yelled above the wind and yells from the giants below. Luckily, they'd lost Loki somewhere in the packed halls, but Sera couldn't help glancing back to check the horizon.

"Can't you go any faster?" Hermes complained.

"Well I *could*, if the ten stone Roman jerk would *get off* me and use his *magic flying sandals*." Phin replied nastily. Hermes obediently fell off backwards, making Sera yelp. But he returned after a few seconds, speeding through the air beside Phin on his winged boots as if he were roller blading along an invisible track.

"They work really well in a straight line!" he shouted as

he zipped along beside them.

"They'll have to!" Sera shouted back "We've got company!"

"*What*?" Hermes started, looking behind him, which sent him tumbling head over heels. He recovered control quickly but didn't dare try to take a second look. Sera was looking though;

"There's a falcon following us!"

"So? Maybe it's one of mine!"

"Trust me, it isn't!"

"Could it be Freya?"

"It could be, but I doubt it!" Hermes made up his mind.

"Right!" he said and whistled sharply. Two of his Lightning Hawks materialised in the air next to them. "Keep up with us!" he told them "If that falcon does anything funny, knock it out of the sky!"

The falcon got closer and closer. Finally, it put on a burst of speed and dived at them. It caught Sera on the cheek, drawing blood and then dived again, hitting Phin full in the flank. She roared in pain and dropped sharply. Sera beat at the falcon until it let go, injuring her hand, but Phin recovered and caught back up with Hermes. The falcon dived again, but this time Hermes' hawks were ready for it. They were much bigger than the falcon and they took it out easily. It transformed into Loki, who fell away, clutching at Freya's falcon cloak.

"Get the cloak!" Sera yelled desperately at the nearest hawk "Don't let him keep hold of it!" The hawk dove towards Loki, seizing the cloak and easily pulling it out of his slippery, blood-stained fingers. He tumbled away towards the ground, screaming with rage.

They broke through the mist that still shrouded Sera's

castle. They ran to the doors and wrenched them open. The three of them squeezed inside, then leaned as hard as they could on the doors to close them. With a creak and a bang, the doors were shut.

"How do we lock them?" Hermes asked.

"I don't know!" Sera said in a panicky voice "I've only been in here one or two times and-"

"Ah, there you are!" came a sand papery voice from down the hall. Ambling down from the other end of the huge table, waving a chicken leg, was the old man Sera had brought back from Midgard.

"No apples." he told her sadly, indicating the oven at the far end.

"Who's this?" Hermes asked, half-curious, half-crazed "Is he supposed to be here? We're fleeing from an army of giants!" he told the old man desperately "Now is not the time to worry about apples!"

"No apples." repeated the man, giving Hermes a baleful look.

"Oh no!" Sera smacked herself in the head "He's the old man I brought back from that meeting! If I'd known Ragnarok was coming, I wouldn't have bothered!" she banged her head against the wall and regretted it. The old man stirred from his daydreams of apples.

"Ragnarok?" he said sharply. Then his tone softened again "I would make it back for Ragnarok." He caught sight of the bundle of feathers in Sera's arms. She'd taken Freya's cloak from the hawk as they landed. The old man tugged it out of her unresisting hand. He turned it this way and that. "It's torn..." he said sadly, shaking his head "I'll fix it." He wandered back off up the hall and into one of the stairways.

"Wait!" Sera called after him "Now isn't the time to be fixing things! You need to get somewhere safe!" She looked

230

pleadingly at Hermes who merely shrugged.

"One place in the castle is as safe as any other, isn't it?" he asked "You don't even know the castle yet, right? And he's been here all night. He probably knows the place better than you."

"I suppose, but-" Sera replied, fretting. Then the ground began to rumble. "They're coming *here?*" she exclaimed "Just because we ran away? There are only *two* of us!" Phin coughed. "OK, *three* of us. But we hardly constitute a threat, do we?"

"It's probably Loki's doing." Hermes replied darkly "I heard he bears a grudge." Then he looked around desperately. "We have to find something to lock or block the door!" They looked around and quickly found the huge, wooden bar that was the locking bar for the castle door. They heaved at it, but they couldn't budge it.

"How did they think I could move this?" Sera complained, frustrated. Then her face lit up. "I know!" she shouted all of a sudden and dashed across the hall "My stuff!"

"Now isn't the time to worry about your stuff!" Hermes yelled after her, exasperated.

"No, I mean the stuff the dwarves made for me!" Sera yelled back "We can use them as weapons!"

"But I thought it was pudding-based!" he yelled back.

"It *is!*" came Sera's reply, now echoing from right across the hall "Just wait there!"

Hermes paced up and down beside the doors for several minutes; all the time the rumbling was getting louder. High above the long table, the chandelier began to tinkle. Hermes watched it nervously and then, not being able to stand it any more, he flew up to one of the windows to see what was happening. Even as he watched, the first few

231

giants lurched out of the mist.

"SERA!!" he yelled down the hall. He heard footsteps and saw Sera hurtling down the hall, red in the face, waving her rucksack in the air. "Sera, what are you-" Sera waved him away and rummaged through her bag. She dumped things out of it onto the floor occasionally, muttering to herself. Finally, she found what she was looking for.

"*A fork*?" Hermes exclaimed "What good is a bloody fork?"

"It's the Fork of Infinite Strength!" she said and stabbed at him. He dodged, about to yell, but realised she'd been aiming for the wooden door slab. "Now let's see if it works-" she lifted up the fork and the slab easily, as if were nothing more than a tiny piece of balsa wood. She manoeuvred it into place, just in time. The doors rattled;

"Doors that big shouldn't rattle!" Hermes hissed "They must be outside! What'll we *do*?"

"Do you think they'll hold?" Sera whispered back. They both looked at the doors. They shook even more violently.

"Not for long." Hermes whispered back "You'd better find something else to block it with." Sera looked around the empty hall.

"Like what?" she hissed. She looked around the hall. It was completely empty, apart from-

"Can you lift that?" Hermes indicated the table. Sera didn't answer; instead she ran across the hall and stabbed the table with the fork. She lifted it. It was light as a feather. As the doors shuddered again she ran across and brought her arm over, throwing the table against the door. Hermes flew up to the window to take a look and immediately ducked down again as a stone smashed through it and flew across the hall. With the thick window gone, the war cries and general yelling of the giants could be heard clearly. Hermes

232

flew back down to Sera;

"There's hundreds of them out there!" he hissed "And they've got a battering ram! We're done for!" Sera bit her lip. Then she came to a decision.

"It's not over 'til the fat lady sings!" she shouted gathering up her dwarven artefacts. "Or until the fat lady doesn't get reinforcements and gets stepped on by a giant, in my case! Here, take a weapon or two."

"*Weapon*?" Hermes scoffed as he was handed a couple of artefacts "This is a whisk!" he looked at the thing in his other hand "And this is a *spatula!*"

"Is it?" Sera peered at the spatula in Hermes' hand "So it is. I'd be careful, if I were you. It's probably the Spatula of Creaming Your Enemies and Scraping Them Off the Floor Afterwards or something. I don't remember being shown that one, so I don't know what it does. Some of the dwarves hadn't finished when I got there."

"Er... I found a label." Hermes said in rather strangled voice.

"And? What does it say?" Sera replied rummaging around in the sack to find all the other things the dwarves had given her.

"It's the Spatula of Decapitation, actually."

"I wasn't far off, then."

"So what about the whisk?"

"It whisks anything into a light, fluffy paste."

"That doesn't sound too deadly."

"I said *anything*. And I was told not to use it for cooking. It's also got a knife in the handle."

"Oh." Hermes had turned a rather unpleasant shade of green. "We're not going to fight them with this stuff?"

"We're going to have to." Sera replied matter-of-factly "We've not got much choice. At least until the reinforcements come." There was a huge bang as something hit the door. They both snapped round to look at it.

"I'm a lover, not a fighter..." Hermes mumbled.

"Tough." Sera shrugged. It was amazing what a castle and a few deadly, pudding-based weapons could do for your attitude. She tossed him a hand whisk "Here, have this one instead. It says 'Hand Whisk of Confusion', so it's probably less deadly, although I wouldn't quote me on that. I'll have the Whisk of Destruction. I'm keeping hold of this fork, too." There was another bang and the door began to splinter. "I hope there's something else in here..." her hand closed on a bar of cold metal. She pulled it out.

"What does that do?" he said eyeing it nervously. The doors began to buckle inwards, sending lethal shards of wood flying across the hall.

"Says here 'Ladle of Smiting'." she replied, reading the label. Meanwhile, Phin was eyeing the door.

"I hate to interrupt your little treasure hunt-" she began "-but we'd better retreat to a safe distance if we don't want to be flattened!" she yelled, running flat out past them "Come on!"

Hermes and Sera grabbed their artefacts and ran; they'd just reached the previous location of the carved table when it flew across the hall, propelled by the force of the battering ram that had just obliterated the doors, and smashed on the floor; all four of its legs spun off in different directions, one of them narrowly missing Hermes, who had flung himself to the floor just in time.

The giants poured into the castle, or tried to, there were so many of them trying to get in that they got themselves stuck. But the ones that did surrounded Sera, Hermes and Phin, who were all stood back-to-back in a shrinking circle of space.

"Get back!" Sera yelled at them "We've got weapons! And we'll use them!"

"Yeah!" Hermes added "Don't make me use this!" He brandished the spatula at them.

The giants roared with laughter.

"He's going to attack us with a terrible plastic stick!" one of them roared.

"Look out men, they've got a ladle!" another one leered. There was a new outbreak of laughter in response to these comedic gems. Sera shrugged.

"You asked for it." she said, and jammed the Whisk of Destruction into the nearest giant's boot. She jiggled it a little. The giant began to laugh but stopped abruptly as his boot was turned rapidly into something like dark brown candy floss. He screamed and hopped away backwards, toppling some of the giants that had managed to unclog themselves from around the door. As another giant stooped forward to take the whisk from Sera, Hermes stepped in front of him, cranking the handle of the Hand Whisk of Confusion as fast as he could. It squeaked furiously. At first, it looked like nothing had happened. The approaching giant just stared at the whisk. The watching giants waited for something to happen and then one of them asked cautiously;

"Are you OK, Gyfod?" The other giant looked at him;

"*What did you say about my MOTHER?!*" he screamed and flung himself at his concerned comrade in a rage. The two brawling giants took several others with them, including some of the ones just recovering from being hit by the hopping maniac with one boot.

"Right!" Sera yelled, smacking another giant in the shin with the Ladle of Smiting. The effect was rather dramatic, he vibrated right across the floor backwards, like a cartoon character who stood too close to a sounding gong, causing a mad scramble to get out of his way. He hit the wall and a chunk fell off and hit him on the head.

All hell broke loose.

The brawling giants merely fought back out of habit and anger, having forgotten why they were in the castle. Some of the ones who hadn't lost their senses tried to knock some sense into the fighting ones - literally - by clonking them on the head and screaming at them to stop. This only made things worse, and Sera, Hermes and Phin lost each other amongst the chaotic mass of giants.

A few still remembered the task at hand and whilst Sera was distracted trying to catch sight of the others, one of them spied his chance and grabbed her.

Sera struggled in vain, unable to break free, but then something brown attached itself to the giant's arm. He screamed and tried to fling it away, but it clung on, drawing blood.

Sera was flung to the ground. As she struggled to her feet a voice said;

"Wotcha, Missus." Sera looked round and located the source of the voice "Thanks for freeing my foot the other day!" the fox added and grinned, insofar as a fox can grin. Then it sped away and up the trousers of the next giant who fell to the ground, eyes crossed and howling in pain. There were more screams from around the doorway.

Foxes were pouring into the hall, biting and scratching and running all over the giants. They were followed by an army of women, dressed in green. The dryads had a most odd fighting tactic. They bunched together, nodded to each other and then smacked whatever was in front of them all at once. Sera saw a group of them back-hand a giant, sending him flying horizontally across the hall, taking out several giants along the way. Getting hit in the knee by one tree was probably very painful, getting hit by the whole wood was probably a whole lot worse.

Then the gods arrived. They were followed shortly after by the dwarves, dressed in special armour so that they wouldn't be turned to stone by the sunlight. It was black, and it covered every inch of their bodies. There was a barely visible slit for their eyes so that they could see out.

A huge man with striking red hair that could only be Thor screamed and rampaged along the hall, mercilessly smashing giants with his hammer as he went. Zeus had also joined the fray, accompanied by more Greek and Roman gods, spinning a sword around over his head and thrusting randomly at the giants when they least expected it. There were a myriad of gods and goddesses that Sera didn't recognise at all.

Sera spotted Hermes and Phin and battled her way to them, using the Fork of Infinite Strength to lift giants up and hurl them out of her way. Just as she got near them, she was narrowly missed by a giant that had been toppled by Thor, and was knocked to the ground; her weapons skidded away across the floor.

A giant spied his chance and bore down on her; Sera flung her arms over her head. Then there was a nasty thwack and a gurgling noise. Sera looked up to see Heimdall's 24 carat grin and, thankfully, the rest of him still attached to it. The giant had been smacked right in the stomach and was now groaning on the floor, not far away.

"Don't you worry Miss Sera!" he shouted above the din, giving her a respectful salute "We'll get 'em! By the way, you haven't seen Loki, have you?"

"I think he's probably hurt out on the plains somewhere!" she shouted back "He was wearing Freya's cloak and we damaged it and he fell out of the sky!"

"Right you are, Miss Sera! I'll get him! He's caused trouble for the last time!" he shouted, saluting at her again and leaping back into the fray.

"Sera!" Hermes yelled, catching up with her, closely followed by Phin "We need to get out of here! Look!"

Some of the giants, after having examined the shards of ceiling that had fallen down, had worked out that it was icing and had started to tear at the walls on either side of the hall.

"Rip it out!" roared one of the leading giants "Eat it up! We'll see how they all like it when the whole place crashes down on their heads!"

"No, don't eat it!" Sera yelled at them remembering what the dwarves had told her "It'll kill you!" They ignored her.

"Keep at it! We'll lose unless we can bury them all!" the lead giant bellowed. Sera searched for her artefacts. They seemed to be intact, although it looked like someone had trod on the Whisk of Destruction and regretted it.

She ran towards the giants who were clawing at the walls, despite Hermes' yells telling her to stop. The giants knocked her away, and just as she was desperately groping for her artefacts, the walls gave a threatening groan and the watching giants cheered, the light elves streamed into the room.

They had pale blonde, flowing hair and their eyes were golden. They wore simple clothes and gold armour that couldn't possibly have been any use in battle. Sera quickly saw why. They wore useless armour because they didn't expect to be hit. As the giants swung at them they *flowed* out of the way, loosing arrows and felling the attacking giants from behind. They dodged and weaved around the giants, lining up at the back of the hall. They worked together, unleashing barrage upon barrage of arrows with unbelievable accuracy, hitting only the giants, sweeping forward and driving them towards the smashed doors and out.

When all the giants were purged from the hall, save those that were injured, unconscious or wisely choosing not to move, plus those that had eaten some of the walls were rolling around and groaning, the whole hall erupted in a huge cheer that rattled the chandelier.

Everyone rushed outside to see the remaining giants retreating into the distance, heading for the safety of Jotunheim.

When the injured and sickened giants had been dragged away and the hall cleaned up, everyone sat around the remains of the carved table and ate and drank and celebrated. They had to stop for a while at one point, because the magic oven couldn't handle all its orders and started to smoke and turn out weird things like pickled cake with ketchup topping. Sera went around the hall, making sure to thank at least every group and thanking every individual she could, especially the light elves, who had owed her no debt and had come to help anyway. She thanked every light elf she saw and told them they were most welcome to her castle and if they wanted anything from her they had only to ask.

The dwarves actually apologised to Sera for not fortifying her castle enough to hold back giants and set about repairing it straight after the celebration.

Freya, her valkyries and the einherjar joined them later, having purged the rest of the giants from the halls of Sessrymnir and Valhalla.

Both the light elves and the dwarves offered to fix Bifrost, saying they would start on it first thing in the morning.

Everyone went to bed happy, relieved and tired, partly from the battle but also from consuming more food than ought to be safe from the magic oven, which was still working, despite its bouts of oddness. The dwarves had also offered to fix that when everything else was done.

The next morning, after having had a good night's sleep in her own castle, which the dwarves had been able to patch up in no time, Sera stood and stared blearily at the oven. It had still managed to produce a decent selection of food for breakfast, although it was clearly still feeling temperamental and had made something neon green and gooey with glowing purple currants in it.

'What the Hel.' Sera thought and forked plenty of pancakes onto her plate, although she wasn't cheerful enough to try the green goo. Just as she had sat down on one the less damaged chairs to eat, she heard a familiar cough. Sera looked up to see Ellis standing on the other side of the table, alone and twisting the hem of her apron.

"Heimdall said to tell you that they've got Loki and that he's been locked up on the edge of Nifelheim. I think." She was managing to mumble snootily, somehow. "The tall blonde one with the gold teeth. And the place where the dead who are bad go... I thought I wouldn't be able to remember the names, so they said tell you that, if I got them wrong."

"No, you got them right." Sera answered, with her fork still halfway to her mouth.

"They said that you sort of helped save the day, a lot in fact." Ellis mumbled, still clutching her apron and trying to look at her knees "So, well, anyway. Thank you, I suppose." She looked up at Sera with a red face and Sera was shocked to see that she seemed to have been crying. Sera's pancake slid off her fork. "Well... anyway... it's a nice castle." she said, pursing her lips. She looked for all the world like a child about to scream.

"Um. Thanks." Sera replied and waited. Ellis made no attempt to leave. The awkward silence continued. She bit her lip and then finally exploded;

"It's not fair!" she shouted "I've been here *ages*, and I've got hardly any friends, and you've got lots and everyone likes you and you've got a castle and all these nice things and I tried, I really *tried* to fit in and get people to follow me, but it was no good and you've only been here five minutes and all I had was my Domestic Goddess title and you messed it up and I *hate you*, only now you've saved everybody and that *includes* my friends, *and* me, so now I can't even hate you and it's ... *Just. Not. Fair!*" she glared defiantly at Sera.

"If it helps, it was my fault that this happened in the first place, so... so it balances out." Sera explained "So you can hate me."

"Oh. Well. G-good." Ellis sniffled. She still looked unhappy.

"I expect Freya and the girls will be cleaning up the bar. They'd really appreciate some help." Sera tried "And she was talking about expanding..." Sera was now Making Things Up but she could have a quiet word with Freya later "You'd look good in a valkyrie outfit. And they need people who are good at cooking-"

"Th-thank you." Ellis muttered, wiping her eyes. She turned and ran. Sera tried to locate the pancake that had fallen off her fork. She'd just got it on her fork again when she heard footsteps running back towards her.

"I STILL HATE YOU!" Ellis yelled from the doorway.

"What's all this yelling, so early in the morning?" Phin

241

complained, trotting down the stairs "What was *she* doing here?"

"Venting, I think." Sera shrugged. After surviving a second Ragnarok, snobby girls were simply not a problem. She turned back to her breakfast once more, but barely managed to get the fork to her mouth before Phin interrupted her again.

"Oh yeah. Him." Sera turned to see what Phin was talking about and saw the old man ambling downstairs, carrying the feather cloak. In all the excitement, Sera had once again completely forgotten about him. He held up the cloak.

It was spotless and seamless, the blood stains gone, the tear perfectly repaired.

"It's fixed now." he said happily "Don't remember why... but it makes me sad to see it damaged. So I fixed it." He looked all over the remains of the table and once more turned a sad, baleful expression on Sera. "No apples." he said sadly.

"Who *are* you?" she asked him suspiciously "How did you know how to fix the cloak?"

"No apples." he said again. Then he seemed to register the question and replied "I'm Od."

"You're... odd?" Sera tried, confused "You're a god? What do you mean?"

"Don't you recognise me? I'm Od." he repeated. Sera looked blank. "Od." he repeated again, hopefully.

"I think..." Sera began "That it's high time we saw Idunn."

Idunn looked up in surprise as Sera and the old man approached. She was back to wearing pink.

"You're that girl. You were one of Freya's trollop waitresses, and then you got yourself a stupid job as Goddess

of Cutlery or something. You were at that game night, too."
she said tilting her head to one side "What do you want?"
Again, after having survived a second Ragnarok Sera was
unperturbed by such a display of rudeness and merely
replied;

"That's right. Except it's puddings, not cutlery. Not a
bad idea for an extension, though." she replied and indicated
the old man "This old man wants one of your apples. He
keeps saying he's odd. I think he means god."

"Od?" Idunn replied, genuinely shocked "As in Odur?"

"*Who?*" said Phin and Sera together. They looked at
each other and then back at Idunn. She didn't seem inclined
to explain. She wordlessly handed them an apple. When
they turned to go she shouted;

"Wait!"

They stopped.

"I want to go with you!" she shouted, suddenly
grinning "This ought to be good -"

Freya frowned at the old man, bent over, clutching his
ancient walking stick as if he'd blow away on the wind if he
didn't. It might even have been the case; he was shaking like
a leaf and his skin was like rice paper over an ornate
drumstick collection. Sera produced the apple from the folds
of her dress. Idunn had forbidden them to give it to Od until
they got to Freya's hall, despite handing it over. Sera would
have ignored her, but Idunn insisted it would be 'worth it'.

The old man, frail as he was, snatched at the apple and
ate it with gusto. Nature may have robbed him of everything
else, but he either had all his own teeth or the best dentures
in the world.

The apple took effect and he started to regain his
youth; his skin flooded with colour, his hair grew shorter and

thicker and took on a golden hue akin to Freya's own shining locks, his thin arms bulged with muscles...

Freya, whose face had gone from puzzled to shocked and everything in between, was now stood with her hands over her mouth looking amazed, and unsure of whether she should laugh or cry. Then, quite suddenly, and before the apple had completely taken effect, she stepped forward and slapped him as hard as she could across his face.

"YOU SAID YOU WERE GOING OUT TO GET SOME MILK, YOU IDIOT!!" she screamed at the top of her lungs "DO YOU HAVE ANY IDEA HOW BLOODY WORRIED I'VE BEEN?! AND HOW BLOODY LONG I SPENT LOOKING FOR YOU?!"

"I'm sorry sweetheart, I got lost." Odur tried to apologise, his voice now the aural equivalent of thick golden syrup instead of sounding like a bad bout of laryngitis.

"*For over a thousand bloody years?!* Who takes over a thousand bloody years to get some bloody milk?!" Freya screamed.

"Well, pumpkin, I accidentally ended up in a desert and I couldn't find my way back to Bifrost and by the time I got out of the desert I was getting old and I got confused and forgot what I was doing and -"

Odur babbled his story, punctuated by screams of rage and a lot of cursing from Freya, until they had both run out of breath.

"And that's what happened, lamb chop." he finished "I'm terribly sorry. There's no rainbow bridge reception down there, you know." Freya had screamed herself out and had run out of curse words, so she said the only thing she could think of:

"We'll send someone else to get the milk next time. Welcome home, darling."

Sera, having completed the last item on her To-Do List

of Happiness for now, headed to Midgard once again - to tell her parents where they *really* didn't have any mobile phone reception.

Meanwhile, in a community centre near one of the few remaining forests where red squirrels can be found, a few nervous returnees dressed in yellow and brown - and three rather confused people who had thought they were going to a baking contest - began the first ever real Meeting of the Sacred Pudding Community...